The Mother Lode
by A.C. Lyons

The Mother Lode

Ghostwritten by Megan Kerr
Edited by Carole A. Ward
Cover Design by Andrew Kerr & Ron Warren

ISBN: 100984729801
ISBN-13: 978-0-9847298-0-7

DEDICATION

This book is dedicated to the Mothers of the world who provide unconditional love to their children. May this unconditional love spread throughout the world as we all are truly just children seeking to love and be loved.

And to my mother who has loved me unconditionally throughout my life.

I love you, Mom.

"Being unwanted, unloved, uncared for, forgotten by everybody, I think that is a much greater hunger, a much greater poverty than the person who has nothing to eat." ~Mother Theresa

1

Samantha St. Clair sat at her desk, a picture of chic middle-aged efficiency. Her suit was neat, subdued and expensive; her jewelry equally as understated. Her make-up, applied with the expertise of thirty years' experience, drew attention to her large eyes. Lip liner and natural lipstick helped her to avoid the pitfall of bright colors bleeding into the trace of lines that began to entrench themselves around her lips. When she looked in the mirror these days, she could still see shades of the young girl she'd been; somewhere beneath the now prominent bones lay a face that was once softened by the plumpness of youth. She could also see - amidst the emerging wrinkles, the slight sinking of her eyelids, and the deepening of her chin - the old woman she would become; how her face would eventually crumple and fold with age.

At times, she felt a flicker of envy for that twenty-year-old who hadn't appreciated the purity of her skin, the smooth curve of her young shoulders, or her unmarked hands. She knew one day she would envy her present skin; free of liver-spots and still, after all, quite taut. Her high-necked blouse hid the feathering that had started to creep around her cleavage. Her knee-length skirt exhibited her brand-new shapely legs – better legs, in fact, than her twenty-year-old self had enjoyed. From behind, she could pass as much younger, just as at one time she passed as older, matronly, and competent.

With everything a modern woman had at her disposal to create a youthful appearance, however, her hands still betrayed her. Science had yet to perfect a technique for "freshening" the hands. Samantha gazed down at hers, studying them. Veins began to stand out over the tendons, like blue string under her skin. The pores were larger now than even two years ago. Fine hairs contrasted with a curiously blotchy color – pink, yellow and red, mixed with purple undertones. The flesh of her ring finger had swollen up to bite around her gold wedding band, as if trying to swallow it. Like Lady Macbeth, she avoided looking at her hands too much. At the moment, these aging hands turned a bottle of pills around and around. Her eyes lowered to examine the print. Last year she'd bought bifocals, paying extra for lenses that hid the telltale line.

Every morning, she arrived at her desk, swallowed her morning medication with her first sip of coffee, and began her day. Routine was a useful tool for remembering things; keeping everything in its proper place, making sure things got done without having to fuss or think about it much. Some routines were now changing, however. Her best friend Marilyn persuading her to join the gym had initiated this change. Now when she shopped for clothes, she no longer reached for a 14 automatically – she began to have to try things on. She no longer knew what size she wore. At the moment, it seemed to vary between ten and eight. Her newfound litheness had an animal energy of its own; her limbs demanding near constant use and exertion. Nowadays, instead of relaxing on the sofa every evening, she cleaned out cupboards and rearranged shelves. She wondered if it was 'the change' that was inspiring this newfound activity.

This morning, in the middle of opening her pill bottle, she stopped and read the writing; something she hadn't done for years. She wondered if she still needed them. She'd been feeling much better lately; more serene and able to handle her daily ration of chaos like a pro. With elaborate caution, as if the bottle might suddenly bite, she dropped it in the wastepaper basket. Without a backward glance, her routine resumed as she spread out the *New York Times* and speed-read the day's news.

"With another lackluster performance last night by the candidates in the Democratic primary debates," read the editorial, *"the party as a whole seems to be stuck in the mud and no one candidate is generating enough momentum to pull them out."*

She clicked her tongue. *Fair enough,* she thought. *We're treading water and it's getting dull for everyone.*

A double-rap on the open door announced Ruth's presence. At one time, Samantha would have called her faithful assistant elderly. Now, she studied her covertly for tips on how to look good in your sixties. Good hair dye was obviously part of it. Ruth's hair, salt-and-pepper a few years back, now boasted an immaculate chestnut bob. She stood in the doorway tapping her notebook on her palm.

"Hardball wants you for tonight's show," said the older woman. "You want it?"

"What's the subject?"

"The public's lethargic response to the snooze-fest we like to call debates."

Samantha chuckled and glanced back at the article. "I'll do it," she grinned.

"You just love being on camera, don't you?" Ruth's tone was dry but amused.

"I like speaking out," Samantha corrected. "Email the details over – I'll need to make some notes…" Her voice was drifting into a self-directed mumble of planning as Ruth turned to leave. "Oh, and can you get my husband on the phone?"

Ruth gave a short, mock bow from the waist. "Yes, Congresswoman, I'll see if we are worthy enough to get through to the omnipotent one."

A minute later, Samantha's phone rang. "The stars must be aligned," said Ruth on the other end, "His Lordship is on line one."

Samantha hit the button and at the first 'h' of her 'Hello,' Richard cut in.

"This better be good – you know how busy I am."

"My women's conference was cancelled this weekend, and I thought I'd come home," she replied briskly. Richard liked people to get straight to the point on the phone. He employed techniques for eliminating time-wasters.

He huffed in irritation. "Sam – you're a grown woman. You don't need my permission to come home. Is there anything else?"

"Well – I just thought you'd want to know," she said uncomfortably, aware that she was now drifting into time-wasting non-essential information. "We haven't seen each other for over a month and I thought you might be a little more enthusiastic."

"Okay. I'm enthused. Now please, I'm busy." A dial tone signaled the end of the call. Richard was efficient and lengthy goodbyes were not.

"Asshole!" she muttered, hanging up.

"I heard that…" called Ruth.

She winced inwardly and tapped her lips with the length of her index finger. A woman's magazine had recently suggested it as a way to avoid crying and so far it seemed to work. At least he'd said he was enthused. He didn't sound like it, but maybe showing excitement wouldn't be good for his work-image. *You're fretting like a sixteen year-old,* Samantha chastised herself, finger tapping faster. *Get on with your own life. Plan your interview. Now come on, what's your angle? They say our debates are boring and we don't really say anything, and they are right. So what will you say?*

When Samantha was fourteen, she gave the most memorable debate speech of her life. The local Rotary club organized competitions between the local schools, called the 'Round Robin' debates, and they were the highlight of her time at Jefferson Middle School. She knew everything there was to know about their primitive art of rhetoric: Introduction, A-B-C, and Conclusion; first speaker introduces the topic, speakers and argument; second speaker gives the bulk of the information; third speaker rebuts and concludes the argument. Her orderly, elegant phrasing and meticulous research made her a perfect second speaker. She was the substantial filling between Andy and Kelly, the more dramatic personalities who opened and closed their arguments with what resembled fireworks and flair. The three of them marched up the ranks round after round.

In the final round, they were up against three boys from Grosse Pointe South high school, all a grade or two above their own team, who stood shining in their smart, designer clothing. GPS boys were known as gentlemanly, clever, and quite a catch. James Laughton was the star of the school and therefore exuded a confident charm. Samantha recognized all of them from previous encounters – the GPS teachers coached them assiduously and whenever the boys weren't speaking, they were chauffeured off to watch other debates and to examine their opponent's strengths and weaknesses. In half a dozen school libraries, Samantha hovered nervously near the beverage table and watched his lordly, easy demeanor while her stomach churned and contracted. His narrow, strongly-defined face boasted plump lips and dark eyes. Tall and elegant; he resembled a young God. She'd always felt too shy to talk to him; far too plump, she didn't want to draw attention to her ungainly figure.

Now she was to debate against him, and dual disasters struck her team: Kelly developed laryngitis and they were opposing 'This house believes marriage should be for love'. A hastily-drafted new team member, Ann, had been given Samantha's speech while Samantha took the third speaker's chair...opposing *him*.

James, the midnight idol of her single bed. James, the unopposed ruler of her wildly orbiting innards. Towering, magnificent, slow-smiling James...the curve of whose lips suggested his little fingernail held more knowledge than the whole of her. James, who stood up, denounced, trounced, and collapsed all her carefully constructed arguments which Ann actually delivered. James, who burst forth in a flow of mesmerizing rhetoric on the nature of love, staring out at the audience with impassioned sincerity, then turning to spear her with his eyes and final words: "If the opposite team can prove now that I lied, I never lived nor no men ever loved." His laser-gaze kept its focus, melting her down to a small puddle, and as he took his seat, a tiny conspiratorial smile crept over his lips.

Why, why, why? Wailed Samantha in her heart. *Why, the first time I hear a boy wax lyrical about love, am I destined to argue against him?*

The audience's lengthy applause gave her time to reshuffle her scrawled cards. She'd scribbled down their arguments, but could find no ripostes to them. Nothing could drown out the repetitive chant in her head: *He's right, he's right, he's right.* When her name was called, she walked to the front, opened her mouth, and the words just fell out. "Maybe he's right."

The audience stared, frozen. She held the pause, feeling their attention stretch like elastic, knowing instantly just how far to pull it. "Maybe they're right," she said again. This wasn't the parliamentary style of debate she would learn later in college; no one on the opposing team or in the audience could leap up and call her to order for agreeing with the other team.

"Maybe they're right that love creates the best possible home environment..." She enumerated their points, flipping through her cards, conceding each one. She was sufficiently experienced at this point to speak and think at the same time, which bought her two precious extra minutes.

"When the proposition says 'should', though," she said at last, "are they talking about an imaginary dream or a real ideal to which we should aspire?" Methodically, she resurrected her team's argument: the fickleness of idealized romantic love, the necessity of trying hard, considering the children, making it work even when it felt stale. These philosophies came from her mother and the glib solutions rolled off her tongue with teenage sincerity.

"Maybe," she concluded, "you could define all of this as 'love'. And then the other team would be right. But James," she had said his name, in public, with proprietary familiarity, "left us in no doubt what they meant by love: that leap in your heart, that squirming in your stomach, that shaking in your hands, the longing to just look at one person forever." She methodically described her own feelings for him, heart thumping in her chest. "If that was the solution, there wouldn't be a problem. We look at the world, and we know it's not that simple." Oh, the worldly-wise fourteen year-old! "Love is lovely," – laughter – "but it's not the only or the main purpose of marriage. We need to look to more stable virtues and less selfish ideals for that." Dramatic, solemn pause. "Thank you." Thunderous applause.

A slew of images swirled about her then; the debating cup for their school landing in her left hand, and more importantly, James shaking her right hand in congratulation, his deep eyes seeing her at last, and saying "You were amazing," while she jabbered every self-deprecating comment she could think of. She thought of it afterwards as her 'Maybe They're Right' speech and felt she had uncovered some essential tool of argument: attack by surrender.

   To keep herself calm, Samantha focused on whether Chris Matthews's perfectly brushed blonde hair was a toupee. His forehead glinted in the spotlight. Her own face was coated an inch-deep with make-up, which kept her from shining or going red with anger.

   "While your party is slipping in the mud and falling flat on their faces," he was saying, "the Republicans are marching in step with a clear, distinct message that unites their base and gives independents an option to choose from. Why can't the Democratic party get their act together like the Republicans?"

   She gave him a composed smile. "You're right, Chris – the Republican message is very clear – so simple I can sum it up in three words: God, guns, and gays." She'd been saving that line for weeks. "Running a country is a complex business, but the Republicans aren't interested in that. They just want a moral crusade. That's a fine thing, but not when we should actually be talking about the country's economy, its foreign affairs, its education system, social welfare, the legal system, and trade laws. These are complicated things and the Republicans don't seem to like complicated things very much. Their moral stance is very clear, but what I want to know is – where are their policies for actually running the country – and I don't mean running it into the ground, as they have been doing."

   The rest of the panel's discussion, with occasional prods from her, turned against the Republican policies, which by the end of the evening looked far muddier. Their time was drawing to a close before Chris could fix her with his beady little blue eyes again, and say, "Okay, enough about the Republicans – Samantha, what do the Democrats plan, in one sentence?"

   "I think running the country is far more complex than a sound bite will give me time for," Samantha said, still smiling sweetly. "What we stand for is a safe nation and expanding opportunity for every American. How we plan to create that is detailed very clearly on our website." She turned to face the camera directly. "Anyone who thinks they can handle some real information about this country's future leaders, instead of just Republican slogans, come check us out." Daringly, she winked.

Samantha timed it perfectly. Chris was forced to sum up after her final word. By the time she got off the set, three missed calls from the party headquarters were listed on her cell. Her phone rang again as she was checking it.

"Congresswoman St. Clair? Ben Morehouse, from DNC."

Her stomach lurched with fear at the sound of the party chairman's voice. *You shouldn't have winked!*

"Hello, Mr. Morehouse. How can I help you?" she said with forced calm.

"I'm wondering if you could join me for dinner tomorrow night. Eight o'clock? The Georgetown Inn?"

"Of course," she said, while scrambling in her purse for her Blackberry. Her heavy schedule and incessant demands on her time necessitated lugging about two phones; the Blackberry doubling as a handy PDA. "I believe I'm available. May I ask what this is about?"

"I'd prefer to discuss this in person, if you don't mind."

"No, I don't mind." She did, but the words came as naturally as breathing.

"Great, I'll see you tomorrow at eight then. Good night."

"Good night." She snapped the phone closed, started biting the inside of her lip, and forced herself to stop.

She and Marilyn moved around the toning circuit together, Samantha taking Marilyn's place each time the red light and chime indicated, while her friend moved on to the next machine. She only needed to change the weights for the arm and thigh exercises. Their standing joke every morning was that Samantha's arms were stronger from paper-pushing, while Marilyn's thighs gained from her energetic sex life.

"What do you think he wants?" asked Marilyn, breathing deeply as her inner thighs squeezed off a hundred pounds. Where Samantha was now all neat trimness, with small, sloping breasts and slender thighs, Marilyn was a feast of curves from her wildly curling hair on down. Sweat was sliding between her generous cleavage, and her face shone with the joy of using her strength.

"I have no idea. He wouldn't say." Samantha's reply was broken into chunks as she strained her outer thighs.

"Come on, there must be some reason he wants to have dinner with you."

The chime sounded and they stood, wiping down their machines and faces. Samantha started lightening the weights on the next machine as Marilyn settled herself onto another with a slight smirk.

"You're getting stronger – soon you'll have a regular pair of man-crushing pins there."

"Yeah, like that's going to make any difference to my life," retorted Samantha. "But this dinner – till now the DNC hasn't taken me seriously enough for a cup of coffee, let alone a whole dinner." She watched her thigh muscles contract smoothly as the weights rose behind her.

"Well – you've been getting a lot of air time. Maybe they want you to tow a better party line than you have been?"

Samantha winced. "That's probably it. On Hardball, I basically agreed with Chris Matthews that the Democrats don't have a cohesive message. I tried to turn it back on the Republicans – I thought I'd managed, but maybe not. Or maybe it was that wink at the end. I bet they're pissed and he's going to lecture me on being a better team player and portraying the party in a better light."

She glanced up from her legs at Marilyn, who stared entranced at a young man walking past in bicycle shorts.

"Hello? Can we stay focused here?"

"Sorry," chuckled Marilyn. "I thought UPS was here with a package delivery." She shook her head to clear it. "I missed that whole round – do you mind if we stay on these machines for the next one?"

Samantha shrugged. The machine behind her was empty. She took a few deep breaths while the chime sounded and the light flicked to red again.

"So where's the dinner?" Marilyn pushed against her machine again.

"The Georgetown Inn."

"Oh wow… Nice. Check out the bar before you leave."

"Why?"

"Because the hottest and most eligible men in DC hang out there on Thursday nights…" She dragged the words out like an ad describing chocolate ice-cream.

Samantha's thighs were straining and she eased the weights back down, breathing heavily.

"You're forgetting something," she said, waving her ring finger in the air. "I'm married, remember?"

"Yeah, to a prick."

Samantha glared at her friend, but Marilyn was wiping herself down and moving on to the pec-machine.

"I'm not telling you to pick up a guy, just check out the bar – do a once-around."

"Why? What's the point?"

Marilyn settled her arms in place, admiring her cleavage as her muscles swelled and rippled. "Just to see what kind of commotion this new body of yours can generate. That's all."

"Oh," said Samantha. She looked down at herself then at the wall-length mirror opposite her. For the first time in her life, she was as limber and slim as she wanted to be. She'd probably been slimmer in college, but had loathed the rounded curve of her belly, the slight droop of her bum. They were still there, but didn't seem to matter anymore. She looked good – and she had great legs. *An admiring glance or two wouldn't hurt you,* she told herself. *A little attention before you wither away completely would be nice.* "You really think I look good?"

"Truly fuckable." grinned Marilyn. Samantha blushed and looked at the floor.

The circuit was taking its toll and both were too breathless to speak for the last few machines. The Stairmaster took all her energy and Samantha mused silently on Marilyn's words as her lungs burned and legs ached. *Fuckable.* She was starting to feel desirable; sloughing off inertia with the excess weight, while regaining her libido with this new sense of energy. *What's the point in looking hot and feeling sexy? Richard never wants you. And if you're honest, you've given up trying until you don't even want him so much either. What a waste – cultivating this shapely sexiness only to sit around watching what womanliness you have left decay and droop, unused, unappreciated. The last beauty you have will fade, long untasted. You don't have so much time before menopause steps in. He's wasting your last little space of fecundity.*

"You okay?"

She blinked, realizing her eyes had misted over. "Yeah," she said, exhaling heavily and switching the machine off. "Just worn out. I think I need to hit the showers before my legs give way completely."

On Marilyn's advice, she changed before dinner from her smart two-piece into a plain grey tailored dress; demure and slender, with a discreet slit up the back. A push-up bra restored her breasts to their sixteen-year-old position, instead of halfway down her torso where they appeared to have settled. They seemed to have moved four inches south in the last thirty years – if she made it to ninety, they might reach her navel. *When did this new obsession with your looks start?* She challenged her reflection. *For years you never gave it a second thought – why the sudden vanity? Get over yourself, this is a business meeting.*

Later that evening over dinner, Ben's news drove all thoughts of her appearance from her mind.

"You want me to do *what?*" she sputtered over the appetizer.

"We want you to run for president," he repeated. In sharp contrast to her painstaking grooming, he was disheveled and crumpled – the original mussed-up liberal who wielded his power too easily to bother with ironed shirts.

"The United States Presidency?" she confirmed, disbelievingly. "Me? A second term representative from Michigan, and someone the DNC has totally ignored until now?"

She took a discomfited swig of her white wine while he and Cynthia, his assistant, exchanged sharp glances.

"We want new blood out there," said Cynthia brusquely. She was a hard-edged woman in her late thirties, whose large bones didn't carry a spare ounce of fat. Everything about her declared fierce determination. "We can't keep sending the same old retreads to get their asses kicked over and over again."

"But why me? Why all of a sudden? Pardon me, but I am probably the least credentialed member of Congress, so I'm a little baffled as to why you are choosing me." Samantha knew she was looking a gift horse in the mouth and pointing out her own flaws, but she didn't care. She needed to understand. The game of appearing powerful or hiding weaknesses had never been one she played well.

"We've been tracking your favorables on the news programs," said Cynthia. "Your numbers are very impressive." *Don't throw this away*, her eyes warned.

"So your message must be hitting home somewhere," said Ben, pushing three spears of asparagus into his mouth at once. He threw in a chunk of bacon and blue cheese to keep them company, and Samantha looked down to avoid seeing the half-masticated mash.

"Samantha – you're the only liberal who's getting any kind of a pulse out there with the voters," said Cynthia.

Samantha straightened her incredulous face and put her glass down, newly serious. "This is unexpected news," she said, "and something I'd very much like to consider carefully."

"Well, we're not expecting an answer today, but we sure would like you to think about it and get back to us fairly soon."

"If I do run, you will fund my campaign – correct?" said Samantha cautiously. "You're not expecting my husband to back this financially, are you?"

"It's you we want, not the family fortune," said Ben. "As long as your campaign gathers momentum, we'll fund it. But can you let us know by mid-week, latest? The sooner we get some spark out there, the better."

Samantha nodded. She thought she hadn't decided yet, but her mind was racing ahead to outline her platform. All the ideals and practical solutions she'd come up with over the years would step into the public arena properly, at last. She could expose new ways of doing things, workable solutions to the age-old social ills... For the rest of dinner, her mouth moved in polite auto-pilot while she drafted public service plans and fragments of speeches. Fizzing euphoria was rising in her as if she might suddenly grow wings and shoot up into the sky. As they were leaving the hotel, she remembered Marilyn's suggestion and paused.

"I think I'm going to visit the lady's room before I head out," she said, stopping them in the lobby. "You two go ahead."

"Okay, Samantha. Good night." Ben paused, then continued, "And please, seriously consider running. You would be a wonderful candidate and a credit to our party." The two shook hands warmly.

As Cynthia leaned in for an air-kiss, she hissed *Think about it!*" in Samantha's ear and drew away with a conspiratorial glance.

Samantha stood in the lobby, watching them go. *You are a presidential candidate.* She glanced at her face in the mirrored wall to her right. The eyes that peered back were a swirling fusion of panic and exhilaration. A few deep breaths and they resumed their serene countenance. Samantha then rewarded her reflection with a confident, official smile. *Look at you – a smart, stylish slim woman, a presidential candidate, powerful and ready to show her stuff!*

A tendril of excitement began creeping back into her mind as she rummaged around in her Fendi bag for her phone, "Marilyn, if there is a God you'll pick up this time!" She muttered through clenched teeth. She couldn't tear open the device fast enough and stood in the lobby, breathing hard and punching the numbers. As a stoic series of rings teased her ears, Samantha struggled to regain her composure. *It simply would not do for a presidential candidate to lose it in the lobby of an upscale Washington hotel. Buck up, babe...you've got a country to charm.*

As usual, Marilyn wasn't picking up. After leaving a staccato message that implored her friend to call her *immediately*, Samantha snapped the phone shut and just stood there. The sound of her breath seemed too much to bear and she eyed the door to the hotel lounge across the lobby. *One more drink to calm the nerves won't hurt.*

Samantha crossed the lobby, her back straighter than usual, high heels thumping neatly onto the heavy carpeting. As she moved through the crowded bar pretending to look for a friend, glances followed her. Marilyn was right – the bright young things of business thronged the room, exuding power and youth through their smart suits. *So this is where they've all been hiding.* Her mouth pressed down over a sudden giggle as she saw a dark-haired Don Juan flash a curious smile in her direction. Perhaps she should stay for a drink and a little eye-candy, to celebrate.

"I don't like doing this," said Cynthia, as Ben maneuvered his car through downtown DC. "She's going to get crushed."

"Oh, she might not do that poorly," said Ben casually. "She really does get decent favorables on those programs."

"Come on, Ben," said Cynthia, frowning. "She's not much more than a few years removed from being a housewife. Politically, our guys will crucify her." Samantha was a strong woman, but too good-natured for such a cut-throat game. As a team member she was a Godsend, but as a potential leader? It wasn't fair to get her hopes up.

"She will bring sex appeal to the race," said Ben, lifting his index finger. "That means media attention, which means exposure to our guys, which means we might actually put some blood into the limp, lifeless race we're witnessing. Our core issues just aren't provocative enough – so if we have to show a little leg and some cleavage to get attention, that's what we'll do. And you must admit, she's gotten to be pretty easy on the eyes lately."

Cynthia shook her head. "Sheep to the wolves," she said sadly, but part of her mind also echoed, *pearls before the swine.*

2

In Junior High, with her barely-there breasts and thick waist, Samantha's spandex leotard made her look like a sparkly potato. By the time she'd entered Lakeview High School, she'd lost most of her puppy fat and had tiny, but clearly defined breasts. When gathered cheesecloth blouses came in style, she leapt at them, complementing them with long peasant skirts, matching headbands, and an armory of bracelets on each arm.

Her look was loosely floating, but her personality was not: she worked furiously. Before all their tests, Marilyn would photocopy Samantha's immaculate notes, only beginning to study when Samantha was already revising her outlines. Samantha earned Bs, for which she worked hard; Marilyn fluctuated between As and Ds, depending on the state of her love-life.

Theirs was a cross-tribes friendship; Marilyn as part of the emerging punk crowd, tearing rips in her jeans and cutting her hair with blunt scissors. Samantha sewed her own clothes, mending any rips with a tiny stitch-in-time. She sat with the other good girls and listened to Abba while studying in her pink bedroom. She knew all the words to *Dancing Queen* and swayed in front of the mirror, imagining herself at the magical age of seventeen - when her stomach would miraculously flatten - being swirled around a disco by James.

Marilyn painted her room black and was allowed to invite boys in; she lay on her bed with them, listening to Blondie and speculating on the endless question of where to draw the line as their fumbling fingers strove to make it past various elastic boundaries. Samantha's mother had very clear rules – no boys in the bedroom and no sitting with a boy behind closed doors – but at that point, this policy was purely theoretical. Marilyn lost her virginity on her sixteenth birthday; Samantha attained sweet-sixteen-and-never-been-kissed. Somehow, their friendship survived the dichotomy. The one time it nearly shattered, Samantha's mother and her iron-clad decorum stepped in to save it.

For a special treat, Samantha and her mother were enjoying a mother/daughter outing to a smart, British-style café that boasted scones, tea and ambiance. Samantha wore an olive-green jumper over a long, cuffed blouse and felt sophisticated and stylish...until she witnessed Marilyn lingering on the sidewalk outside the café.

Overnight, her best friend's punk-look had vanished. The shaggy hair was trimmed into a short bob while a richly-colored caftan scooped low over her plump breasts. Standing next to her, in an aquamarine three-piece suit, his right arm around her shoulders, left hand lifting her chin and leaning in for a kiss, was James. Samantha's James. Suddenly Samantha realized how childish her own clothes were and how stupid it appeared to be hanging out with one's mother.

Marilyn walked in, spotted them and ran up with surprised, effervescent greetings. Samantha regarded her friend through squinted eyes, replied icily, and dismissively turned back to her mother. Her heart hammered so fast she felt faint while her hands shook with rage. *She knows – she* knows *you like James – the traitorous bitch!* The teapot spout rattled against the fragile edge of her china cup as Samantha poured a fresh round and looked up to see her mother's lips set in a tight line.

"What was that display of rudeness?" her mother demanded tensely. "That is your friend."

"She's not my friend anymore," said Samantha, feeling tears begin to run down her face. "She's with James – she knows I like him..." She began to sob behind her hands.

"Pull yourself together!" hissed her mother, shoving a napkin into her hand. "Stop crying this *instant* and wipe your face. Now you are going to walk over there and apologize for your behavior..."

"But I liked him first!" wailed Samantha. "It's not fair..."

"Keep your voice *down*! A lady does not cry in public. And just because this young man chose your friend over you is no reason to behave rudely and cause a scene."

Samantha obeyed, as always. Marilyn and James saw the sparkle in her eyes, not knowing that tears were making them shine. They both readily accepted her explanation that she and her mother had been "right in the middle of a really serious conversation" and beamed their way through the next few moments. After a few more pleasantries, Samantha resumed her seat with her mother and was rewarded with an approving look.

"That's my girl."

Being sweet sixteen had its own rewards, only because it fulfilled a custom. Unkissed seventeen wasn't so sweet and she didn't feel 'only seventeen' at all. She felt left on the shelf. The age of seventeen contained no magic...none of the miracles she'd imagined. Following her mother's example, Samantha swallowed the jagged little pill of betrayal and grimly steered her way into adulthood.

"How much do I owe you?"

The bartender set down the glass of amber whisky. "That won't be necessary – the drink is compliments of the tall gentleman in the dark suit."

Samantha's eyes followed his gesturing thumb down the length of the wooden and brass bar to the man who'd flashed the disarming smile as she walked in. Her eyes performed a startled double-take – he was a thirty-something version of James. She reminded herself that the real James would be a couple of years older than her and pushing fifty. Apparently, Samantha's tastes hadn't changed so much over the years: tall, dark-haired, with an air of quietly flamboyant authority. Men possessing these traits had always been her weakness. She was one of the few who actually approved of Timothy Dalton as James Bond. Demurely, she raised her glass in a gesture of thanks. Her outward composure shifted slightly as her stomach suddenly clenched. He was squeezing through the crowd towards her. She took a hasty swig of the whiskey that burned her throat.

"Hello, I'm Thomas."

"Samantha," she said hoarsely, extending her hand with studied composure. His eyes, almost too blue to look at, held hers a moment too long to be considered polite before drifting appreciatively downwards.

"I hope I wasn't too forward buying you that drink." His eyes recaptured hers. "Was I?" His words seemed humble, but his smile was more certain.

"Oh – no – you're perfectly fine," she faltered.

"Because I didn't see your wedding ring from across the room, and I certainly don't want to be inappropriate."

Her breath caught. "No, I think buying me a drink is innocent enough. Don't you?"

"For now it is."

Samantha covered her mouth against an embarrassing teenager's giggle. She cursed herself as his eyes drifted away, towards the door.

"Will your husband be joining you?" His glance spun back.

"Oh, well…no. I'm just here on business, got an interesting proposal, and I thought I'd come in here and celebrate with a drink."

"Can you share with me what we're celebrating?" His hand cupped her elbow as he steered her from the bar towards a seat on the leather banquette that rippled around the length of the room.

"I really can't," she said regretfully, "but it's a very promising proposal – worth thinking over."

He lifted his glass in a toast and she copied his gesture.

"To Samantha's new proposal. May it be as attractive and captivating as the lady it was proposed to."

Their glasses met with a soft chink of glass, ice rattling, and she studied him as she took a sip. Their patch of seating was only enough for one and a half people, so she kept her knees crossed, trying to prevent her thighs from touching his, and instead exposed half her leg. They talked lightly, without revealing too much. Samantha said she was 'in politics' and avoided any topic that led to Richard and her marriage. Thomas was 'in law' and slid his business card into her palm, the tips of his fingers brushing the inside of hers, lingering there.

Either he had a pact with the Devil or he tipped small fortunes, because the bartender kept their drinks flowing even when the crush around the bar was three-deep. She laughed, made witty remarks, and shivered with delight to feel his eyes roving her body in appreciation. *If you're not actually doing anything, you can't be doing anything wrong,* she told herself. She kept her legs neatly crossed, but the curve of the banquette and press of people on either side pushed them closer together. When she tried to change her legs over, her knee accidentally hooked over his thigh.

"Sorry," she muttered, appalled, trying to untangle herself.

His hand closed over her knee. "Why be sorry? I don't know when I last had such a shapely leg draped over mine." His palm was warm and whispered over her sheer pantyhose. A swarm of butterflies rose from her stomach, sealing her throat with delicate multicolored wings. She sat in sudden silence, trembling, pretending that his hand wasn't stroking under the hem of her dress and that she couldn't feel a sudden glowing coal between her legs. She glanced around; concerned that someone may see what was going on under their table. It wouldn't do to have a married congresswoman who is running for president to be cavorting around in such a manner.

"So what cases are you working on at the moment?" she said in a thin voice as she continued her reconnaissance mission. Deciding that no one seemed to notice their flirtation, and enjoying how good it felt to be touched this way, Samantha took a deep, shuddering breath and simply went with it.

Thomas smiled slowly, sensing blood in the water, and looked directly at her. "Right now?" He raised an eyebrow. His fingers drifted over the inside of her thigh, just above her knee, and he watched her lips part in a quick, quiet gasp. "Right now – I'm working on…" His fingertips traced small circles, punctuating his words. Her eyes darted briefly around the room again; half panicked, half enjoying the titillation of the moment. His gaze slid down and fixed on her lips. He cleared his throat. "I'm working on trying to concentrate when all I can think about is your lips."

She laughed nervously and weakly blocked his hand from roaming further.

"Well, that's not quite true," he went on, removing his hand and lifting his drink. "I'm also thinking about your sexy legs and what the rest of you might look like under that demure little dress." He grinned. When she couldn't meet his eyes anymore, Samantha glanced away and saw the warm tanned sheen of his chest where his tie had loosened.

Abruptly, she was visited by a complete vision of that naked chest hovering above her and she blinked in panic. *Is this really happening?*

"Cat got your tongue?" His hand slid back onto her leg as a small groan escaped her throat.

"It's – very hard to talk…" she murmured.

"Very hard," he agreed, suddenly breaking their closeness and sliding out from the booth. "Excuse me – I'll be right back…"

He disappeared into the throng of suits. Alone at the table, she took a determined sip of whisky and several deep breaths while she tried to talk sense into herself.

He wants to see your naked body.

But I'm married!

You promised fidelity – not celibacy. You're still sexy and you won't always be. Enjoy it while it lasts.

I am enjoying it. But it can't go further than this. I'm a fricken' congresswoman, for God's sake!

When were you last touched like that? His hands give you back the sense of your own skin.

So long – God, it's been so long. But I mustn't sleep with him.

You probably shouldn't.

I don't want to leave. Not just yet.

Just a little more.

"I was afraid you'd run away." Thomas was slipping into his seat next to her again, even closer than before. His knuckles brushed her collarbone.

"I'm not sure I could run if I tried," she laughed shakily. "My legs seem to have ceased functioning."

"So I'll have to carry you upstairs?" he said softly, laying his room keycard on the table. She stared at the plastic rectangle with its metallic strip and everything it represented.

I mustn't sleep with him.

But let him touch you more – feel hands on your breasts again. Better in private than here.

His fingers softly traced the curve of her neck…right in the back; her submissive spot. He'd found it. Her resolve and most of her carefully constructed sensibilities melted away as he helped her up and guided her towards the elevator.

"We shouldn't be doing this," she said, gently nudging him away as the doors closed on them and he attempted to close on her.

"I know," he said softly, leaning in…his lips close enough to taste.

"I'm married," she reminded him, turning her face away while placing one more tiny step between them. Her mind screamed, *Oh God, oh God, oh God...*

"I know," he said against her ear. Her knees briefly caved and he caught her between his body and the elevator wall. "But I can't shake the feeling your body is screaming to be touched as much as mine is screaming to touch you."

Samantha gathered up any remaining sense she possessed against the din of desire and again pushed him away. "Not here. Cameras." She motioned with her eyes the smoky-colored glass bubble positioned discreetly in the back corner. Sighing, Thomas assumed a respectful distance just as the elevator chimed.

Just a little more, just a little more, her mind recited frantically as the doors slid open again and he led her to a numbered door. *You won't go all the way, but just taste a little more – it's not fair to never be touched.*

Being folded in his arms while his mouth hotly opened hers was just a little more. His hand sliding down the long zipper at the back of her dress was just a little more and meant that at last *someone* would see and admire the body she'd worked so hard to acquire. His mouth and hands murmured speechless admiration all over her. They only ended up on the bed because a wave of lust crumpled her legs. He laid her gently back; her knees slung over the edge, and kissed her skin back into womanliness. That too was just a little more. She swam in his touch and the golden tides of sensation. When one deft finger hooked her panties to the side and his mouth descended, her body claimed it as her birthright which she could no longer accept being denied. The moment she began moaning and screaming on his fingers, exploding under his tongue, the line was irrevocably crossed. If she had just stolen this illicit cup of freedom, she would drink it down to the last drop. She ceased her struggle to just passively accept his gift of bliss and began to meet his passion with her own.

In the cold white of dawn, shot through with golden spears of sensation, she drove back to her little DC apartment and packed a small suitcase for her weekend trip home. Soon she would accede to the guilt, but for now her body still hummed with joy and her mind spun through a flashback kaleidoscope of perfect moments. She was late getting to the gym and Marilyn had already left. Samantha climbed onto a treadmill, but couldn't bring herself to punish her body with its usual straining effort. After a few minutes of desultory strolling, she settled for a hot shower. Afterward, in the bright lights of the gym bathroom, she applied concealer to the dark circles under her eyes, painted a workaday face over her transformed skin, and drove to her office. When she still hadn't heard from Marilyn by mid-morning, she sent her errant best friend a text to meet for lunch.

"Well, well, well," said Marilyn dryly as Samantha sat down opposite her. "Missed the gym… dreamy smile… guilty spark… shining eyes…" She ticked the symptoms off on her fingers. "The doctor diagnoses – sex. You got laid last night, didn't you?"

Samantha's face froze in an alarmed expression that didn't quite wipe the smile off.

"Oh my God. You did. Didn't you? Is that what you called me about last night?"

"Why would you say such a thing?" Samantha picked up the menu and studied it. Her face was on fire.

"Come off it, you may as well have a flashing sign above your head. You're *glowing*."

"I might just be having a good hair day," smirked Samantha.

"You look exhausted *and* you look fantastic – I don't think that was an all-nighter of paper work."

Samantha giggled. Glancing around the room, she leaned forward and whispered, "Okay – I had sex last night. Lots and lots."

"I *knew* it," said Marilyn, "so go on – spill the details!"

"Okay… Well – I went to the hotel bar like you told me to, and was picked up by this incredibly sexy, young and virile romantic man – mmm…" Her eyes glazed as the events flowed past in her mind like a film only she could see.

"And?" Marilyn snapped her fingers. "Stay with me, girlfriend."

"And he got a room and we had the most amazing, passionate, tender sex I've ever had." The words didn't do it justice.

"Whoa – rewind – how did you get from the bar to the room?"

Squirmy with embarrassment and delight, Samantha quietly unraveled the evening. The guilt still waited, just out of sight; it would get its turn in due course, but not yet. "And then," she whispered over her salad, "he made me come over and over, but he hadn't – I mean, it was bizarre, I've never met a guy who – well, anyway, he started disappearing under the covers and I said, 'Where are you going?' and he said, 'You'll find out' – obviously I knew, because he'd been there before, but… And oh my God, I've never felt anything so wonderful, I was all still glowing with orgasm and then he – ah." She gave a small shudder.

"Oh my – he trimmed the bushes. I *like* this guy."

"Well, if he trimmed the bushes, I watered them like they've never been watered before!"

Marilyn snorted with laughter and Samantha's hand rose to cover her own ladylike giggles.

"I am so proud of you, Samantha. You needed a night like that."

The guilt slammed in at last, cold and bitter. "You shouldn't be proud of this behavior. I'm a grown, married woman, not a college student. I should've known better." Its acidity ate away at her stomach like too much coffee.

"Oh come on," said Marilyn impatiently. "Don't tell me you regret it already."

"But doesn't it make me a slut?" said Samantha. "A whore? An adulteress? All of the above?"

"Are you suddenly a different person than who you were when you decided to engage with him? You made a decision, you carried it out, so what did you think about it then?"

"That I deserve it," answered Samantha in a small voice. "That for so long I hadn't had any – well, I hadn't had any of it; no love, no touching, nothing. I felt that somehow the universe owed me that much and I had a right to it. I felt starved – for passion, for love, for tenderness, and to feel desirable."

"Then I think that makes you a typical woman," said Marilyn resolutely. "But in the middle of all that passion, how did you find time to call me? You sounded so urgent in your message, but I had no idea how urgent it was!" Marilyn was confused but beaming.

"Message?" Samantha said distantly, a look of confusion crossing her face before realization slammed her eyes wide open. "Oh my God! I forgot about the meeting with Ben last night!" She hissed, gripping Marilyn's arm.

"You mean you didn't go? This guy must have been good!"

Shocked, Samantha shook her head. "No – no I went! But I just can't believe that even an amazing romp in the hay made me forget that the DNC asked me to run in the presidential primaries last night!"

Marilyn's mouth fell open. "Seriously? Was this before or after the guy made you cum?"

"Marilyn!" Samantha gasped and then lowered her voice again, "Uh…before."

"And you're considering it?"

"Yes."

"Did you tell the Prick yet?"

"No."

"Oh my, talk about a sticky wicket! When are you going to tell him?"

"This weekend – I'm going home for a couple days. You know, he might even be pleased for me, he was very supportive of my becoming a representative – and he is my husband, he'll want me to do well…" Marilyn let Samantha continue reassuring herself without contradiction. By mutual consent, criticism of Samantha's marriage was off-limits, although Marilyn did get away with calling him the Prick. The cost of curing Samantha's blind spot would probably be the end of their friendship and neither was prepared to pay that price.

By nightfall, during Samantha's flight home, the guilt had taken root like a red weed and developed a voice that was eerily similar to her mother's. *Thinking you need sex is no excuse for adultery and infidelity. Sex is not a need like water or food; no one dies from lack of sex. Calling it a need is just an excuse for weak-willed self-indulgence. If you 'need' it so much, go to your husband, not some random Tom, Dick or Harry you've just picked up in a bar – that's disgusting. And you're a public servant! How do you think your 'public' would feel about your indiscretion? Put some effort into your marriage. You haven't seen Richard for a month; what kind of wife are you? He has needs, which you aren't there to meet, then you go running off screwing strangers because you say your needs aren't being met?*

He doesn't meet my needs whether I'm there or not. Samantha faced off against her conscience. *We haven't had sex in years.*

And whose fault is that, young lady? Her guilt continued its assault. *Put some effort in. Make yourself attractive. A good marriage doesn't just happen, you know.*

Samantha slumped in her seat. All the effort she made receded suddenly into the distant past, and her new guilt flowed fresh. She'd convinced herself anew that it was indeed her fault and she could make it better. With penitential care, she began to make a plan.

Even coming from DC, Samantha reached their marital home before her husband. This gave her time to shower, dress up – or down as it were, light candles and put some music on. Her lacy teddy hid the stretch marks on her stomach and showed off the slender lines of her body. It also, discreetly, held her breasts up. The small flickering flames were kind to her aging skin. With her hair combed out, in this glowing half-light, she could even pass for youthful. Her stomach flipped with nerves as she heard the key grate in the door.

Richard strode in the room, bulky in his suit, a sheaf of mail in his hand. He looked at Samantha, then at the candles.

"What's all this?" He dumped his briefcase next to the spindly legs of the antique side-table and stared at her.

"I wanted to make it pretty – as a surprise – it's been a long time since we've seen each other…" She was unsure whether the 'it' she referred to was the room or herself.

"Well, a better surprise would be heating me up some dinner. I'm starved." He turned his attention to the envelopes in his hand as he walked on. At the doorway, he stopped dead and looked at her with slight distaste.

"And put some clothes on, will you? It's slutty, wearing your underwear in the living room. Make some effort at decorum, why don't you?"

He just got in from work. He's probably tired and stressed. You can't expect him to feel aroused just because you are.

Samantha moved on to Plan B, which consisted of a gracefully flung-together dinner by candlelight; providing an opportunity for them to reconnect through conversation. Richard switched the light on as he entered the dining room and laid some papers next to his place setting. He liked to see his food. As he chewed, he flipped through the documents. Samantha remained invisible to him. After only one mouthful, she lost her appetite and just sat staring at him.

He's probably used to working over dinner. He has routines when you're not here, you know.

But I'm here now.

"You know, we haven't seen each other in over a month," she said, as if observing the weather.

"Yes, I believe you already pointed that out." He didn't look up from his food.

Pretending she could still eat, Samantha twirled her food around her plate.

Try talking about his *life. He's sure to respond to that.*

"I've been watching the financial news. It sounds like the public offering is going well."

"Yes – very, very well. Actually better than I could have ever dreamed, and you know me, I dream big." His eyes hadn't left his papers.

She wished their table were smaller, so that she could take his hand. She sipped her wine instead. "I'm thinking of running for President of the United States."

After a few seconds, Richard looked up from his papers. "What did you say?"

She straightened in her chair and rested her hand on her glass again as she repeated herself. He took off his reading glasses to look at her.

"Oh I see, you're trying to be funny. You think I'm not listening to you."

"No, I'm completely serious. The DNC approached me and asked me to run."

"What are they on, crack?"

Her stomach, cold all evening, burnt abruptly with anger. "No!" she exclaimed, defensively.

"Then are they that desperate to run just anyone?"

"How can you say that?" She was surprised that she wasn't outraged by his reaction – part of her must have been expecting it, after all.

"Well, they asked you, didn't they?" he said reasonably. "So just tell them no, you're not interested or even qualified."

"Actually, I'm thinking of telling them yes." She was well-trained in controlling her voice by her years on the debate team, and would not allow her quaking fear to make it tremble now. Richard leapt to his feet, angrily. His fork clattered on the plate.

"Who the hell do you think you are? Do you actually think you're capable of being President of the United States?"

"Well, I think I'm a pretty good representative." Her voice was mild.

"And the only reason you're a *representative,*" he spat out her official title as if it were fraudulent, "is because I financially backed your campaign and you were able to milk my good name in the community!" He remained standing, fists on the table. She knew better than to show fear, which was like a red rag to a bull.

"I was elected because I have good ideas," she replied quietly.

"You were *elected* because you were my wife. Period."
His finger jabbed the air. "And they thought they were
electing an extension of *me* to be *my surrogate* in DC."

"But I'm on TV, Richard – people actually listen to my
ideas."

"Oh my God, you're so naïve." He sat down heavily, to
her relief. "Did you ever notice they only started calling you
to be on their shows once you got this new look of yours?
They're showcasing some T&A, not your so-called *ideas*."

"Why are you talking to me like this?" She could no
longer keep the tears out of her words.

"Because I want to put some common sense into that
head of yours and get it off this stupid idea."

"But you're hurting me…"

"And you hurt me with these ridiculous ideas, you'll
embarrass me and you'll hurt my company. Listen – the only
reason I got you that house seat is because without Faith here
anymore you just moped around the house crying all the time
and I couldn't stand it any longer." He shoved a few more
mouthfuls in and chewed angrily.

She held the stem of her wine glass between two fingers
and a thumb, wondering how much pressure would snap it.
"I'm a good representative," she said tremulously. "I don't
care what you say."

"No, you're nothing more than a bored housewife filling
the time and pretending to make a difference. As soon as
you get that straight, your crazy ideas of being able to lead a
country will go away and you can go back to your women
conferences and tea parties and whatever else it is you do to
stay busy."

If there had been no truth at all in his words, she
reasoned, tears would not have started rolling down her face.
She sniffed surreptitiously and he glanced up in disgust.

"Oh for chrissakes, don't start crying. You say you want
to be president and then your defense is to *cry*? Word to the
wise – presidents don't cry."

"Well, maybe they should!" she burst out, but he ignored that.

Simply sleeping in the same bed as him that night was the hardest thing in the world for Samantha to do. Her intentions to seduce him were met with scorn and ridicule; now she couldn't even stand having his body a foot away under the same duvet. He seemed to emanate violence, contempt and malice from his pores.

For better or worse, that was their only conversation on the subject that weekend. It was, in fact, their only conversation. She spruced up the garden, he washed his car, she watched TV, he read the papers, she ran on the treadmill, he gesticulated and bellowed his way through a karate routine. She remembered that really, this was how it was between them. Anything else would have involved confrontation, which she'd never win, and scenes, which she hated. His presence in her life was constrictive. Allowing Richard to see the expression on her face made Samantha feel too vulnerable, so the habitual mask of calm settled over her features. Nothing had changed between them, except the belief that it was okay to go on like this or that things might somehow improve. The only difference was that the little feathered bird of hope lay dead at the bottom of its cage. It didn't bear thinking about, so she thought about her work instead.

At mid-seventeen, Samantha acquired a boyfriend and was kissed, in that order. She met Matthew while working on the school newspaper, The Lakeview Gazette. For their first date he took her to see *Grease* and held her hand in the cinema. Samantha identified painfully with Sandy and was aghast when she sacrificed her own true personality to win her man. Over milkshakes, she and Matthew discussed the film's morality. To her delight, he agreed with her.

"Giving up your beliefs for love – that's a very worrying message to send out," he said.

"She changed who she *was* – that can't ever be right...right?" said Samantha.

Once they'd drunk enough sugar to make them slightly hysterical, and roundly condemned the film, they walked to her house hand-in-hand, humming the tunes. She hoped for a kiss, which wasn't forthcoming, but he did say stiffly, "I'd like to see you again," clearly not meaning Monday's editorial meeting.

"Yes, I'd like that," she said awkwardly.

On their third date, he officially asked her to be his girlfriend and when she said yes, brushed her lips with his.

Matthew, as it turned out, was saving himself for marriage. Samantha was disappointed, but determined to respect his choice. She changed her fantasies from stolen embraces in his bedroom, or in unspecified meadows, to tender wedding-night passion in which he slowly stripped away the layers of tulle, gauze and lace in which virginity is traditionally wrapped.

He did eventually kiss her with more enthusiasm. His house overlooked the shore of Lake St. Clair and one sultry August night, they walked together through the scrubby dune grass and stood listening to the water as the sun set. Their solitude, and the thought of everything it could mean, made her veins hammer. When the darkness was complete, they kissed and he 'gave into his lust', as he later put it. They ran their tongues over each other's, licked each other's jaws and necks with exquisite delicacy, and pressed their bodies restlessly together. When they sank onto the sand, his hand skimmed her breast and he leapt away, panting, as if she'd slapped him.

"No – we can't – this is wrong!" he exclaimed hoarsely. He turned his back resolutely and began to walk back to the house. Ashamed and hurt, Samantha stood up, dusted the sand from her dress, and trailed after him.

His church's explanations about 'where to draw the line' was so breathtakingly logical that it would have fitted neatly into *Alice In Wonderland.* Premarital sex being wrong, they argued, anything that led to premarital sex was also wrong, if only through causing lustful thoughts – God's thought-crime. Closed-mouthed kissing did not cause lustful thoughts, because one could kiss family members and friends like that. French kissing and any kind of fondling did. Therefore, until marriage, only closed-mouthed kissing was appropriate.

The flaw in that logic was that being a teenager, being alive, simply having a pulse, all caused lustful thoughts. Nature's determination to reproduce life was not so easily sidestepped. Matthew avoided Samantha's erogenous zones so assiduously that his touch on the inside of her wrist could instantly make her swoon with desire. He only ever 'gave into his lust' (hers was never spoken of) in the dark, then agonized with a guilt that made it all seem ugly and sordid. Living with the sting of frustrated desire, with the emotional slap of abrupt rejection, became normal and even noble in Samantha's world. Once, tentatively, she said, "It hurts me when you suddenly stop and leap away – like we're being disgusting..."

"Then you shouldn't let me start," he snapped, doubled over his aching erection. She knew it only as a bulge in his pants that caused him suffering. Her hands were not welcome to explore or discover its shape, much less ease its longing.

The easy times of working on the paper, chatting over milkshakes, walking together and sharing chaste kisses, were gradually overshadowed by the tug-o-war between desire and refusal. Soon, every date they had was darkened by their furious, furtive longing. Samantha secretly thought it might be simpler if they gave in a little, but to Matthew heavy petting was out of the question. She suspected, rightly, that they couldn't go on in that state.

School work was a relief. The cool order of facts, arguments and logic flowed over her turbulent thoughts, realigning and ordering her. Proving math theorems and finishing with a neat 'Q.E.D.' was satisfying and conclusive; her dates and arguments with Matthew never were.

3

Given that she'd chosen every stick of furniture and thread of soft furnishing in their marital home, Samantha should have liked it more than she did. It was a proper home; of the sort to which her mother's clapboard house had always aspired without having the money to realize. It was well-appointed; deep carpets in pale colors, heavy curtains and covered valances in corresponding shades, polished wood antique furniture, large gilt mirrors, occasional tables bearing lamps, a range of lighting 'scenarios', spotlit works of art on the walls, cushions, and bowls of flowers. It was a show-home, as her marriage was a show-marriage and her face a show-face, under which no throb of life hummed. Her DC apartment, to which she did not invite company, was plain, with unresolved décor. It contained idiosyncratic choices that served practical purposes, not design decisions – a painting which no longer suited the living room in the marital home and which she didn't much like served to liven up a blank wall, a shelf of mismatched books which she wanted in easy reach of her workspace, a blue blanket folded up on the sofa which she wrapped around her in the evenings, and so on. From time to time, she thought she ought to make it more of a home, so that people could drop by and say, "I like what you've done with the place." People said it was women who cared about aesthetics – stylish homes, makeup, clothes, and so on – but it wasn't true, she reflected. Women cared, as men did, about other people's opinions. The marital home was as much Richard's display as it was hers, even if she was the one who organized it.

On Monday evening in her DC apartment, Samantha chewed on salad and stared into the middle distance. She was thinking about Faith, the inequality of the education system, and what the federal government could do to support state governments in fixing it, when the doorbell rang. The sound was so unfamiliar that she checked her phone before hurrying to the door.

"Faith!" Her face lit up as she threw open the door. "Baby – I was just thinking about you. What are you doing here?"

"I just thought it would be a good time to visit my mom." Her daughter grinned and the vibrant, unshakeable *youth* of her caught in Samantha's throat. She hid her sudden emotion in a long hug, after which Faith produced a bottle of Shiraz.

"Every moment is a good time to visit your mom. Come in, sweetheart." Samantha received the offered bottle of wine with a bow.

Faith had recently cut her long black hair close to her head and spiky, making her elfin in appearance. Her layers of flimsy clothes, a compilation more than an outfit, made Samantha smile.

"I had a top like this once," she said, fingering the threadbare cheesecloth sleeve.

"This is yours," Faith said, grinning. "Hold onto clothes long enough, they come back into fashion. Hey, this lighting is harsh – do you have any candles?"

Later, once they'd exhausted Faith's latest college-girl news – and most of the wine consumed in the soft glow of candlelight, Samantha shyly admitted her own.

"Oh, Mom!" Impulsively, Faith leapt over and gave her another hug, planting a fat kiss on her cheek. "I'm so proud of you! You would make a wonderful president!"

"You really think so?"

"I can't imagine anyone better!"

"I wasn't sure it was such a good idea…"

Faith's expression darkened. "Dad?"

Samantha lowered her head. "He did make some good points, honey… I'm not exactly qualified."

"Not qualified?" Her daughter's voice rose in righteous anger.

"Even though I'm in public office, I'm just a junior representative...nothing impressive. I'm still basically just a mother. I mean, there's all my charity work, but everyone does that..."

She watched Faith struggle to master her anger. "Mom, think about it," she said. "In a world where hate brings on more hate and violence brings on more violence, where we have terrorism, suicide bombers, global warming, starvation, poverty, AIDS epidemics – don't you think the world's kind of overdue for some mothering? And charity, for that matter?"

"But it's so feeble..."

"No!' Faith set her glass down abruptly, arms flying as she tried to explain. "You have the skills – you *know* you have the skills, and the intelligence, and Goddammit you have a purity of *desire* to do it that no one else in the race has! It's challenging work, but it's not rocket science – it's for people who understand people and know how to make people work together, and it's not like you don't understand finance and economics – Dad's a prick and you *know* it..."

"Faith..." began Samantha warningly.

"Please – let me finish. You are *qualified*. You are *perfect*. You are exactly what this country needs. And you're drinking my wine."

Samantha laughed. "Thank you, baby. Come here." She extended her arm and Faith snuggled up to lean on her shoulder. "Who's mothering who now?" she teased lightly.

"I suppose I owe you some," said Faith.

Samantha woke up with a throbbing headache as if her skull had been sawed in half. Her breath offended even herself. It must be age catching up – half a bottle of wine never had that effect in her youth. Perhaps it was her change in diet; a salad probably didn't line her stomach as much as a generous helping of meatloaf. As she washed an aspirin down with three glasses of water, she remembered her medication. She seemed to be doing fine without it. Sure she'd slept with a strange man and induced a horrific hangover, but then she'd also given a great interview, raced through her paperwork, and was now in the running for the presidential primaries. Samantha grinned, and then winced with the pain.

There are some advantages to being a woman, after all. At least you get to hide these purple swollen eyelids and blotchy face. Men have to go to work looking as hung-over as they were.

"What the hell... I'm in." She smiled up at Ruth, who stood in the doorway.

"Great!" Ben's voice boomed out of the speakerphone. "You'll be a wonderful candidate."

"Okay, so what do I do first?"

"You'll need to make an announcement. I'll get something set up."

"Great."

"Oh, and we'll have to get you assigned some secret service agents."

Samantha frowned and raised an eyebrow at Ruth, who nodded ruefully.

"Is that really necessary?"

"Absolutely. Okay – catch you later." He hung up and Samantha hit the disconnect button.

"So how do you feel?" said Ruth.

"Honestly? Like I never want to see another drop of wine again. I didn't even have that much – I must be losing my edge..."

"Or perhaps you're not drowning your sorrows so often these days?" suggested Ruth. "You just rest there, Mrs. President. I'll get you another coffee."

"Thanks, Ruth." Samantha smiled gratefully. "Can you hold my calls for a couple hours? I have some planning to do." Despite the purple cloud permeating it, her mind was racing. Faith's comment about the country needing a mother resonated deeply with her. The country wasn't really a business after all; it was a home to three hundred million people. Like a home, it needed good financial management, but also proper care, concern for people's welfare, education and development. Akin to the charities she used to run, it was a not-for-profit organization. Specific practical solutions existed to its problems, if only one assumed that those problems *should* be solved. Even if she didn't get to be president, she could give these plans to the country. It didn't matter who did the work, as long as it got done. She began to scribble, tap on her laptop, run quick calculations through Excel, and make lists.

"Shopping-list for a better future," she wrote at the top of a piece of paper and laughed. It really was as simple as mothering – which was to say, extremely complex.

Ben didn't waste any time. At the press conference the next morning, Samantha stood at the podium, beautifully groomed and dressed, and thought of Faith. Her smile was warm and sincere, illuminating her whole face.

"As of today," she said clearly, "I'm throwing my hat into the ring to become the next President of the United States."

The handful of reporters that had bothered to show up looked back blandly as if waiting for the real news. When no questions followed, she glanced at Ben uncertainly.

"Don't worry," said Ben. "It's just the calm before the storm."

She smiled again, but this time it didn't reach her eyes.

When she got back to the office, a present from Marilyn was lying on her desk next to a huge bunch of exceptionally phallic lilies. The card read: *Sisters are doing it for themselves!* and inside Marilyn had written "You go, girl! So proud of you, future President Friend. Here's something to encourage your new-found independence." She opened the package to find a book with a woman sensuously biting the hand of some off-stage man. *The Ten Visions*, by Olivia Knight, it said in massive text, and then a small subtitle: "An Erotic Romance". She blushed and shoved it in her bag before Ruth's sharp eyes could fall on it. Only Marilyn would consider pornography to be the perfect present for a presidential candidate.

That evening, she pulled the book out again and studied the cover, which declared it 'Erotic Fiction by Women'. By *women*? No one was around to see, so she snuggled herself up on the sofa, pulled a blanket over her legs, and began to read. By the second chapter, the heroine had had sex with two different men, one of whom may or may not have been a ghost. By the third chapter, Samantha was hooked and squirming against the cushions. By the fourth chapter, she was too flushed to read, too excited not to, and thinking longingly of her night with Thomas. Phoning him was out of the question, obviously, but… Up to the age of forty-seven, she'd only slept with two men, and whether the first even counted was entirely subjective. Now it was three.

The prom was held a few months before their exams, in an effort to "get it out the way" before serious studying began. It took her five hours to get ready; showering, shaving, plucking her eyebrows, curling her hair, painting her toenails and fingernails peach to match her dress, applying the full range of makeup before finally fixing her hair. Her mother then zipped her into her dress and they sat together in the living room waiting for Matthew.

"Now, Samantha," began her mom somberly. "I know you're very much in love..."

Samantha's insides recoiled in terror. It was coming: either the don't-have-sex speech or, more appallingly, a stilted, modern conversation about being "careful".

"But don't forget to think about other people, too. Love can make us very selfish, when two people only think about each other. A proper lady always considers the feelings of other people around her and makes an effort to talk to everybody."

Somewhere in the house, Samantha believed, was a little volume entitled "A Proper Lady" from which these pronouncements came.

"Okay, Mom"

Matthew did everything according to every mother's checklist for a true gentleman; he arrived with a corsage (check) and told her she looked very nice (check). He held the car door open (check), but not her chair at dinner (cross). He helped her to her feet for the first dance (check), but stared at his feet the whole time (cross). When the formal waltz finished, the disco music started and he sat out the songs whose lyrics he didn't approve. Samantha vacillated between being an attentive partner and obeying her mother's injunction to pay attention to other people. Leaving Matthew's side to dance with other boys didn't seem right, so she chatted brightly to the other wallflowers and complimented their dresses. Someone had spiked the punch; Samantha recognized the taste of brandy from sips she had stolen at home. She drank it cautiously; interspersed with lots of water (a proper lady is never drunk). Matthew either didn't notice, or he had a better head for alcohol than she did.

The after-party was at Carolyn Schaeffer's house, with colored lights strung all over the huge lawn, tin buckets full of cold beer, tables heaped with candy and punch, floating candles in the pool, and even a hired DJ to keep the records spinning. Samantha was all dressed-up, seventeen, and they played *Dancing Queen*. Matthew thought the lyrics encouraged promiscuity: "You're a teaser, you turn 'em on, leave them burning and then you're gone, looking out for another, anyone will do..."

Because Matthew wouldn't dance with her, she accepted Brad Holcomb's invitation to dance. He was short, sweaty-handed, and inclined to pull Samantha close to his groin, but he served as her passport onto the dance-floor. Afterwards, she extricated herself from his embrace and went looking for Matthew, who was standing with a clutch of boys drinking beer. Instead of awkwardly standing around waiting for Matthew's attention, Samantha mingled. She flitted from group to group, attentive to everyone, a compliment on her lips for every girl, making conversation and socializing properly. An hour or two later, Matthew was nowhere to be found. At two o'clock, the party was thinning, her specially-extended curfew was approaching, and she still couldn't find him. Marilyn's date offered her a lift home, and she accepted. While Samantha hunted for the hostess to say goodbye and leave a message for Matthew, she opened the door to Carolyn's darkened bedroom, and found them both inside.

It took her confused vision a few seconds to even work out what she was seeing in the tangle of limbs, thumping pelvises, and grabbing hands. Nails suddenly dug into buttocks, both heads flung back, two barely-recognizable faces twisted, eyes shut, and mouths open and wailing thinly. Carolyn's breasts were bare and wobbling. As their eyes opened, both heads spun in unison to the rectangle of light.

"I'm sorry – I didn't realize," said Samantha automatically, shutting the door again. Marilyn and her date were already waiting outside, and she was out of the house before Matthew could even find his trousers. Only at home, in her own bed, did she realize that what she had witnessed must have been the moment of their climax.

Numb, she visited Marilyn the next day. Her friend's bedroom was orange at this point; patchy and dark where the black still showed through, with colorful Indian silk scarves pinned on the walls. They sat together on the unmade bed and Marilyn was outraged in a way Samantha couldn't bring herself to be.

"I didn't want to be responsible for him going against his beliefs, though," said Samantha. "So even if he did, at least it's not my fault – I don't think I could have lived with that."

"Screw his beliefs!" bellowed Marilyn in disbelief. "He's gone against *you* – he's a two-timing jerk!"

"But it was probably easier for him to screw the village slut instead of me, he saw us as so pure..."

"Samantha Anderson, that's the first time I've heard you say something downright *mean*. Well done! Now if you can just be that mean about Matthew..."

"But I don't *want* to!" She twisted the blankets between her hands in misery. "And I even know why he did it – we both wanted to do it so much, but it had become impossible to do it together."

"You know what your problem is? You're too understanding."

Marilyn had hit the nail on the head. The problem with understanding people was that one could never just get mad, pure and simple. Everyone knew that men's sexual drives were voracious and uncontrollable. She'd wanted sex so much she could hardly restrain herself, what must he have been feeling? To take her virginity would have been a crime against the purity of their relationship. To get relief with the easy-come-easy-go Carolyn was just that; physical. She understood his logic even before his explanations. By the time he came to beg her forgiveness (which he did by defending his behavior), God had already granted *His* forgiveness, so her own was just a formality and her Christian duty.

"It's humbled me," he said. "I realize now my pride was a sin – I thought I was better than other people because I could resist the sins of the flesh, but now I realize I'm as weak as everyone else."

Alone in her room, she sang along tearfully to *Stand by your man* and *Bridge over troubled water*, again and again. In forgiving his infidelity, she had joined a new grown-up club of sorrowful, understanding women. She had, she felt, ascended to Womanhood.

When his briefly-sated physical needs soon reasserted themselves, they agreed to have sex. His mother worked outside of the home, so his chilly bedroom was to be the scene of their passion. He lit a candle, which had no effect in the pale daylight, and put *Love Song* on the record player. Ironically, after all the months of furnace-hot lust, they were both awkward and unresponsive. He had to make himself ready with his hand. It was the first time she'd seen a penis and was surprised by its ordinariness. They both assumed Samantha required no preparation, which made penetration clumsy and difficult. Carolyn must have known what she was doing when they got together, because Matthew certainly didn't. He could only get a couple of inches in and when he rubbed back and forth, it hurt. Samantha was dry and didn't know she should be wet. She lay on her back, waiting for her virginity to be gone, and he gave a little groan with an orgasm that

49

was more like a sneeze. The song finished shortly after he did. Her hymen remained intact. Samantha surmised that they should have given in when they really wanted each other – it would have been nicer and more natural.

The dictionary defined sex as "penetration and male orgasm", but its definition of 'penetration' didn't specify how much of the penis should be inserted into the vagina in order to count. As a result, Samantha was never certain whether she and Matthew had even had sex. After that abortive experience, they finally broke up and she could mourn the lost perfection of their love without having to confront its reality anymore. To ease her heartache, she flung herself into studying, and that was that.

Or it was almost that. Thanks to Matthew's ineptitude, the results of Samantha's finals surpassed everyone's expectations, including her own. She flew to the top of her class with straight A's in all the preliminary exams. She barely had a chance to even think about college before the counselor called her and her mother in to discuss the merits of various studies and universities.

"She's our top debater, her memory is clearly excellent – while this is not a traditional choice for females, I think your daughter should seriously consider undergraduate studies in pre-law and then eventually seek a law degree," he said to her mother.

"Isn't it too late to apply?" asked Samantha.

He looked over his glasses at her, as if surprised that she was even in the room.

"Not if you work hard on your applications," he said sternly before returning his attention to her mother. "Now..." He opened a drawer and pulled out some brochures. "She might want to consider a state college as opposed to a private university..."

Samantha sat in stunned silence as the counselor and her mother leaned over the brochures and mapped out her future. *Her* future, which apparently she had no say in whatsoever.

Marilyn was already changed for gym and rearranging her leotard straps when Samantha rushed into the locker room and quickly stripped.

"Thanks for the book – I think," she said with a grin. "It didn't exactly make it easy to sleep, but... Where do you *find* this stuff?"

"Oh – here and there," said Marilyn vaguely, digging in her gym bag.

"I'm so excited!" Samantha went on. "I have so many great ideas for my campaign. Okay, the press conference was dry, but I'm sure it's just the beginning. Did you see it, by the way?"

"Yeah," said Marilyn, her face still averted. "It was in the paper – page twenty-seven. Yup, I read it."

Samantha sat down in her leotard, deflated. "You don't seem very excited for me."

"I am, Sam, really." Marilyn met her eyes briefly and looked away again. "But I'm afraid I've got some bad news."

"Oh, Marilyn..." Samantha laid a hand gently on her shoulder. "What is it, honey? Is it man-trouble?" Her friend didn't respond. "Or has something happened at work?"

"No," said Marilyn reluctantly. "The bad news is about you."

Samantha froze. Marilyn pulled her hand out of her bag and handed over a few printed sheets of paper. Samantha glanced at them, did a double-take, and looked closer. Her hand rose to cover her mouth.

"Shit..." she whispered. "*Shit!* Where did you get these?"

Marilyn pointed to the internet address printed at the top of each page. www.babesblowingbigones.com

"Shit..." said Samantha again. "How did this happen? Whose website is this?" Her voice began to rise in panicked pitch as she turned the pages over hoping to find an answer there.

"I don't know, honey. It popped up on my screen last night while I was doing some...research."

Samantha's blood was vacillating between hot and cold as she looked at the image of her own face embracing Thomas's swollen member. "But – it must be a trick – I didn't see a camera."

"Maybe a camera-phone?" suggested Marilyn bleakly. "I mean, you look kind of preoccupied in the pictures."

Samantha covered her face, her voice muffled by her palms. "I just announced I'm running for president and now I'm on the internet giving a guy a... a..."

"A blow job," supplied Marilyn.

"For the whole country to see!" Her voice had now reached a level best described as shrill.

"Maybe not – we might be able to get these taken down – do you have his number? His name, at least?"

"Of course I have his name," snapped Samantha, "I'm not that much of a slut! I've got his card." She dug around in her purse and slid it out. "He's a lawyer at Mason, Peterson and Steinborn."

"Call him...now," said Marilyn, offering her iPhone for the call...just in case it was traced. "If he's the one that posted these pics, you might be able to convince him to take them down by threatening a slander suit. Trust me, I know this firm. He can't afford this kind of publicity."

"What should I say?"

Marilyn shot her a look. "Samantha, your career may very well be hanging in the balance. I'm sure you'll think of something."

"I can't call here." She said, glancing around. "It's too public."

"Come on," said Marilyn, throwing her clothes on over her leotard. "Quick, get dressed. My office is just around the corner. You can call from there."

Samantha was fully dressed in record time, her stomach knotted with panic. Every second they lingered might mean someone else saw the pictures.

"Let's go," said Marilyn. She'd slipped her black office-attire skirt and jacket over her leotard, which showed in a neat plunging strip.

"You're kind of pouring out of your leotard," said Samantha.

"Yes, I know. It looks hot. I'm not the only one with a reputation to maintain." She winked.

"That's not funny."

"I know. I'm sorry, honey. You know how I resort to levity in intense situations."

Samantha spent the car journey groaning, staring out the window in disbelief, burying her face in her hands, and swearing under her breath.

"I know you were kind of blown away by the whole experience," said Marilyn, "but think, Samantha...did you at any time notice a camera nearby?"

"No. I mean, I haven't given a...umm..." began Samantha tensely.

"Blow job."

"Yes – blow-job... in over fifteen years. I was really, really focused on returning his – umm..."

"His penis."

"Yes – his, um, penis – in one piece." She banged her finger hard against her lips. "Oh please, please, don't let the papers get hold of this – please let us get it off this stupid site in time..."

4

Samantha stood in the elevator, clutching her elbows, watching the numbers slowly rise. Every second counted. With each passing moment, someone could be stumbling across that site and recognizing her face. Marilyn stole curious sidelong glances at her. Samantha had always been such a prude that it was difficult, even with pictures as evidence, to imagine her giving head.

"So why didn't you tell me he was so big?" she asked.

"Oh – yeah," Samantha replied distractedly. Her body was straining upwards as if she could encourage the elevator to go faster. "Very tall. Probably over six foot three, I guess."

"No – I mean his package. It was huge."

"Oh, my God, yes!" Samantha turned abruptly. "I wasn't sure – I mean, I'm not actually that experienced – but I didn't know they got that big. Is that normal?"

"In my *substantial* experience, that's about as big as they come."

"I'd hope so. I can't imagine it getting much bigger." Her eyes drifted back to the numbers, which had stopped at forty. "Come on, come *on*," she muttered, as the doors slid open.

She moved aside to let someone step in without taking her eyes off the numbers. Marilyn glanced at the man's ruffled blonde hair, smooth young face and smart suit, then at the buttons next to her.

"Can I help you out here?" she murmured.

"69, please." He winked. "No kidding."

"Oh, I think I can help you out there…"

Samantha glared at her, but Marilyn's eyes were locked on the elevator's other occupant, a cat-getting-the-canary smile creeping across her face. As the two women stepped out onto Marilyn's office floor, Samantha's smooth friend pocketed his business card with a smirk.

"And you didn't want me to wear the leotard."

Samantha ignored her. Marilyn's predatory approach to sex never ceased to amaze her, but right now she was too uptight to comment. Throughout the entire rush over here, all she could think about was the pictures. It had only just struck her that she was about to speak to Thomas again for the first time since their night together and her panic was mingling with school-girlish nerves.

After entering Marilyn's office and securing the door, Samantha dialed Thomas's office. She stood there, using her friend as a point of focus while she listened to the repetitive ring on the line. Just before she lost it completely and flung the phone against the wall, she heard a click that replaced the ringing with his voice on the other end.

"This is Thomas." His voice sounded cocky, relaxed. It annoyed her to no end.

"Thomas? Samantha." She waited for the sound of recognition in his voice. Her eyes narrowed as it took a moment longer than she liked.

"Samantha! What a surprise! How are you?" Why didn't he sound ashamed? He could at least have the decency to act as if he were.

"Well, let's see…I've been better, actually. It appears that we've both become quite the hot item on the internet these days." She could barely keep herself from screaming. It took another moment for Thomas to respond.

"I'm afraid I don't follow you. The Internet?"

"Yes Thomas, the Internet. At this moment, I'm looking at some pretty graphic images of you and I doing…what we did…at the Georgetown Inn the other night, and they're printed from this classy little website called," Samantha had to squint to read the small print, "www.babesblowingbigones.com."

"I-I..don't understand."

"Did you have anything to do with this? Did you actually do this to me?" Her voice was again bordering on shrill. She struggled to dial it back. The adrenalin of her panic translated more easily into anger than she would ever have thought possible.

"Me? Wait, I-"

"Because if you had anything to do with this, Thomas – anything at all - I will have your *ass* in a sling! You're not the only one who has access to an entire legal team, you know." Marilyn stood at the door, mouth agape, watching her typically diffident friend transform before her very eyes into a tigress on wheels.

"Hold on, Samantha, I-"

"I'm a congresswoman for God's sake…a *congresswoman*, Thomas. Do you have any idea what this will do to my career?" She paused a moment, breathing heavily, heart pounding.

The momentary silence on the line was deafening.

"Are you finished?" When Samantha didn't respond right away, Thomas continued, "Okay, I'm going to speak now, and I need you to listen. Will you do that for me, Samantha?"

"Yes."

"First off, I had nothing to do with pictures of us being published on the Internet. What's more, I have no idea how they were even taken. Seriously, Samantha, you're not the only one whose career is on the line here." After a few seconds of silence, he ventured further, "Are you sure they're even us? I mean, sometimes people alter images and put people's heads on other people's bodies."

"Yes Thomas. They are most definitely of us." She let out a long sigh then, deflated. "I don't know what to do now. If you didn't post them, who did? Who took them?"

"I don't know."

Their conversation was abruptly interrupted by the ringing of her own cell phone. "Excuse me," she said stiffly, pulling it out to check the caller ID. *Ben Morehouse* flashed on her screen. Her hand shook as she stared at it. "Oh… shit…" she whispered slowly, handing Marilyn her iPhone with Thomas still waiting on the other end and flipping open her own. Samantha swallowed hard before uttering, "Hello?"

Ben didn't blast her over the phone, just requested her immediate attendance at an emergency meeting. His tone of voice said it all.

"He wants to execute me in person," said Samantha to Marilyn.

"She'll call you back." Marilyn clicked the "end call" button and regarded her friend carefully. "How are you doing, Samantha? Do you need to sit down?"

An hour later, Samantha's face was attentive and contrite as Ben bellowed his way through a tirade. She sat in her own visitor's chair while he pounded her desk and strode up and down her office. Her years of experience at listening to angry men taught Samantha they usually needed to shout for a while before any solution could be raised. Cynthia sat in similar silence.

"Okay," he said at last, calming down and rumpling his hair. "We need to do some major damage-control here."

"For me?" asked Samantha.

"No, for the party. You're toast. We just have to distance ourselves from you as soon as possible and just hope we have some celebrity break-up that the press can stay focused on for a while."

"Brad and Angelina?" suggested Cynthia.

Ben stopped abruptly and gave her a sharp look. "Would they do it?"

"Who knows? They're very loyal to the party – but there are the children to consider."

"What should I do?" Samantha tried to keep her voice practical.

"You're going to withdraw from the race, resign your seat, go back to Michigan and live off your husband's millions in obscurity," said Ben acidly. "What do *you* want?"

Samantha was about to reply, when she realized he didn't mean her. Ruth hovered anxiously in the doorway.

"Sam – if you've finished – it's your husband on line two," Ruth said bleakly.

Ben and Cynthia looked at each other, then Samantha, and took their cue to leave. As the door closed behind them, Samantha picked up the phone and closed her eyes. Richard began to shout almost immediately. She sat with one hand over her face while the other held the phone a few inches away from her ear – partly to lower the volume of her husband's yelling, partly to hide the sound of her sobs.

Even after he hung up, she couldn't stop the torrential tears. She wept for the lie that her marriage had become and that she could see no choice but to return to it. She wept for the damage she'd caused to the party and her shredded hopes. Mostly, she wept for all the people she thought her plans could have helped, that might not get that chance of schooling, training, health care, and public transport she had planned to offer them, just because some middle-aged woman had experienced a serious lapse in judgment.

Outside, Ruth's heart wrenched as she listened to the tiny, telltale sounds. After half-an-hour, she pulled a bottle of Rescue Remedy out her bag and stepped into Samantha's office, closing the door behind her. Samantha looked up, her face ruined, tears streaming.

"All those people," she choked out. "All those people whose lives might have been better and now will be worse… Oh, Ruth, what have I *done*?"

Ruth bit her lip. "It's nothing Ben hasn't done himself, I'll wager," she said with thinly veiled anger. "Now open up…" She squirted the remedy into Samantha's mouth and patted her shoulder. "Come on, now. It's not the end of the world. Go wash your face; it'll make you feel better."

Some work still needed doing, as a member of congress if not as a presidential candidate. Even if she resigned tomorrow, today she still needed to reply to her constituents' mail and finish drafting the monthly newsletter; someone else might deliver her proposed bill on maternity leave, but she'd done the research and had to write it; seven local charities had requested federal funds and she should process those before she went. Not answering the various journalists' queries would leave the party open to attack. Leaving immediately, with a cardboard box and a dramatic resignation, would hurt dozens of committees, projects, local businesses, and charities. Not finishing her reports and putting down the results of her research would leave a mess for her successor and a lot of work to repeat. She worked hard and fast until ten o'clock, leaving a neat paper trail for the next person to follow, and finally admitted to herself she'd simply have to carry on during the storm of the next day.

A miserable, windy October morning tore at her hair and clothes as Samantha stepped from her apartment block, gym bag in hand. A young woman with thin ash-blonde hair and a small, neat body was standing with her arms tightly folded against the driving chill wind. Her suit was drenched.

"Congresswoman St. Clair?" She asked.

"Yes?"

The woman extended a frozen hand. "I'm special agent Hope Seward. I've been assigned to be your Secret Service protection."

"Oh, well that's hardly necessary now, since I'm stepping down soon. I'm just heading to the gym, I'll be perfectly safe. You probably need to get yourself dried off."

"I'm sorry, ma'am, that's not an option," replied Hope. "I've been assigned to do whatever it takes to ensure your safety, which includes accompanying you wherever you go."

Hope took Samantha's bag, opened the right rear passenger door of a waiting limousine and motioned for her to enter. Samantha leaned in and stared at the plush interior.

"This is ridiculous, though – I'm about to withdraw from the race – all this security is such a waste. The only person who wants to kill me is me."

Hope didn't smile at her attempted joke. "While that may be the case, Ma'am, until I'm reassigned, I'm your protection."

"At least let me sit up front with you," pleaded Samantha.

"Negative, Ma'am. Protocol dictates that you ride in back." The ghost of a smile flashed across Hope's face as she held the door, waiting. Samantha slid in and looked at her new agent with a rueful smile.

"I feel like such a fraud. This may be your shortest assignment ever."

"Yes, ma'am," said Hope, before closing the door. "Seatbelt, please." Hope placed Samantha's gym bag into the Limo's trunk and quickly slid in to the driver's seat.

"Are you familiar with my situation?" Asked Samantha, clicking the buckle in place.

"Yes, ma'am, I am."

"Please call me Sam."

"No ma'am. Which gym, please?"

Samantha gave Hope the necessary information and settled back in the seat. She regarded Hope's stiff posture and attempted to break the ice a bit. "You must be pretty low down the Secret Service totem pole if they assigned you to me."

"Yes, ma'am. Second year agent."

On each trip to the gym, Samantha and Marilyn worked the toning circuit, then on Mondays came the Stairmaster,

Wednesdays the treadmill, and Fridays the exercise bikes. This particular Friday found them pedaling furiously alongside each other.

"Why do you have to resign your seat? So you had extramarital sex. Welcome to the human race. What's the big deal?"

"What do you mean?" panted Samantha. She had the bike set to the steepest incline, so that the burning pain in her legs would replace any other distress she felt, but it only half-worked. "Infidelity is a big deal."

"Let me tell you this, if every congressman who had extramarital sex resigned today, you could hold their next session in the handicap stall in the women's restroom." She took one hand off the handlebars, her fingers rising and falling as she mentally counted through them.

Samantha's program went onto a cool-down plateau and she took a few deep breaths as the pain eased up. "I appreciate your insight into the sexual behaviors of the US Congress," she said dryly, "however I still have to do what's best for my party and what's best for my marriage."

"Fuck your party and *fuck* your marriage! There, I've said it, and if you ditch me for it you're a goddamned fool. What has the party, or that *prick* you call your husband, done for you lately?"

Sam's bike spun to a halt and she sat up, toweling off her forehead and sipping from her water bottle while she considered her reply.

"I have to take responsibility for my own actions," she said at last. "Let's face it – I humiliated the party and my husband – Richard has the biggest deal in his company's history on the table right now, and this is really bad timing for him. It's bad timing for the party, as well. The best thing I could do for both is to resign and fall off the face of the earth."

"This is *so* unfair," said Marilyn. "Men sleep around like sailors on shore leave and you do it just one time and you have to resign?"

"The difference," Samantha pointed out, "is that my 'one time' is flying around the internet for the whole world to enjoy."

By the end of the day, her mountain of work was barely dented, despite her speediest efforts. Her personal belongings were neatly piled in a cardboard box and sitting on her now-barren desk. She couldn't bear the thought of all that work left unattended to in her absence. Her indiscretion had likely already hit the news, and by Monday, reporters would be camping outside the building. It would surely be better for the party if they didn't see her coming into work – and better for her if they didn't catch her leaving with a box and a potted plant.

Faith was waiting for her outside her apartment.

"You heard then?" said Samantha softly.

Her daughter nodded. "I thought maybe you could use some company tonight."

Samantha unlocked the door, set down the box, and burst into tears as Faith's arms enfolded her.

"I guess Dad's not exactly singing *Stand by your Woman*," she said grimly.

"Oh, baby." Samantha gave a half-smile and touched Faith's face gently. "He's so angry."

"Angry that you had sex with another man or angry that it might hurt his business?"

Samantha shrugged wearily and kicked off her heels. She wandered over to the fridge, opened the door and stared at its disparate contents. Gloom seemed to settle in all the empty spaces. "I had carry-out at the office, but if you're hungry, I can fix up an omelet."

"I've eaten. You don't need to look after me right now, Mom; I'm here to look after *you*."

Samantha began to cry again. "I've got no one left to look after," she said, fumbling blindly in the cupboard for glasses. "I was going to look after the whole country, all my ideas, even if I didn't get elected – I thought I had a platform – I had all these ideas…'

"You've got yourself to look after," said Faith gently. "When did you last do some of that?"

Samantha hid her face in her hands, but Faith pried her fingers away. "There's no shame in sadness, Mom. Come on, you have a good cry and I'll open some wine and we'll chat about it when you're ready."

Twenty minutes later, both women were settled on the sofa with half a glass each of red wine in their bellies. Samantha was more composed. Faith held her free hand, playing with her fingers as she spoke.

"Don't apologize. Don't drop out of the race. Don't resign your seat," she said.

"I have to. I'm a disgrace to the party and to our family. It's the right thing to do."

"Mom, I know how Dad treats you. I know how things have been at home. Do you honestly feel that what you did was wrong?"

Samantha stared at her glass for a long time before lifting her head and meeting Faith's eyes. "Honestly? No, I don't."

"Why?" pressed Faith.

"Because I need affection – I've been starved of love, of passion, of intimacy, for years and years and years. And it suddenly occurred to me that I wasn't prepared to go to my grave without ever feeling any of that again. I didn't leave your Dad because I thought *that* would be the wrong thing to do. Maybe I should've, but I thought it was wrong. And then – being with this other man – others say it was wrong, but it's not as if I'd planned it – I just needed to be touched,

more than I ever realized. If there was any affection or
passion in our marriage, I don't think it would have
happened."

"In a nutshell, then, why?" prompted Faith again.

"Because I'd been starved of passion and taught to accept
it as it stood, and then suddenly realized that I couldn't
anymore."

Faith leaned back on the sofa with an air of resolution.
"So tell the country what you just told me," she said. "Don't
resign."

Samantha shook her head. "They won't understand,
baby. And unless you're in the situation yourself, you can't
possibly understand how it feels."

"Do you really think you're the only woman in the
country that's in this position?"

Samantha stared at her incredulously.

"And thanks to the 19th amendment," Faith went on
brightly, "half the voters are women. Actually, more than
half. Women make up fifty-one percent of the country's
population, and more women tend to vote than men. Mom,
women always feel as if they're alone in their suffering – it's
the same with everything: accidental pregnancies,
miscarriages, abuse, unhappy marriages – because
everyone's so busy keeping up a brave front that they never
admit the truth. And the moment one of us finally steps up
and tells the painful truth, every other woman is going to say
'yes, me too, me too'."

"So what are you saying?"

"That most of your voters will understand all too well
what you're going through. Do this democratically, Mom.
Let *them* decide if you're still a good candidate."

The storm broke on Saturday morning. Once more,
sharing a bottle of wine with Faith had left Samantha's head
pounding. She regretted waking up even more when she saw
the papers. Her official congressional portrait was on every

front page. Obscenity laws prevented them showing the money shot, but the internet was unfettered. Gloom pressed on her shoulders as she Googled her own name and discovered the photos appeared higher up on the list than her congressional home page. She found that even as she flipped through them in a sort of sick fascination, she was intrigued by how lovely she looked.

You're ridiculous! Her inner critic had arrived, right on schedule. *You're more concerned about how you look than if everyone sees you going down on someone?*

No! But if they are going to see it, at least I look alright...

For a whore.

That's cruel!

It's true.

Is not. Whores get paid.

She was pleased at getting the last word in on an argument, until she remembered that she was arguing with herself. Her perplexed expression was broken by Ruth's appearance in her office doorway. Ben was on line one.

"I've ordered a press conference at two p.m.," he informed her brusquely. "This is getting way out of hand – we can't wait until Monday. Our press office is emailing your statement over."

"It's already arrived," said Samantha. "I don't even get to write my own speech?"

"Jesus, Samantha, don't be difficult. I can't prevent you from tweaking it if you want, but don't mess this up any more than you have already, okay?"

She printed out the speech and reviewed it over a strong cup of coffee.

"As of today, I am withdrawing from the presidential race and resigning my position as a member of Congress. This is a decision that has not been undertaken lightly, but in the face of recent news coverage, I feel I have no choice. My actions were rash, and no matter how bitterly I regret them, I cannot undo the damage. The party will survive without me, of course. My main concern right now is my family. With this in mind, I ask for the press's forbearance during the difficult time ahead for us. We will get through this together somehow, God willing. But I would ask you to respect our efforts to recover in privacy. Thank you. Goodbye."

The press office's intentions were clear: dissociate her from the party and persuade the press to leave the story alone. She'd always had a knack for quotations and proverbs, and now they came flooding into her mind: people in glass houses, out of sight out of mind, when lovely woman stoops to folly, let those without sin, the scarlet letter… She paced about the room, smoothed her hair, put on a musical playlist from her computer, and applied her war-paint.

While her announcement of her intention to run for president had been met with relative indifference, the journalists and photographers were out in full force to consume her public disgrace. *Carrion crows*, she mused, keeping her face poised. She tapped the microphone for silence.

"Good afternoon," she began. The right tone of voice now was imperative: calm, a little subdued, low and strong. Just the facts, ma'am.

"First off, I'd like to make it clear that I am neither resigning my congressional seat nor withdrawing from my bid for the Presidency. I have not come here today to step down but to simply explain my actions."

In the corner of her eye, she could see Cynthia and Ben staring at each other in disbelief, but she held her steady gaze for the press.

"No one outside of my situation could possibly understand the reasons I did what I did. I have, however, come to realize that my situation is not unique – although I wish it was. I wish all women felt loved by their husbands. I wish that not one of us felt ourselves slowly dying inside for lack of one tender gesture, one loving kiss, and one concerned or interested word. I wish no marriages were empty shells that we maintain in an effort to appear happy, inspiring others to feel as if they're alone in a void. Well, guess what; it's not only you, and it's not only me.

"You've all seen the photographs of me that appear pornographic. They are, in fact, a private sexual moment that should have never been witnessed by anyone else. I'm not sure who took the photographs, nor who posted them on the internet, but I would like to think that he or she would hesitate if the person in them were their mother or sister. I was unaware that photos were being taken, and I assert that these particular photographs do not show the truth. In reality, the event was not at all pornographic. It was gentle, tender, loving, and beautiful. For one night, I felt like a woman, and that was a wonderful thing for my heart, my mind, and my soul to feel again. I discovered that night that I needed to finally and fully be a woman.

"Maybe there are better ways to find out. But I thought I was doing the right thing by staying with my husband; even after my every effort to make our marriage work had long since failed. I was brought up by my mother to stand by my man, and I swear I tried. I thought I could cope with celibacy for fifteen years – fifteen lonely, heart-breaking, confusing years when everything I tried failed. I thought I could cope without any tender loving care. I thought I could accept withering on the vine, knowing the next embrace I got would be the grave's.

"Well guess what, I was wrong. And I didn't even know it until it was too late. I was so starved of affection, of love, of passion, that when a man showed genuine tender interest in me, when that man found me attractive as a person and a woman, and when that man was enraptured by my body which I had so long considered dead – I fell, hook line and sinker. I fell because while I thought I could survive without love, I finally knew that I couldn't.

"Maybe my discovering this the hard way, and so publicly, will help others who are suffering. I am speaking to the women out there. Maybe you think you don't need love – but you do. Maybe you think you can cope without your husband ever touching you – but you can't. Maybe you think you can manage without a thank you, a how-are-you, a sorry, a kind gesture – but you can't. It hurts. And if you're a married man, think about this: with my example all over the press and the internet, maybe this is a good time to start being loving to your wife again. Because I'm *not* the only one. There are others who can no longer cope with decades of indifference, and they will surface. I've just given them a face."

The questions bubbled up, but she raised a hand for silence.

"I have one more thing to add. I admit having had extramarital sex and I have explained why. This is *all* I have to say about the subject. I will give no intimate details. I will answer no further questions about it. Ever. Thank you."

As she walked away from the uproar, Ben grabbed her arm tightly in full view of the photographers.

"By the time we're done with you," he growled, "Monica Lewinski will be viewed as a saint."

Samantha pried his fingers off her arm as she said coldly, "You do whatever you have to."

Cynthia hurried after her. "Samantha – wait. I totally sympathize with what you did, but I have a job to do, and that will be to destroy you. Do you understand that?" Samantha nodded and left. As she reached the lobby, her cell phone rang, flashing *Home-MI*. Richard had finally found it within himself to pick up a phone. She pressed 'reject' and slipped it back in her purse. At the door, she paused with her hand against the glass, stared at the dreary weather outside, turned around, and headed back up to her office. She had a lot of work to do.

5

The streets were dark as Hope guided the limousine from the office back to Samantha's apartment.

"So, Agent Seward, what did you think of my statement at the press conference today?"

"With all due respect, I'm not allowed to provide my opinion on political issues."

Samantha sighed. Being accompanied everywhere by someone who wasn't allowed to chat was alienating. "If I'm soliciting your opinion, surely it's completely appropriate?"

"It was an interesting and thought-provoking statement, ma'am," Hope said carefully.

"Is that all the opinion you have on the subject?"

Hope took a few moments to choose her words while Samantha sat in patient silence. "I think you hit on something most people will be able to relate to."

"I see." She looked at the agent expectantly, waiting for an elaboration that didn't come. "Well, thank you for your insight, Agent Seward…"

"In fact," Hope continued, "I know my mother would have related to what you said."

"Really? How?"

Hope's eyes stayed firmly on the road while her jaw tightened. "I believe she died of loneliness in the end," she said softly. "My dad abandoned us for some floozy when I was ten and we never heard from him again. They never actually got divorced and my mom had this idea that because she was still married… I tried, you know. I tried to be a friend to her, but she was still so lonely. A daughter can't be a partner, no matter how hard she tries. She should've had someone in her life."

"No woman is an island," Samantha said wryly. "My mom was alone, too. Funny, I never thought about it much when I was growing up."

A warm silence of shared thoughtfulness filled the car for a few blocks.

"She was still a fighter, though, my mom," Hope said. "She was a teacher – in the worst areas with the wildest kids. She was a great teacher, but she wouldn't follow the money to the better schools. She said to always do what matters most, not what pays best. So she drummed it into me to do something that *mattered* with my life."

"Protecting me matters?" said Samantha disbelievingly.

Hope shot her a burning look. "If you're standing up for sexual equality, you *matter*, Samantha St. Clair. "

Hope paused a moment before continuing, "So what did your mom teach you?"

"Well, to be a proper lady, mostly. I'm not so sure she succeeded. And she taught me to put others above myself, which is a dual-edged sword, and I don't seem to be able to kick the habit. Somehow that idea ended up shaping my life, for better or worse." She thought of all the times she'd put Richard's needs ahead of her own, never getting - or asking - for a return on all her habitual self-sacrifice. It hadn't done either of them much good, she reflected.

"Well, you're a congresswoman, and presidential candidate. Not a bad life to have shaped."

Samantha grinned. "There is that. I don't think she'd have liked this publicity much, though. It's not very ladylike."

Samantha arrived at her office at dawn on Monday morning, not wanting any journalists to see her carrying her cardboard box of possessions back in. By the time she returned from the gym, Ruth had already unpacked everything for her. Samantha sat down in her chair and swiveled it around to study the room in satisfaction.

"Thanks, Ruth." She studied her desk, puzzled. "Something's missing."

Ruth disappeared and returned holding a framed photo of Richard. "I took the liberty of removing this – I thought you might not need it. He's phoned three times, by the way."

"Just keep holding his calls – I'll phone him when I'm ready."

"And the photo?" Ruth waggled it in the air and Samantha stretched her hand out for it.

"I like the frame," she called defensively as Ruth left.

She studied the photo, which she'd taken herself ten years ago. Richard's hair was still thick and black, his skin more golden and less lined than now. She realized, as she examined it, that Richard had also aged and not particularly well.

"I don't need you scowling at me day in and day out," she informed the photo, shaking it. She opened the back and pulled it out, returning the empty frame to its usual place. She'd find something else to put in it soon enough. She studied the photograph once more before filing it, and him, in the trash can. His eyes met the camera, frowning, as if to say "What are you doing *now*, woman?" Samantha took a ballpoint pen and poked them out.

"Can I get you anything? A dead chicken, maybe? A ball of wax? Some pins?" Ruth was in the doorway with her coffee and a piece of paper.

Samantha chuckled. "Maybe his head on silver platter," she said.

"How about the numbers instead?"

Thoughts of Richard vanished instantly. "What? How bad?"

"You've moved *up* – from two percent to six percent."

"Are you serious?" Samantha straightened in her chair, eyes wide.

"Of course. You also passed Johnson and Winters, and you're now in sixth place in the polls."

Samantha's chair shot back from her desk as she gave herself a few celebratory spins.

"And that isn't even the best part," Ruth went on, her face now splitting into a grin.

Samantha stopped abruptly. "What do you mean? What else can there be?"

"Donations to your campaign are coming in hand over fist."

"From *who*?"

"I guess the "desperate housewife" constituents have decided to reallocate some of their grocery money so they can participate in the political process."

"*Yes!*" Samantha punched the air and sent her chair into another rotation.

Ruth chuckled. She'd never worked for anyone with so much poise and so little pose.

Outside the office, Ruth's phone started ringing.

"If that's Richard, tell him I'm very busy and important and I can't be disturbed."

Richard was on the news that evening. *It was only a matter of time; you can't avoid hearing what he has to say forever.* Her daughter echoed her words almost as she thought them and squeezed her hand tightly. Samantha flashed a grateful smile.

"Mr. St. Clair," the reporter was asking, "do you have any response to your wife's claim that you drove her to infidelity by neglecting her physical needs?"

Richard leaned forward and spoke into the microphone. "Obviously I'm outraged. My wife gets caught committing an immoral act, and then publicly declares that it's my fault. Apparently, the minimal time she's spent in Washington has already had its effects if she thinks she can spin her depraved behavior into something that's my responsibility."

"But what about her claim that you didn't meet her physical and emotional needs?" persisted the reporter.

Richard's face changed. He was giving the reporter his full attention now. "Samantha and I made love on a regular basis," he said slowly. "Hard as it is for me to talk in public about our private life, that's the facts. What I wouldn't give her was deviant, raunchy sex. Why, just a week ago…" He halted his sentence abruptly, as if reluctant to spill the filthy details. He shook his head. "I think that's why she strayed – what I wouldn't do for her – those kinds of perversions. Excuse me." He left abruptly.

"Bullshit…" breathed Samantha, staring at his tiny figure on screen disappearing into the back of his waiting car. "That filthy *liar*! He hasn't touched in me in God knows how long! Now he's telling the whole world I'm a pervert?"

"Mom…" Faith's arm, slung around her, pulled her into a squeeze. "Don't worry about it… The truth will come out."

"I hope so. Well, at least I don't need to rely on his money."

Faith raised her eyebrows.

"Didn't I tell you? Oh, baby, such exciting news!" She snapped the TV off with the remote and turned to face her daughter. "I'm up to six percent in the polls – I jumped *four percent* in one weekend! – and the money's rolling in, so I don't need the DNC's money – I wouldn't get any by the way, Ben's out for my blood – and I don't need your father's money either – which is just as well, considering I've publicly cuckolded him, while informing world that he wasn't giving me any." She winced, half-laughing. "Of all the ways to hammer a man's ego, I think I just hit the top three."

"I'm so happy for you, Mom – but don't blow it."

"Too late for that," sniggered Samantha, then clapped her hand over her mouth. "I can't believe I just said – you're my *daughter* – sorry, Faith."

Faith was giggling. "You know what I mean – you obviously made a connection with the female voters by showing them you're a woman, so don't mess it up now."

"How would I mess it up?"

"By running for president as a man."

Samantha looked pointedly down at her body and waved an expressive hand. "Uh – Faith – *mother* – your female parent – the one who's a woman…?"

"But don't be a woman pretending to be a man, who says she can behave like a man."

"I'm lost."

Faith crossed her legs as she turned to face her mother directly. Her spiky hair made her thin face appear heart-shaped and Samantha's eyes softened with love.

"Don't go up there and say in a roundabout way, 'I can be as tough as a man, as determined as a man, as strong as a man.' You have to be more authentic than that."

"And what do you want me to say instead?"

Faith's expression grew luminous. "Change the dialogue, Mom. Make it so men have to say, 'I'm as compassionate as a woman, as caring as a woman, as intuitive as a woman.' You can do this. By behaving like the woman you are, you have the power to change the landscape of American politics." She grinned and with feigned nonchalance took a sip of her wine.

"How do I do that?" asked Samantha, bewildered.

"Just follow your heart, Mom. Don't play by their rules, ever. Do what *you* would do, regardless of what they do."

They sat in silence, drinking their wine and twirling their glasses around by the stem, both mother and daughter with the same expression of distant thoughtfulness.

"I don't want to throw money about in a big look-at-me parade," said Samantha, "I really hate the PR bullshit strategy of *creating* photo opportunities instead of actually doing anything."

"A website's cheap," said Faith. "Free, if you do it yourself."

"Oooh – good idea, honey! Hey, do you think you could help me…?"

Faith was grimacing. "I'm really, really sorry, Mom – but I've got finals coming up."

"Of course. You need to study." Samantha felt abruptly downcast. Faith's support was so comforting, like a trampoline beneath her, that it was easy to forget her daughter had a life of her own to live.

"But it's not hard – it's not rocket science, really. If a twelve year-old can build a website, then I'm confident you'll have no problem. There are tons of books available to teach you how, and programs that'll do most of it for you."

When Faith left, Samantha Googled 'web design'. "Start planning on paper," the website advised.

"Good," she said aloud. "I can do that." She got out a pen, a legal pad, and set to work.

6

Senator Brown leaned back in the chair in front of Ben
Morehouse's desk, hands in his pockets, eyes fixed
unsmilingly on Ben's. At first glance, the two men couldn't
be more different: Ben's clothes drooped around him and his
hair floated wildly, while Daniel's suit and hair were smartly
cut, nothing fancy; business-like styles for a business-like
world. While Ben's skin was grey with fatigue, Daniel's was
a hue of orange that only sunless tanning can create. The
hard look in each one's eyes, however, suggested they
understood each other perfectly.

"She's an embarrassment to our party and she's making a
mockery of this race," said Ben. "Serious candidates, such as
you, will continue to be on the back page as long as this sex
scandal stays on the front page."

Daniel concurred grimly. The photographs had arrived in
his inbox the same day that the story broke in the news.
They were stunning shots and had provided some very
satisfying fantasies – who would have thought demure little
Mrs. Goody-Two-Shoes had it in her? He'd grasp her hair in
his hand, guiding her down…

"We need you back in the spotlight," said Ben, swatting
his desk for emphasis. "This is no time to be soft."

Daniel shifted in his seat, uncomfortably aware that he
wasn't.

"I need you to attack her," the chairman continued. "This
stunt she pulled with the press conference – undermine it.
Make her out to be the genuine whore she is."

"How do I do that?" asked Daniel. His aroused mind was
teaming with possibilities, but none of them practical.

Ben stared at him, incredulously. "There are pictures of
her blissfully consuming some guy's cock flying around the

internet," he said slowly. "Use your imagination! How hard can it be?"

Daniel murmured thoughtfully. He slung his blazer casually over his arm, hiding his crotch as he stood. "She's basically arguing that women have a *right* to have sex – no, that they *have* to have it. That can't be right."

"Don't start arguing – just question her morality, remind people about the big picture. And don't forget, some of our voters are women, we don't want to raise anyone's hackles."

Ben stood to see Daniel out. In the doorway, he grabbed the candidate's elbow.

"Daniel," he said in a low voice, "you don't have any skeletons in your closet I have to worry about, do you?"

"Of course I do, but those closets are locked." Daniel's easy smile spread across his face.

"Are you sure?"

"With Deadbolts." He winked.

It was 1984. Garish colors had permeated every shop while thick padding festooned the shoulders of every woman in America. Mondrian topped the art charts and money became fashionable once more. Marilyn, who served as Samantha's stylish canary-in-a-coal-mine, donned purple leggings and bra, topped by a yellow net tunic and matching headband, with Day-Glo orange fingernails completing the ensemble whenever they went out dancing on Friday nights.

Samantha, her BA under her belt, was becoming disillusioned with her law course. She hadn't even chosen it, exactly – after the counselor's original verdict, her mother decided that was what she would do, and Samantha acquiesced. She had initially assumed that law was about helping people. However her studies convinced her that it wasn't: the aim was simply to use the law – twist it, turn it, and stretch it to suit your case and your client. The courtroom was not a place for truth. Lawyers were not permitted to be truthful if it didn't serve their client's interests.

She soon realized that her career would force her to defend the guilty against the innocent, and the better she performed that travesty of justice, the better she would be paid. The hierarchy of creating change was daunting; the way to help people was to create jobs. To create jobs, one needed capital. To get capital, one had to earn good money. To earn good money as a lawyer, she'd have to set criminals free and watch bars slam in front of the guiltless. Catch twenty-two.

She continued to work hard, because her scholarship demanded it, but the workload drained her energy and became a grey and dreary bludgeoning of facts into her brain. She didn't have time to sew clothes, to work a part-time job, or to cook herself proper meals. She was running out of money, living off boxed macaroni and cheese, and felt like Cinderella buckling under the weight of it all. Richard arrived in her life then like Prince Charming, while Marilyn performed well in her role as the Fairy Godmother providing ball gowns and slippers.

On the night they met, Samantha, dressed in Marilyn's cast-offs, attended an alumni frat ball with a guy she'd met in Civil Procedures. When her date drank so much he threw up on the lawn, Richard moved in for the kill.

"So what's a pretty thing like you doing with an ape like that?" He towered over her, his handsome face smirking down, the edge of maturity in his jaw setting him apart from the other students.

"I'll tell you what I'm *not* doing – getting in a car with him." Samantha watched in disgust as her erstwhile date managed to stand up and stagger under a tree before voiding his stomach generously over its trunk and his own hands.

"Absolutely not, you'll be coming home with me," announced Richard. "That is – I'll drop you at home," he amended, with a slight smile.

"Thank you," said Samantha, blushing.

Richard studied her closely. She formed the perfect image of demure – a proper little all-American beauty, with polished nails, neat make-up, and round, rosy cheeks.

"I wanted to marry you from the moment I saw you," he would later tell her. She was too steeped in romance to think logically about this statement – that if he was indeed speaking the truth, his desire had nothing whatsoever to do with her personality. The idea of someone loving her at first sight – someone like Richard; older, wealthy, experienced, sophisticated, and loving someone like her; far from skinny without the benefit of curves, struggling, ordinary – was all too intoxicating.

Richard had recently launched his own company, selling hair-care products, and was wooing the world. He took her to dinner parties, where she shyly shook hands with his new business partners and was later described as "a gem, Richard – a real find. She could charm a monk out of his habit," and Richard would grin proudly. He took her on picnics, unpinned her hair, and brushed it out for her, showing her how to begin slowly from the bottom and work her way up so as not to snap any hairs. She knew that already, but the feeling of being petted was too sweet to interrupt. He took her on drives, roaring down the highways in his sports car. Eventually, when she was sufficiently dazzled by the glamour and refinement of it all, he took her.

The difficulty of entering her and the blood on his sheets answered the question uppermost in both their minds. This was no awkward, fumbled attempt in a schoolboy's bedroom. Richard had his own luxurious apartment, a vast double bed, and more than enough experience for both of them. After Matthew's three-minute sprint from start to finish, Richard's more leisurely and knowing pace, lasting a full quarter of an hour, made him officially the best lover she'd ever had.

By fall, Samantha was falling drastically behind with her schoolwork. Her frustration with the system, coupled with Richard's constant round of social engagements, was proving fatal. One of her professors, loath to part with such a promising student, had a long and honest talk with her about her chances of succeeding if she continued in such a fashion.

Samantha arrived at Richard's apartment that evening in a flood of tears. She sobbed into his chest until he poured her a brandy and helped her to the leather sofa. She appreciated it as a curiously male gesture, which indicated that he respected and treated her as an equal.

"Do you want to be a lawyer?" he said.

"I don't *know* anymore!" she said, crying again. "I thought I did, but it's not how I thought it would be..." She began to reiterate all her problems with the system, but he interrupted her. Gently and firmly, he repeated his question.

"No. Not really," she admitted.

"Then stop." He spread his hands as though the problem had vanished into thin air. The smile that relaxed across his face said it had.

"Drop out?"

"You have a degree already," he reminded her, "so it's not exactly like dropping out."

She hesitated. The idea of shrugging off all that pressure was so appealing, but felt instinctively wrong. Besides, if she wasn't going to be an attorney, what was she going to be? If she stopped studying today, what would she do tomorrow?

"Just think about it," he urged. "I hate to see you making yourself so unhappy when it's so unnecessary."

"But what would I do instead?"

He stood up and left the room. She sat, alone with her question and her brandy, wondering if she'd said something wrong.

"I was planning something different," he said, as he walked back in. "More glamorous, but..." He gave a wry smile and knelt in front of the sofa. "Samantha Anderson," he said, opening his hand to show a small velvet box, "will you be my wife?"

The living room table was covered with sheets of paper. Samantha studied her latest draft and picked up her already worn copy of *Web Design for Dummies*.

"Okay," she muttered to herself, "Preferably no more than six main sections... damn!" She looked at 'The Cost of War', wondering if it could be combined with anything else – 'Do the Math', maybe. The television in the corner broadcast the news to a fragment of her awareness, reminding her that the cost of war was not simply however-many-trillion dollars. Body counts were not a matter of mathematics. "So what else can be combined?" she asked herself pensively. His name on the news caught her full attention.

"Richard St. Clair of St. Clair Industries recently claimed to news reporters that he and his wife, Democratic presidential candidate Samantha St. Clair, share a passionate and monogamous marriage. However, with his wife now the subject of a major sex scandal, women from all over his hair care empire, including models, administrative assistants, and interns, are coming forward claiming they had sexual relations with the millionaire. In addition to debunking Richard St. Clair's statement of a monogamous marriage, these women all claim that Mr. St. Clair's sexual preferences were highly deviant, involving sadomasochistic props and role playing – further contradicting his statement to the press. Mr. St. Clair has so far chosen not to respond to these allegations."

Samantha looked around to the sofa, where Faith sat curled up with a textbook.

"I know you knew," said Faith softly.

"I suppose I did," said Samantha, staring at her sea of paper. "I've wanted to leave him for a long time now."

"I know."

"But he made sure I had no self-esteem, so I'd be afraid to. I was part of the image – part of the deal – part of his show of success."

Faith wandered over and ran her hand gently down her mother's hair.

"And of course," Samantha added, snapping out of her momentary trance, "he was afraid I'd take half the money with me."

She swung the remote towards the TV, switching it off, and turned back to her work. "Okay – how do I link the pages together?"

"Try the index," said Faith from the sofa, where she'd returned to immerse herself once more in her own studies.

"Determined to make me independent, aren't you?" smiled Samantha.

"Yup."

Samantha was still at it as she perched behind her desk the next day. She gave a low groan and bent over until her nose almost touched the keyboard. As she straightened, she saw Ruth's face peering around the door.

"Cramps?" said Ruth, concerned.

"No... damn html! Half my table's vanished and I don't know where it's *gone*. Look – it's there – but it's invisible!

They appear when I skip the cursor over them, so the cells are there, why can't I *see* them otherwise?"

"*Gnōthi seauton*," replied Ruth sagely.

"What?"

"Oh, I'm sorry. You were speaking Greek so I thought I'd join in."

Samantha laughed and waved the boldly-colored book in the air. "For dummies, see? I'm a complete novice at this."

The phone's shrill ring summoned Ruth back to her desk, and she disappeared with the question "Coffee?" floating over her shoulder.

"Yes, *please*," called Samantha, and returned to the bewildering world of HyperText Markup Language.

She was muttering happily to herself when Ruth returned with the coffee.

"Open table, open row, open cell – gotcha, you bastard, SPACE – close cell, close row, open row, open cell – take *that* – close cell…"

"You know, the first sign of madness is talking to yourself," said Ruth, slipping the coffee into Samantha's sightline.

"I'm not talking to myself," she countered, eyes glued to the screen, "I'm *talking* to my *computer*. Anyway, the first sign of madness is looking for hairs on the palm of your hand." Her eyes flicked upwards. Ruth had instinctively turned her hand over. "Gotcha! You're mad."

"Have you noticed that the phone keeps ringing?" said Ruth.

Samantha nodded.

"And you're not curious why we're getting hundreds of calls a day?"

"I assumed it was my new publicity. You know what they say – sex sells…. Actually, I reckoned the entire country was phoning in one by one to denounce me."

A little smile crept across Ruth's mouth. "Not to denounce you – to *pay* you. The money is rolling in,

Samantha St. Clair – left right and center, your war-chest is getting as big as the front runners!"

Samantha's face lit up, radiating her skin. "That's wonderful! They really support me – literally." She sighed happily. "We'll have to return it."

"We'll *what*" Ruth's face fell, her eyes wide as she stared at her smiling boss.

"Return it. I don't want it and I don't need it."

"How are you going to campaign if you don't have any money?"

"I'm not going to campaign," said Samantha contentedly.

"What"' Anger and betrayal blended in Ruth's expression before merging with confusion as Samantha gave her a slow wink.

7

After the first few harrowing days, Samantha realized that web designing – even badly – was addictive, and would quickly chew up all her time if she let it. She decided to restrict herself to an hour a day, plus as much of her lunch break as she liked. That familiar inner critic whispered, *this is ridiculous, who are you trying to fool? You're not a web designer. Who said you can make websites? Don't be so silly, you're wasting time. Pay someone to do it.*

Faith said it was easy – that anyone could. All these kids do, so I can.

You can't teach an old dog new tricks.

Yes, I can *– I'm learning how to do it. I'm getting there. I'm even using templates! And it feels good to be learning something again, so even if it's just a hobby, that's okay.*

Previously, her congressional work had filled her days to overflowing; the torrent of correspondence never letting up, the committee demands while every issue seemed pressing. Now, she'd somehow magically compressed the same work into a few hours less, while planning her presidential platform filled the rest of her day. At eight, she rang Hope, who stood guard outside her outer office door.

"Just another half-hour, honey," she promised.

At a quarter to nine, she rang again. "I'm so sorry Hope, I've still got a pile of stuff here – you go get yourself something to eat if you want, okay? … Oh come on, the building's got security; I won't die if you get a burger… Well how about take-out? … But look, this isn't fair on you; you need your sleep… Oh. Really? Is there? Well, okay. But I don't want to wake you up in the middle of the night, so if it gets past eleven you just sleep, okay? The couch pulls out in the outer office."

She rubbed her eyes as she sat down, forgetting about her make-up until she saw the smear of grey and beige imprinted on her palm. Hope insisted that Samantha keep to her regular schedule, whatever that might be, and that it was Hope's job to fit around it. It still felt unfair to keep the girl out until all hours, but she steadfastly refused to go home.

She looked at her in-tray with a glow of pride. She'd got rid of at least six inches. How did the other candidates manage their work with campaign schedules, all those school-visits, union addresses, jetting around the country tearing through carbon points? Who, while they were striding the national stage, did their work?

"Next for shaving," she muttered, pulling a sheaf of papers in a pink folder over to the middle of her desk. *Food labeling: organic/GM/sat-fat/Es/origin/etc.*

The first heading was "How Much does the Consumer Need to Know?" and she glanced over the opening paragraph: "… danger of incomplete information … need to avoid scare-mongering…" She slapped the desk in frustration.

"Since when did the US government avoid scare-mongering?" she interrogated the report, scrawled a big question mark next to the heading and wrote "Complete right to know – give as much info as poss."

Her cell phone's sudden ring practically knocked her out of her chair.

"Yes Hope."

"Sorry to bother you, ma'am, but there's a gentleman here to see you. He says his name is Thomas and that he's a friend. Should I let him through?"

A jolt of anger, interspersed with excitement coursed through her veins. "What the heck does *he* want?"

"I don't know ma'am, but he comes bearing gifts."

Samantha sat there, knitted brows, tapping the desk with her pen. After a few moments, Hope's voice coaxed her back into the now. "Ma'am?"

Curiosity overtook her finally and she relented, "Let him in…but stand guard."

"Yes ma'am."

A quiet knock on her door soon followed. "Come in!" she yelled, expecting to see Hope. When it didn't open, she looked up. The dull knock came again, as if the door were being kicked. She strode over and whisked it open. On the other side stood Thomas, a rose between his teeth, a bottle of champagne in one hand, two champagne flutes in the other.

"Exactly what are you doing here?" Samantha backed away from the door in surprise. "You absolutely should *not* be here!"

"Grkr knh knh," said Thomas around the rose stem.

"And take that rose out of your mouth!"

He waved the bottle and glasses helplessly, to indicate he had no hands free. She stared in fascination, wondering how he'd picked the rose up with his mouth in the first place. Sitting on the edge of her desk, her hands beneath her, she stared at him implacably. His puppy-dog expression was spoiled by the grimace he needed to keep the flower in place. At last, he spat it out.

"Damn," he said, "That wasn't as romantic as I wanted it to be."

"What are you doing here, Thomas? I've been giving a fresh start to my campaign and if you get caught here it will be *over* for me."

"Why's that?" He walked closer to the desk to set down the bottle and she shrank away from him. "I thought you had wild passionate lovemaking for sexually starved females as part of your political platform."

"Ha. Ha. Ha. Listen, I've managed to rescue my campaign once after our…interlude. Don't ruin it for me again."

"Don't worry. I've commissioned an investigation into who is responsible for shooting and posting the images, and

I'll proceed with action against them if there's enough of a case. With your permission, of course."

Samantha chewed on her lip.

"This is crazy, Sam." He continued, his hand lingering over the champagne cork, not daring to open it yet. "It's all very simple; you want me, I want you. We have the opportunity, the motive, *and* we have the blessing of your demographics, so why don't we just do what we both want to do?"

Samantha reached out and clasped her fingers around his wrists in an attempt to push him away, but the contact with his warm skin made her insides flicker. She brought his wrists together in front - so that he stood as if handcuffed - looked into his chestnut eyes and said with sincerity, "Thomas – as wonderful as making love to you is, and as much as you bring out all the passion in me and give me a sense of complete fulfillment – we still can't do it. It's not *right*."

"Why?" He leaned in, his voice gentle and low. "Please tell me why this isn't right?"

Suddenly struck by his youth, Samantha let go of one wrist and ran the back of her fingers over his chin. She felt his sandpapery evening stubble grazing her skin, and hovered for a moment on the brink of acquiescence. If she gave in, just for a few seconds, he would be stepping closer, pulling her legs around him as he sank down to kiss her. With a deep breath, she took her hands away and sat on them again.

"Because when we got together, I was lonely and needed so badly to be touched. The public could buy that," she said. "This time, I would be perceived as just a whore getting her rocks off for the fun of it."

His face curled in disgust at her words and he stepped backwards. "You don't believe your own message, do you?"

"What does *that* mean?"

"It's just a campaign lie, like any other – you don't really think it's normal to need sex, you're just saying it is to cover your ass. You've been telling the world you're dying of thirst, that you need passion and desire and it's okay to need it, and now you're telling me you don't even want a sip when a fountain is flowing in front of you?"

Samantha turned away to stare at the bookshelf. "Maybe my thirst has been quenched," she said, avoiding his eyes.

Thomas grasped one wrist, pulling her hand free from underneath her bottom. "Has it?"

Unyielding, she looked straight at him. "Yes," she lied, "It has."

He took her other wrist and held them both to his chest, moving so close her knees almost brushed his groin and his body filled her vision. He tilted his head down to look directly into her eyes. "Just to be clear; you're telling me that every part of your being is not dying to be made love to again – you really don't want me to kneel down right now and worship you with my mouth – you don't want me to bring you to the brink of bliss again and again, driving into you, making every cell of your body scream with joy?"

"Sorry, Casanova." The effort to keep her voice from shaking made her tone harsh. "This being is quite content."

Thomas let go of her and stepped back. "You're lying," he said, bewildered. He'd made a life's study of interpreting the signs of desire – lips drying and being moistened, pupils dilating, a sudden intake of air through the nostrils, the twitch of the spine from a twinge deeper within…

"Nope," said Samantha airily. She was so dizzy with hunger for him that it made her giggle. "I'm like a camel. I can handle long periods of time between sips."

He could see she was breathless, shaky and nearly hysterical. "I don't believe that for a second," he said huskily. "I think you are a sexually *alive* woman, who needs passion, and tenderness, and romance all the time, and for you not to have it is a total waste of your beauty and your sensuality." His eyes also suggested that he should be the one to provide it all.

She stood up, sidestepping around him, and folded her arms. "Well, since I'm asking you to leave, obviously you must be wrong. But thanks for stopping by."

As if he were already dismissed, she returned to her chair behind the desk and jerked the mouse, bringing the screen to life.

"Well, maybe I was wrong," he said. "Maybe your moral elitism is actually stronger than your sincerity."

She kept her face expressionless, her eyes on the screen. He picked up the glasses and unopened bottle.

"And with that said, you'll never hear from me again." As he reached the door, he turned back and saw that she was watching him after all. Sullenly, he added "Unless, of course, you want to make an appointment with me in another fifteen years."

She shook her head, her lips tightly compressed. He stepped through the doorway.

"Thomas, wait!"

He hesitated. It was humiliating, to offer oneself so honestly and openly only to be turned down. He wanted to walk off with whatever pride he could salvage, but he lingered, waiting for her next words.

"Is there any chance – I mean, do you know – uh, I don't know how to..." She waved her hands in the air, struggling and blushing to put her request into words. In seconds, he was back in the room, the door slammed behind him, the champagne back on the desk, kneeling by her chair.

"Can I what?" he said tenderly, staring into her eyes. He laid his palm on her thigh and felt it tense and tremble.

"Can you..." Samantha swallowed hard, her nerves shrieking against his close proximity. "Can you do html?"

Thomas breathed deeply through his nose, counting to five in his head. He slipped one hand around her waist and threw himself backward, pulling her on top of him, his other hand rose up under her hair while he kissed her wildly.

"I'm sorry, I lost my head," he gasped, as she wrenched herself free, pinning his arms down and straddling him. "Do you have any *idea* how frustrating you are?"

She laughed. "I know how frustrated I am."

"So you *were* lying?"

She bit her lip, nodding. Her hips slid against him and he groaned, jerking his head back. When he could compose himself enough he asked, "So can I kiss you again?"

Her sudden exhalation had already said yes even as she considered it, and her grip on his wrists slackened.

"But first I have to warn you," he went on. "If you do kiss me, the chances of me making wild love to you, for hours, and hours, and hours, are very high. It's a risk."

"A very serious risk," she added, the corner of her mouth twitching as she studied his lips.

"You probably shouldn't even consider it." His hands slid free of hers and clasped either side of her waist. She could feel his groin stirring underneath her and shivered with desire, which only served to make her flutter enticingly against him and send the whole thing into a vicious circle.

"Just one kiss?" she whispered.

"Would present an intolerable risk of lovemaking, yes," he said regretfully. "Of course, there is about a zero point zero zero zero zero one percent chance that you'll escape unscathed."

She mused on that, pretending their hips weren't already making tiny wiggling circles against each other. "Sounds like good odds to me."

His fingers spread over the center of her back, guiding her upper torso to bend over him. As she brought her lips down to his, the angle of her hips tilted until only their clothes kept them apart.

"God, Sam," he moaned, his hands gripping her hips. "I think your odds just got worse…"

Abruptly, he held her away from him and disentangled himself. Kneeling on the floor, disheveled, she stared at him in surprise.

"I don't want you to regret this," he said. "I want you so much it *hurts*, but I do not want you to turn around afterwards and say you wish you hadn't."

"Oh," she said, bemused. She hadn't known men could do that – stop midway.

"Do you want me?" he asked throatily.

"Yes," she whispered. "It actually hurts."

He closed his eyes, fighting for control. "Will you hate me or yourself afterwards?"

She thought about it. Her marriage no longer existed. It had been a farce for years. The divorce papers would follow, but the union itself had already died – if it had ever really been alive. She looked inside her heart and realized she no longer agreed with society's dictates that legalities were all that mattered. In real terms, she hadn't been married for fifteen years, no matter what the law stated.

"No," she said in surprise.

"Then come here, *now*."

"Morality is not a question of contingencies, or excuses. If killing people is wrong, then killing people is wrong – you can't say that it depends on the situation, you can't argue that it's okay because you really *wanted* to. If adultery is wrong, adultery is wrong. By trying to argue otherwise, by trying to defend the indefensible, Samantha St. Clair is an embarrassment to herself, her family, her party, this congress, and the great country of the United States."

Senator Daniel Brown, despite the lingering hint of orange that the make-up girl hadn't been able to disguise, appeared statesmanlike as he stood behind the podium. The requisite amount of wrinkles (wisdom), lack of grey hair (vigor), and expertly-tailored suit (affluence) allowed him the perfect image of sensible authority.

"It is obvious to me," he continued regretfully, "and I assume it is obvious to the majority of voters, that we cannot let a woman of low morals make a mockery of this race and political process. So I have decided to step forward as a spokesperson for the Democratic Party, on behalf of all people who are serious about politics, to demand that Samantha St. Clair withdraw from this race and let the serious, moral candidates make their messages heard. Thank you for your time."

The sudden uproar of questions faded as the anchor reappeared on screen. Senator Brown's speech was being rebroadcast from earlier that evening

"Ouch," said Thomas.

Samantha looked at him, puzzled. The two were lying on the sofa bed in her office, snuggled under an old blanket. The dawn creeping through the uncurtained windows found them still awake, marveling in the endless delights of nature. When at last they'd collapsed, sated, it was too late to sleep.

"What do you mean, 'ouch'?" she said.

"Well – the morality argument is difficult to counter… I don't mean I'm convinced," he added hastily, "I'm just thinking of your campaign."

Samantha shook her head, sighing. "No one ever listens," she said despairingly. "No one *ever* listens to an argument. Not even an attorney. First of all, argument by analogy proves nothing, right?"

Thomas blinked, and then agreed. "Unless the analogy is precedent," he added.

"His analogy was: killing is always wrong, therefore adultery is always wrong."

"That's not exactly by analogy," interrupted Thomas, "it's extending it to a general principle – that ethics, in general, are not contingent."

"And he proves that with the argument of killing?' said Samantha.

Thomas shrugged, not understanding where she was going.

"You see?" She flopped back onto the couch, groaning theatrically. "No one listens and no one thinks, not even you. You think killing is always wrong?"

"Well…"

"So you're a passionate anti-war campaigner, I assume?" she persisted. "And therefore would like federal law to ban the death sentence in all states, correct? I can safely assume that you're one hundred percent pacifist in other words?"

"Well…" he began again, but she interrupted swiftly, still staring at the ceiling.

"You see – I *am* opposed to the war, this one, and I *am* opposed to the death sentence, and there are very few situations in which I would argue for a non-pacifist solution, but even I – touchy-feely anti-war largely-pacifist liberal that I am – see that there are times when killing might, just might, be necessary and morally justified. And there's an entire *country* out there, most of whom back the war, back the death sentence, and scorn pacifism, and they're all nodding sagely over their breakfast cereal saying, 'Yeah, exactly, if killing's always wrong, then adultery's always wrong, the man's got a point.' Nobody listens; they just thread the words through their ears and agree with whatever comes last."

"Wow," said Thomas, who was propped up on one elbow and staring down at her.

"Wow what?" challenged Samantha defensively.

"Wow, you sure can rant, and wow, you have *great* breasts."

"Did you listen to a *word* I said?"

"Yes." As his hand reached for her nipple, he rattled off swiftly, "You argued that all morality is contingent, with yourself an extreme example of the opposite possible viewpoint which nevertheless failed to prove their position, elegantly demolishing their argument without constructing one of your own, leaving the opposition without anything to attack which makes you appear infallible."

"Oh. So you were listening."

"Mmmhmm."

"I should get up and get dressed."

"Mmmhmm."

"Thomas – I really should be getting back to work."

"Mmm-mmm…"

"Look, this is – we really don't have time – dear God, you can't possibly…"

"Mmm…"

"Ah. You can. Oh God. Oh God… Thomas…"

Hope glanced at Samantha's reflection in the rear-view mirror, the hint of a smirk in her eyes.

"What?" said Samantha.

Returning her gaze to their usual forward position, Hope replied, "Nothing, ma'am."

"You're thinking something, I can tell."

"My mind is completely empty, ma'am."

Samantha flipped open her compact to check her appearance. She'd washed off and reapplied her make-up in the office bathroom, combed her hair and straightened her clothes.

"I have a big day today; I needed to pull an all-nighter."

"Yes, ma'am. Just an F.Y.I., however; security expressed their concern over the level of noise your all-nighter created."

"The *what*?" Samantha's skin crawled.

"The night security staff became alarmed by the loud howling and screeching from your office, ma'am. As your SS agent, I had to assure them that your well-being was in no way being threatened."

Samantha hid a suddenly scarlet face in her hands. "Was I that loud?" she whispered.

"Only for those in the same building. I don't think the next block heard anything."

"I was actually howling?"

"The correct term might be ululating, I'm not exactly sure."

"And everyone *knows*?"

Hope shot her a sly look. "Only me and night security, ma'am – and from what they were telling me, there's barely an office in the building that's never had a WIOP."

"WIOP?"

Hope replied, "Their term, ma'am. It means, Welcome Intruder On Premises. In your case, they put down VVVWIOP."

Despite her embarrassment, Samantha chuckled. "Promise me you won't tell a soul," she pleaded.

"I am discreet, ma'am, it's my job."

"Okay, then that'll be that."

Samantha looked out over the room of reporters, resisting the urge to adjust her suit. *Never touch your hair or clothes*; it was one of the first rules of public speaking she'd ever learned. This was her first appearance since she'd defended her right to blow strangers – *your right to have a sexual existence,* she corrected herself primly – and she needed to make an impression that would drive out all thoughts of sex scandals. On Marilyn's advice, she wore a trim blue suit.

"If it worked for the Virgin Mary, it can work for you," her friend had commented snidely. "Combine it with gold jewelry and you've got the complete look."

"Silver suits me better," Samantha had replied absentmindedly. The suit was exquisite: grey slate-blue, the color of the sky before a thunderstorm; raw silk, expensive without being shiny or ostentatious; cut to emphasize her long waist and darted to suggest her breasts were pert and held high. "I look so elegant…"

"Don't sound so damned surprised."

Her make-up was subtle, her fingernails cut short ("Long fingernails say fuck me, short fingernails say I'm sensible," explained Marilyn). The photographer's bulbs were flashing all over the room as she stood, a calm smile in place, her fingers resting lightly on her notes. Samantha raised one hand for silence and the crowd hushed.

"I'm here to announce that I will not be campaigning for the Presidency of the United States," she said clearly. That stirred them up. She held both hands up, this time, as if in saintly benediction. "Please – one at a time. Yes?"

"So you're taking Senator Brown's advice and withdrawing from the race?"

"No. I'm not withdrawing. I'm just not campaigning in the traditional sense."

"What exactly does that mean?"

"I will engage in debates, press conferences, and interviews, but I won't be flying from one end of the country to the other and I won't be doing commercials. I believe those campaign aspects would waste good people's money and keep me from my work as a member of congress."

"So how will you get your message out?"

"Commercials don't get a message out – they get slogans out. I am not a slogan campaigner – I have a real message. Voters can visit my website, at www.SamanthaStClair.com or they can call 1-800-362-8008 to have the information mailed to them. And of course, they'll be able to compare me against other candidates by watching the televised debates."

"Does this mean you won't have any slogans?"

"What do you have against commercials?"

"Why are you not doing stump speeches?"

Rather than raise her own voice or lift her hands yet again for silence, Samantha stood patiently, waiting for the reporters' questions to die down. When the room hushed, she gave a little smile.

"How about I tell you *everything* I can think of about how I intend to run," she suggested, a thread of laughter in her voice, "and when I'm finished, if I've left out anything, you can ask your questions then?"

A chuckle ran around the room.

"Okay – here's the plan. As I've said before, running the country is more complex than a slogan, and someone's ideas on how to run the country should never be reduced to a slogan. Commercials do exactly that – they turn a presidential contest into a competition between marketing teams, not candidates, and determine who can sling the most mud at their opponent. I want this campaign to be about my *message*, and as I've said earlier, my message can be easily accessed by visiting my website, or calling my 800 number.

"I'm also considering the financial aspect in my decision not to campaign. Filming commercials and stumping across the country use an inordinate amount of campaign funds. As of this press conference, I've been given a great deal of money for campaign finance. That money was given to me by hardworking people who probably made significant sacrifices to donate it. I value their support deeply and I am currently in the process of returning those donations. I'd like anyone who donated to my campaign and who really doesn't want their money back to know that there's a list of charities on my website that would benefit from your support and that really *need* that money. I don't need it – I'm simply giving information, and information's free."

She fell silent and raised her eyebrows expectantly. After a pause, one reporter lifted a hand and asked hesitantly, "Do you really believe it can be that simple?"

"It is that simple," laughed Samantha. "So why complicate it by running commercial after commercial that only bankrolls some marketing firm and carries on *ad nauseum* until the voters are just that, nauseous? Go to my website, call for my literature, watch the debates, digest the information, and then decide."

"What about Senator Brown's comments from yesterday's press conference?" someone called from the back. The question set off a new avalanche of queries.

"Do you consider yourself immoral?"

"Do you agree that you're an embarrassment to your party?"

"Do you have anything to say to him?"

"Would you say you're making a mockery of the political process?"

"Do you agree you should withdraw from the race?"

"Now who asked *that*?" snapped Samantha. "Do I agree I should withdraw from the *race*?" Her tone was suddenly withering. "Whoever that was, get yourself another coffee, it appears as if you've slept through the entire press conference so far." She looked at them all with the same intensity that a teacher looks at students who are just not paying attention. Despite her best efforts, she just couldn't take the media circus seriously.

"As for saying anything to Senator Brown – I prefer to speak to people either directly or on the phone, not passing messages through the press. But thanks for the offer. And thanks very much for coming today. It's lovely to see you all again. And *do* help yourself to coffee."

The polite hostess comments flowed out of her mouth unbidden, and the atmosphere in the room relaxed a bit in response. Samantha switched off the microphone and muttered through the side of her mouth to Ruth, "Okay, that was weird. Did I just come off all 'Mom' on their asses?"

Ruth nodded. "I think they quite liked it though. Good gamble. Now go mingle."

8

Perching cross-legged on the floor, Samantha tapped figures into Excel on her laptop, turning from time to time to flip through the slab of budget documents at her side. As usual, the television was on in the corner of the living room – partly to fill the silence of her quiet apartment, partly to keep an eye on the news. On a pad of paper, she scribbled reminders to herself. *No deficit = static debt. Rate of inflation forecast? Mandatory payments not sustainable. Risk of top-heavy pop?*

A commercial break came on and she irritably punched a button on the remote, flipping channels.

Interactive? she wrote. *Compare household budget? Defense: Education = 11:1! War > defense budget (cf extra costs).*

"Democratic Senator Daniel Brown has declared his Legislative constituent Representative Samantha St. Clair to be immoral," announced an authoritative voice from the TV. She jerked her head up to see a picture of her own face. Of course, they couldn't use *those* shots, but the newshounds had chosen to share a decisive moment when she'd leaned towards the microphone with her lips parted to speak. She shook her head in frustration. *You'd better not put anything in your mouth in public, girl – not a fingernail, not even a pen. Eat a hotdog and you're dead meat.*

The anchor's next words, however, raised her spirits. "So it's even *more* bad news for Senator Brown's camp that a former volunteer has come forward claiming she had sexual relations with Senator Brown during his last campaign. Beth Elder, a single stay-at-home mother of two, claims that she performed a variety of sexual favors for Senator Brown on several occasions."

Samantha gasped and then glanced from the TV to her laptop again. "*More* bad news? Have I been missing something?"

"Senator Daniel Brown," she typed in the Google textbox and hit search.

Samantha shook her head slowly in disbelief as she scrolled through the results. She knew Senator Brown – not well, but enough to greet him and his wife socially. He was typical in demeanor for a powerful man; always exuding an air of being slightly too busy for a conversation, but if one made it quick he'd be polite and patient about it. He didn't seem approachable enough for someone to successfully get his trousers down.

Then again, maybe you're just not his type – these women are all a lot younger, and poorer.

She clicked on one of the tabloid-oriented articles.

"A sobering blow today for Senator Brown's presidential campaign: just twenty-four hours after he demanded that Congresswoman Samantha St. Clair step down from her presidential bid to make way for serious, moral candidates, a female limousine driver has come forward claiming to have had sex with the Senator en route to a political fundraiser. Holly James, a driver for Elite Limo services, claims money wasn't the only thing Brown raised that night. Now that's elite service!"

She hit 'back' and scrolled down the screen. How had she missed these stories? Every newspaper, tabloid and information channel seemed to be carrying them.

"Oh, Danny-boy," she muttered and laughed as the music struck up in her head. "Oh Danny-boy," she sang, "the girls, the girls are calling... from state to state and down the coastal side... The news is out, and all the papers crying..." She hesitated, floundering for the next words.

"'Tis you, 'tis you must go and I must bide," piped up Faith from the sofa.

"Poor man," said Samantha. "I know *just* how he feels."
She burst out laughing.

The next morning held another surprise for Senator
Brown. Samantha drank her pre-gym smoothie to the news
that he and a flight attendant had (allegedly) had sex in the
bathroom while in-flight. "Please note," added the anchor
dryly, "we called the airline and they confirmed this service
is not standard with a first class ticket fare."

"Told you so," were Marilyn's words of greeting as
Samantha walked into the locker-room.

"Told me what?"

"Told you the whole of congress had their pants down
and their stuff hanging out."

Two women gave Marilyn frosty stares as Samantha
nudged her with an elbow.

"Keep your voice *down*," she hissed.

"Why?" said Marilyn, even louder. "Is there someone
who *doesn't* know Senator Daniel Brown's been putting it in
anywhere he can?"

"For heaven's *sake*," whispered Samantha. "Show some
discretion!"

"*You* need to show some gloating, girl," retorted Marilyn.
"Come on, the man bawled you out on morality and it turns
out he's a hypocrite! And at least you were screwing your
equal, not some underpaid floozy too scared to say no."

"Yes, but I'm trying to run a serious *presidential*
campaign here. Please tone it down!"

"Pish-posh."

They headed for the toning circuit, Marilyn still pushing
buttons.

"So?" she said at last.

"So what?" said Samantha.

"I'm waiting for you to say something uncharitable. As
your psychiatrist…"

"You are *not* my psychiatrist!"

"Okay, as *a* psychiatrist, I feel it's necessary for your emotional development."

"Truthfully?" said Samantha, curling her arms. "I feel quite sorry for him. I mean – maybe his wife wasn't providing any... you-know..."

Marilyn stalled mid-pump, staring at her friend open-mouthed. "As far as you're concerned, feminism is just something that's happened to other people, isn't it?" she said in disbelief. "Honey, he's been boning anything that moves and you say it's his *wife's* fault?"

"Well – that was pretty much my own justification with Richard," said Samantha uncomfortably. "I mean, it's not really so different..."

"Bullshit!" spat Marilyn while leaping up from her machine. Samantha shrank back in horror. "The similarities between you and this buffoon in an Armani suit are like apples and oranges! Samantha, this is not a man who spent twenty-five years desperately trying to make his marriage work! This man did *not* do everything in his power to attract his wife! He would *not* ditch his closest friends if they said a word against her! So do not even *begin* to put yourself in the same league as a womanizer like him, Samantha, because it is most definitely *not the same!*" Her voice had risen in volume with each enunciated sentence to the point of yelling.

"Excuse me – ma'am – can you keep your voice down?" One of the instructors hovered nervously behind Marilyn, who was flushed with Amazonian fury. "I'm afraid I'll – have to ask you to leave, unless..."

Marilyn's transformation took a moment, but as she noted his golden tan, taut muscles and shock of blonde hair, the huntress had returned.

"Unless?" she purred.

"Um... unless you can keep quiet, ma'am."

"I've never been able to keep quiet," she murmured, dead-pan.

He blushed to the roots of his hair and said, "Uh – great – uh, thanks – yeah, much appreciated," and fled.

The bell sounded and Samantha changed machines as if nothing had happened.

"Hey – I haven't done that machine," objected Marilyn.

"I'm sorry. Do I know you?"

"Okay, so I was a bit loud," laughed Marilyn, moving on to the next one. "But you've got to admit – it's not the same."

"Of course it's not," said Samantha unexpectedly. "We're completely different people, in different situations, and we're different genders. But think about it – I was going out of my *mind* for lack of – well, sex, to put it bluntly – and I'm a woman, so…"

"*So?*" cut in Marilyn, belligerently.

"Well, everyone knows men have higher sex drives."

"Oh, *do* they."

Samantha glanced at Marilyn's face, which was reddening – with anger or exertion, she wasn't sure. She seemed to be working against the toning machine with unnecessary force.

"Don't they?" Samantha asked uncertainly.

"If I get onto *this* topic," said Marilyn grimly, "I'll definitely get thrown out, because there is no *way* I will be able to keep my voice down."

Marilyn managed to keep quiet for two whole machines before she burst out, "I can't *believe* you, Samantha! Do you really just buy every bit of gender-shit you've ever been fed?"

"If you're just going to insult me, I don't see that we need to continue this conversation," said Samantha coldly.

"Sorry – sorry – don't get uppity – I just get frustrated. Look, we're all told these lies, and they're not true. That's it."

"Are you speaking personally or professionally here?"

"Both. This idea that women are frigid and just into having babies and staying home – that is *new*, Sam, it's brand-spanking-shiny *new*, on evolutionary terms. People have tried to explain why it would make sense from caveman times, but actually, just five hundred years ago *everyone* knew that women were fickle horny little fuckers and men were loyal and constant! Read any Renaissance poet and you'll see! Read *Shakespeare*, and you'll see it. I see it in my clients, I see it in research papers and scientific studies, and yes, I see it in my own personal life."

"But then…" Samantha was bemused. She'd stopped exercising and just sat, staring at Marilyn. "But then…"

"They don't want sex more than we do," said Marilyn, also letting go of the weights and leaning forward. "We're just in this situation where women ignore what they want and men feel obliged to pretend it's all they ever think about. Women play hard-to-get and men play predator-predator – but that's all it is – playing – make-believe."

"Excuse me," said the woman behind them. "Are you two moving on?"

"Sorry," they said in unison, hurrying to the next machine.

"Like I said," Marilyn went on, "I've seen the research, proper research, and I've conducted a few informal experiments of my own."

"A *few*?" queried Samantha pointedly.

Marilyn laughed. "Okay – lots, but not a representative sample by scientific standards...even I have to sleep! The thing is," she went on, "guys pretend all they want is sex and they're just in it for the sex and their world would be paradise if women were easier to lay – then you just try coming on to a couple of men for a change, and see how they react. Suddenly, they're all shy and retiring. Suddenly, when you're horny, they're saying they feel used, that you just want them for their body, blah blah blah… They all behave as if they're howling at the moon, but they don't know what to do with a tallow candle."

For a few more minutes, they worked out in silence while Samantha tried to digest what Marilyn was saying. Her entire sex life, up until Thomas, had been predicated on the assumption that her partner needed sex and she didn't really but was being kind enough to provide it. She thought of all the times she'd made herself available to Richard, assuming that if she was horny he'd be chomping at the bit.

"I suppose you do have to feel sorry for them," said Marilyn. "Think of the image they're trying to live up to. No wonder Viagra sells so well!"

The late-night shows were having a field day with the Daniel Brown stories. Samantha watched them between her fingers, not knowing whether to be glad that her rival was getting his come-uppance or mortified by the comments still flung in her direction.

"Now wouldn't Senator Brown and Congresswoman St. Clair be the perfect ticket for the Democratic Party?" began Bill Maher with relish. The audience burst into applause, hooting with delight at the thought of jokes to come. He kept his face almost straight, just his eyes twinkling with cupidity as he went on. "Playboy and Penthouse would be in the press corps. Dignitary balls, Head of State and Vice President would all have new meanings – and the country's job market would grow immediately." He let the audience flounder for a moment before adding, "Well – in hand jobs and blow jobs, certainly!" His expression feigned regret while the audience roared and clapped, before at last he conceded a momentary smirk.

Jay Leno was less subtle. Hands deep in his pocket, jaw facing the camera, he intoned, "We all know about the sexy picture of Democratic presidential hopeful, Samantha St. Clair, giving one of her constituents some special attention – I'm sorry, sir," he gestured off the stage, "Could you lower that flagpole? Oh – sorry – my mistake." The whoops that followed, thought Samantha, sounded fake.

"But now it looks like *another* Democratic presidential hopeful, Senator Daniel Brown, got a little action in the back seat of a limo on *his* way to a fundraiser." He raised his eyebrows, bobbing his head firmly, as if to say, you better believe it.

"With all this sexual activity going on with the Democrats," he went on, "when they ask for an oral debate it might actually be swallowing versus non-swallowing!"

"Well, that was labored," said Faith.

"Mmm, I know," said Samantha critically. "He'd have done better with a one-liner. I thought of a good one myself, actually…"

"This is no laughing matter!" yelled Ben. "I thought the closets were locked! 'Dead bolted', you said!"

Daniel's head was buried in his hands as the chairman roared in anger. "I had them all paid off, honest," he said. "None of them ever spoke out before."

"So what changed?" snapped Ben. "Why are they all creeping out of the woodwork all of a sudden?"

"It's that fucking St. Clair." Daniel was defensive. "It's not my fault she's their fucking idol. They'd sooner defend her from my attacks than take my money. She's like some scorned woman's superhero – the more wounded the woman is, the more they see her as their inspiration. It's sick, that's what it is."

Ben sat down, running his hand through his hair. "Okay," he said. "The women's groups are going crazy over this one. They all love St. Clair too, but…" He held up a warning finger. "They *don't* see her as a viable presidential candidate; nobody's treating her like a candidate – so let's not make her into one, okay?"

Daniel nodded his head.

"And we're lucky – only the tabloid journalists and late-night guys have picked up on it so far. The mainstream media seems to be keeping their distance for the moment; that means *they're* not taking St. Clair seriously either."

"What do you want me to do?" said Daniel morosely.

"Can you deny these allegations?"

"Yes."

"And none of them have proof?"

"No."

"No stained dresses anywhere?"

"Either they swallowed, or it was – you know…" He made an obscure gesture.

Ben stared at him. "No, I don't know. What?"

"Inside… a condom… in their – uh…" muttered Daniel shamefacedly.

"Spare me the details. You disposed of the condoms?"

"Yes."

"Good thinking." He huffed and knuckled the desk in frustration. "Are there any others that might come forward?"

"Well, I'm not sure if they…"

"I *mean*," interrupted Ben, "have you screwed anyone *else* besides your wife?"

"God, yeah," said Daniel. He covered his face briefly then stared up again. "But none of them have proof, I swear. I've been incredibly careful."

"Okay – we're not going to throw you aside. You're a good candidate. You go out and lie your *ass* off and make it look good, and I'll go out and destroy the women's credibility, so we can get you elected and do some good for this country. Got it?"

"Got it."

Samantha was a grown-up – at last. She had a stylish apartment, a nice car, tasteful furniture, matching dishes, multiple sets of bed linen, and regular appointments at the hairdresser. She considered her grooming, cooking and cleaning to be part of being a proper wife, and prided herself on her organizational skills. She enjoyed the feeling of sliding her shiny car into a parking space in the mall and the click of her heels as she strode across the pavement, tucking the keys into her leather bag. Samantha took her appearance seriously, making sure her lipstick didn't fade and an extra pair of stockings remained tucked in her bag at all times. She learned to make cucumber mousse, stuffed peppers, and quiche. When Richard invited people for dinner, she would mark the date on a calendar in the kitchen, plan the menu a week in advance, sketch out the table décor several days before, and spend hours sourcing the right color flowers, napkins, and candles. She hoarded housewifely tips as her mother had hoarded coupons and even – briefly – began a collection of these fragments of wisdom. Under 'dinner parties' were the following gems: set the table first thing in the morning; always have one dish that can be made in advance with no last-minute preparation; never repeat an ingredient; never serve a heavy dessert after a heavy main course; finish dressing half an hour before guests arrive; rinse and stack dishes, then wash them in the morning.

She'd leapt from never having run a household or held a dinner party to being solely responsible for their shopping, cooking, cleaning, laundry, décor, mending, ironing, and attending at least one function a week. Richard was thirty and a businessman; their guests were important people; she couldn't just muddle through like her friends, laughing off burnt meals and dashing out for Chinese. She was proud of her competence. She was, in short, a model little housewife.

By the end of their first year of marriage, she'd learned to cook more easily: meals that had initially taken her three hours to prepare now took forty-five minutes. She'd learned how to keep a house clean and its bills paid with a minimum of fuss. She didn't need to look at every care label when she did the laundry. She could shop on auto-pilot, not staring for ten minutes at different types of coffee, wondering which represented the best quality / value for money, changing her mind four times, finally choosing a brand, and then repeating the whole procedure for every item on her list. She could throw together a soup or stew without opening a recipe book. She started setting herself new challenges: soufflés, bread, croissants, homemade pasta. Marilyn dropped in once while the kitchen was festooned with drying lasagna sheets.

"What the hell is this?" she said.

"It's lasagna," said Samantha proudly.

"You entering some cook-of-the-year competition?" said Marilyn. "Because I thought you were going to be an attorney."

"Don't start," said Samantha. Marilyn had recently discovered *The Women's Room* and, not feeling oppressed in her own relationship, had decided to liberate Samantha instead.

"Funny." Marilyn lit a cigarette. "The valedictorian in our school gets a job as a housekeeper."

"I am *not* a housekeeper," said Samantha grimly. "I am Richard's *wife*."

"Oh – sorry. Housekeeper-come-whore."

Samantha's hand sailed through the air, slapping Marilyn hard across the face. Absolutely stunned, Marilyn just stared at her. Samantha, whatever her faults, was not aggressive or melodramatic, and did not lose her temper. She was also – usually – not hysterical, though now she sank into a chair and wailed into her arms.

"The stupid lasagna's not even working," she wept, "How can I be so smart if I can't even make stupid lasagna? Everyone mocks homemakers as lacking ambition and the reality is that running a household is so *difficult*; there's so much you have to do and no one teaches you how to do it, you're just expected to know everything. I don't think Richard even *realizes* it's difficult. He thinks I just lie around all day combing my hair like some damn pet mermaid, when I'm trying so *hard*! I still have to cook half the meals twice because the first time around it gets ruined and I have to throw it all away. I wish I *was* his whore, because maybe then we'd have sex more often. It's been a whole month and I don't know what's wrong. I'm scared, and I'm so lonely; I feel so sick, and I'm tired *all the time*, everything's a massive effort – it's all I can do to get out of bed but I just keep on making myself do everything..."

Marilyn sat in bewildered silence, gently stroking Samantha's hair and issuing vague comforting murmurs. She could think of no advice with which to meet her friend's litany of woes.

"I'm sorry..." said Samantha, leaping up and opening the back door onto the fire escape. "That cigarette's making me feel really sick..." She fanned her tear-stained face, her other hand at her throat.

Marilyn frowned. "How long have you been feeling sick?" she said.

"What, you're a doctor already?" snapped Samantha and burst into tears again, before vomiting over the side of the fire-escape.

Marilyn was only in her second year of medical school, but she didn't need credentials to diagnose Samantha's pregnancy. She ran a cloth under the tap and held it out to Samantha to wipe her face.

"Sweetie, when was your last period?" she asked gently.

Samantha frowned, opened her eyes very wide, and began to cry some more.

9

Samantha flipped through the *New York Times*, her eyes rapidly scanning the day's issues and questing, fruitlessly, for some mention of her candidacy. While the tabloids couldn't let a day pass without some reference to her hair, figure, sexual proclivities, possible partners, and so forth, the serious newspapers seemed to be keeping their distance. She lifted her coffee, sighing heavily as she did and steaming up her reading glasses.

"You won't believe this," said Ruth.

"What?" said Samantha, gazing at her through a fog and then removing her glasses to wipe them.

"We're getting so many hits on your website, the server's almost reaching capacity."

Samantha put her glasses back on and took the extended print-out. Her eyes glanced critically at the graphs, and then did a double-take at the figures marked on the y-axis.

"Holy *cow*!" she blurted out. "I have this many people visiting?"

Ruth nodded with satisfaction.

"We'd better increase our capacity. If the late-night guys get hold of it, they'll have a field day."

"What do they have to do with anything?"

With a slight smirk, Samantha replied, "What do Samantha St. Clair and her server have in common? They both go down on you."

Ruth chuckled despite herself. "I'll get onto it. Oh – and um – good news or bad news…"

"Good news," grinned Samantha. "No – bad news, then the good news can cheer me up after."

"I meant – I'm not sure if this is good or bad news – for you, personally, I mean. Have you seen the financial pages? Okay, you take a look; I'll phone the IT people."

Samantha rifled through the flimsy paper to find her own name blaring out of the business section – or rather, Richard's name. *Picket blow to St. Clair Industries* read the headline, accompanied by a shot of women crowded outside the headquarters, carrying signs. "Cheats are bad business" read one. Peering closer, Samantha made out "St. Clair won't touch *my* hair" and "No more public offering" on others.

"St. Clair Industries' forthcoming public offering is being soured by protests from its largely female customers against CEO and founder Richard St. Clair's alleged extramarital affairs," read the article. It went on to remind readers that while Richard may or may not have slept with his secretaries and several models, his wife was also a Democratic presidential candidate who had also been involved in a sexual scandal. Samantha shook her head slowly.

When one read these articles about other people, everything was distinct; the formal, familiar phrases seemed to cut straight through a morass of complex human behavior to the core truth. Messy details, like who put what where, how they felt before, during and after, how they had reacted since, that entire tangle belonged to tabloids who gleefully paraded humanity in all its disorder. Serious newspapers, she'd always thought, stated dispassionate facts: a sexual scandal; alleged extramarital affairs. Now she marveled at the distance between these supposedly accurate words and the actual experiences. Her night with Thomas, born of a desperate fear of ageing and the sudden shocking realization of just how *much* she needed to be touched, the ways he had touched her and how much she resisted before succumbing and joining in, her guilt and failure to regret it, were all summed up authoritatively by the *New York Times* as "a sexual scandal". The thronging incompatible emotions about

Richard's infidelities – revulsion, hurt, vindication, confirmation of a long-held suspicion, anger both self-righteous and unjustified – were tidied away with that one word, 'extramarital'. She thought of all the times she'd read those words about other people and formed opinions, thought she had a handle on the facts, without the *least* idea of the real situation.

She blinked, returning her focus to the article in front of her. One of the protesters was quoted as saying "Considering women are the majority of St. Clair industry customers, Richard St. Clair Industries should treat women better." Another had declared "Richard St. Clair should understand that women need more than beautiful hair – and if you attack one, you attack us all." That brought a warm glow and a smile to Samantha, although she suspected it was rarely true. A spokesperson for St. Clair Industries had said that "a handful of angry housewives won't ruin the financial success of our public offering'". Samantha winced. She'd been telling Richard for years that his PR wasn't the best, but he'd refused to listen. That dismissive phrase would slap half their customers in the face.

Samantha sat on the sofa, holding the baby and waiting for the sound of the key in the door. She was painfully aware that this was a cliché, as her whole life had become a cliché of "the little woman at home, left holding the baby." She, however, was *not* a cliché: she was Samantha St. Clair, née Anderson, whose very specific biography had led her to this moment and whose still-sharp mind analyzed and dissected her position from every angle. She just couldn't work out how *not* to be sitting on the sofa, holding the baby, waiting for the sound of the key in the door. Marilyn said she should leave him, but that seemed an extreme reaction.

Faith was good all day. She was a year old now, not walking, but dragging herself along the edges of chairs and shuffling on her padded bottom across the floor. She could wield a spoon and use it to bang the underside of a pot, accompanying her percussion with burbles of laughter. She could say "mamma", with distorted vowels, and "hooza", which Samantha translated as "Who's a..." as in "Who's a good girl, then? Who's a pretty thing? Who's a lovely baby?" It could also just be meaningless babble.

While this good baby banged pots, dragged herself around the room, and gurgled, Samantha was able to get the whole apartment immaculate. At the supermarket, other shoppers turned in delight to see the giggling smiling creature in her shopping cart and Samantha beamed. Unlike her typical routine, Faith stayed awake in the car, babbling at the images rushing past, her mother echoing her half-formed sounds. At home, Samantha prepared a casserole between games of peek-a-boo that made her little daughter shriek with laughter and amazement. As the casserole went into the oven, Faith stood up under the coffee table, banged her head on the wooden strut, and began to scream.

She was inconsolable. Samantha cradled her, kissed the bruised skin with its fine dusting of hair, and sang *rock-a-bye baby* over and over, but Faith would not be soothed. She howled herself red in the face, anguish and a sense of betrayal in her streaming tears; a world of impotence and helpless misery in her tiny, banging fists. Samantha *knew* it was just a bump on the head with no damage done, she *knew* Faith had missed her midday nap and was just overtired, and she *knew* Faith was just working herself into a state of crying, which perpetuated more crying. Knowing this, however, was of no use. She still felt her baby's grief as if it were her own and could not believe how much she was a captive to this little creature's feelings. Faith's small hands clutched her mother's heartstrings, ripping at emotion. Samantha lifted the baby's face to her shoulder and laid her cheek against the baby's head as her own tears merged with her daughter's.

They sat on the sofa together, the tiny helpless one held by the bigger helpless one, until at last Faith cried herself to sleep and Samantha cried herself calm. The baby was sleeping restlessly, though, and every time Samantha tried to move to check the casserole, she'd wake again and burst out crying afresh. It was half-past six: Richard would be home any moment. He could check the casserole when he came in. If she didn't disturb Faith, the baby would have time to sink into a deeper sleep and another bout of tears could be avoided. So she sat on the sofa, holding Faith, waiting for the sound of the key in the door so that the baby could sleep and the casserole could be checked.

At half-past seven, Faith was breathing steadily and soundly. Cautiously, Samantha stood up. The little eyelids didn't flicker. As if balancing a glass of water on the back of a spoon, she carried Faith into the nursery and laid her in the cradle. She stepped back, holding her breath, waiting for the explosion. When it didn't come, she tiptoed back out of the room, sped up in the corridor, and dashed into the kitchen. The casserole had over-baked and was stuck on the bottom and sides of the casserole dish. Samantha scraped what she felt could be salvaged off the walls of the casserole dish with a wooden spoon, scooping the resulting mush in another dish. She continued scraping and a large black chunk dislodged itself from the bottom.

"Shit, shit, shit," she muttered to herself, desperate to save the dinner she'd worked hard to prepare. She continued transferring the remainder of casserole to the dish, trying to avoid including the crusty parts. As she lifted the casserole dish to scrape the last of it out, her fingers slipped beneath the potholder and touched the hot Pyrex glass, burning her fingers. The casserole dish slid out of her grip, bashed onto the counter, bounced between her grabbing hands, and sailed off onto the floor where it shattered. She stood frozen, shards of glass and smears of casserole at her feet, waiting for the howl to rise from the nursery and break the silence. Instead, she heard the key in the lock.

Options scampered through her head, like rabbits flushed out of the undergrowth by a snarling dog. She could run into the foyer to greet Richard and try to keep him out of the kitchen until she'd cleaned up. She could grab a dustpan and brush and try to clear up before he walked into the kitchen. She could make a joke of it and hope he saw the funny side. In the end, she stood in front of the mess, hoping her long skirts would hide it.

Richard walked into the kitchen, breathing heavy and tugging at his tie. He stopped short and sniffed the air.

"What's that smell? It smells like something's burning."

"Dinner got a bit burnt," admitted Samantha, not moving from her pose in the middle of the floor.

"For fuck's sake," he muttered, slamming his briefcase onto the counter. "I really don't need this today." He snapped the clasps open and took out a sheaf of papers. "What was it?"

"Casserole."

He stared at her in disbelief. "You managed to *burn* a *casserole*? Don't we have a kitchen timer?"

"I didn't use it and I couldn't check the casserole – I was holding the baby." Her voice sounded whiny and defensive when she wanted it to sound rational.

He rolled his eyes. "I don't know. I thought women held babies on their hips, or something – or put them down, occasionally."

"She was crying, she kept waking up..."

Richard's mouth shifted into a vague smile, still half-disapproving as he shook his head and sighed. He was indulging her. She was being forgiven.

"Sometimes I wonder about you," he said, sounding amused. "Okay, so why are you standing in the middle of the room like that?"

Samantha shrugged. Curiously, he stepped forward and peered at the floor around her. His face lost its smile. The wry expression became quizzical then disgusted as he looked from the broken dish to her and back again. Without a word, he left the room. As she heard the tinkle of his whisky sloshing into its glass, she bent and started picking up the pieces.

A severe mental dialog ensued: *He treats me like a child. Why do I behave like such a child? Accidents happen. Things break. People get cross. It doesn't mean* anything. *It was just a stupid dish. It's not like we can't afford a dish. I hate being treated like a child. I hate feeling like a child. I'm his* wife. *Why do I behave like a guilty child, then?*

The heat, although constant, seemed to wash over her body in repetitive waves, each one pressing deeper, kneading into the dark-red imagined world of tight muscles that slowly succumbed and untangled themselves under the hot, unrelenting force. Sweat gathered on her flat center where no fat or muscle overlaid the bone, then trickled straight downwards to either pool in her navel or rest in the crease between her breasts. A violent hissing sound came from somewhere outside her body. The air became still thicker with heat, which had seemed impossible. Sweat streamed freely over her skin, the air and her body equally damp.

"Sam?"

"Mmph." She didn't want to break the spell. She was enjoying the sensation of swimming in the depths of her own body.

"Sam…" The voice was insistent and she opened her eyes, allowing the narrow wooden roof of the sauna to appear in her vision.

"What is it?"

Marilyn was leaning against the far wall, head tilted back, her normally firm and bouncy body yielding and turning flaccid in the heat.

"I was thinking… I don't get it. It's crazy. You're giving back all the money, you're not campaigning, what are you going to do next, offer fellacio to guys in exchange for their votes?"

Samantha smiled lazily. "Don't be crass. Although it's not a bad idea," she murmured. "Not so feasible, though – I'll have to make you my running mate to pick up the slack."

Marilyn chuckled. The two of them were like divers or astronauts; all their thoughts and gestures slow and purposeful, as if they were wading through the ferocious humidity.

"It may work," she replied. "Give me the eighteen to forties, and you handle the Viagra generation…"

Samantha emitted a soft chuckle.

The silence and moisture weighed down on them.

"But seriously, what are you doing?"

Reluctantly, Samantha opened her eyes again. "You know that lucky blue dress of yours?"

"Uh-huh."

"It's like that. It doesn't seem like your sexiest come-get-me dress – you've got dresses that are way more provocative, but…"

"It never fails," grinned Marilyn. "It's not what you show…"

"It's what you don't show, and how you don't show it," completed Samantha. "That's what I'm doing. Showing just enough to make people want to see more, find out more. Being intriguing and unorthodox, instead of rushing out and being in their face and saying…"

"Take me, take me?" cut in Marilyn.

"Well – vote for me, at any rate. In the land of political tarts, I'm the only one playing hard to get."

Marilyn raised an eyebrow. "You manipulative seductress, you. I'm impressed. Especially if it works."

"It's working. Why go chasing them when they can chase you?"

"My whole sex life is based on that strategy," said Marilyn. "You're basing your election campaign on my *sex life*."

"Hey, if it's that successful, why not copy it?"

"I did not have sexual relations with these women."

Senator Daniel Brown was standing at the podium, his tie matching his wife's magenta dress in a show of solidarity.

"Are you refuting *all* the women's statements that've come forward?" pressed a reporter from the back, her strident voice cutting through the babble and hum of the others.

Daniel put an arm around his wife, pressing her unresponsive body against his. "Yes," he said. "I have enjoyed a loving, monogamous relationship with my wife of twenty-one years." He looked down at her tenderly. When she didn't raise her eyes to his, he lifted her chin gently with his hand and said into her face, "And I'd never do anything to threaten the wonderful life we have together." He beamed and she gave a small, tight smile in reply. "Obviously, this is all very upsetting for both of us," he added, losing his own smile.

"So why would these women lie?" persisted the same piercing voice. "Why would they *say* they had sex with you when they didn't?" She sounded scornful, as though no woman in her right mind would admit to bedding the Senator. He barely flinched: just the skin around his eyelids tightened a little.

"I can't read their minds," he retorted, "but personally? I believe they're supporters of Congresswoman Samantha St. Clair and will stoop to anything to help her campaign."

"Do you *really* think these women would do this for Representative St. Clair?" The same derisory tone came again. This time Daniel's eyes flashed to the corner of the room with momentary anger.

"Samantha St. Clair is like a cult leader for bitter women," he said, addressing the questioner directly. "So yes, I think they'd do anything for her."

"So are you saying that Congresswoman St. Clair is putting these women up to this?" The room's attention was divided now between the front and the far back corner.

"She did try to put the blame on her husband when she was caught cheating on him," said Daniel, "so who knows what she's capable of doing?"

A thoughtful silence came over the room. Just then he remembered that St. Clair's husband was accused of far more incidences of adultery than she was. Perhaps it wasn't the most foolproof argument, but no one seemed to have noticed.

"If there are no more questions," he said hurriedly, "I thank you for your time, everyone."

He jerked his head with a tough-man smile to the room at large. With his arm around his wife, he walked away from the podium. Suddenly, their posture became awkward – his arm was being tugged; she wasn't moving in step with him. In a confused scuffle, she broke out of his embrace and darted the few steps back to the podium.

"Wait!" she yelped to the group, who were already packing their notepads away and dismantling their cameras. Some were filing out the door. "I can't sit back and watch him lie again!"

An electric stillness came over the room, as if its occupants were afraid to dislodge the moment by moving. Daniel was still midstride, half-turned back towards his wife. His lips had parted a fraction and his eyes widened with horror. A quick photographer snapped his look of guilty dismay in the same shot as his wife stood despairingly at the podium, one hand half-covering her mouth. That was the photograph which would grace the nation's newspapers the next morning.

"My husband is insulting these women by calling them *liars* – while I can't be expected to like them, they're not liars! They shouldn't have slept with him, but they did. I know my husband very well; he preys on people – look at them, they're babies, babies with no money, he's powerful and threatening, of course they succumbed…"

She realized she was babbling and took a deep breath, organizing her thoughts. In the firmer voice with which the public was more familiar, she said, "My husband has been unfaithful since the birth of our first child, consistently and repeatedly. He has slept with interns, volunteers, administrative assistants, nannies, and I'm sure countless others I don't know about. Many other young women have turned to *me* for support, upset by my husband's inappropriate advances. He is both unfaithful and guilty of repetitive sexual harassment. I am not going to stand by and watch him attack a woman whose sexual unfaithfulness arose after what appears to be years and years of pain and neglect! Because I know how she feels."

For the first time, she turned to look at her husband. When she'd rushed to the podium, her eyes were wild and tearful. Now the look she gave him was implacable and pitiless.

"Did you *think*," she said slowly, "that I didn't need love? That I didn't need to be held? That I didn't need passion?" Her eyebrows rose and she wrinkled her nose in disdain. "Like I said, I can relate to what Congresswoman St. Clair went through. She is an inspiration to me. So she had sex with a man, after fifteen years of forced celibacy by a philandering husband? Good for her! And shame on you, Daniel."

Her last four words were to be the headline, above the photo. She walked off the stage, eyes firmly in the distance, brushing past an expressionless Ben and Cynthia. Abruptly, Daniel bolted after her and the photographers craned their necks to see behind the curtains to where the door slammed shut.

10

"Shame on You, Daniel," Ruth read aloud. She held the paper up with a flourish so that Samantha could appreciate Daniel's horrified profile on the far right, juxtaposed with his wife's grief-stricken face in full frontal on the far left. "Well, that's one less for you to worry about," she went on, scanning the columns. "He's pulled out of the race – taken down by his own wife."

Samantha raised her eyebrows. "She confirmed the accusations? In public?"

"Worse – she added to them. She even mentioned that some girls came to her complaining of sexual harassment. She's basically accused him of screwing everything in sight for the last – how old is their daughter? Oh yes…twenty years."

"Mr. step-aside-for-the-moral-candidates?" Samantha shook her head, caught between satisfaction and bewilderment. "Why do these guys in glass houses think that no one is ever going to throw something back?"

"And the last rock came from inside the house," added Ruth. She set the paper in front of Samantha. "I'll get you some coffee."

Alone again, Samantha leaned forward on her elbows, as engrossed in the dirty details of Daniel's downfall as everyone else in the nation.

Is it so interesting because it's not you for a change?
Come on, he's a hypocrite…
And that's better than a slut?
Look at what Mrs. Brown said, "sexual unfaithfulness arose after…"
So what was last night, then?

Samantha grinned and twitched uncomfortably in her seat. *So I've slept with the same man more than once. That kind of makes me less of a slut – it's not a considered one-night stand anymore.*

But it's not exactly one desperate act, is it?

No – it's multiple. Multiple acts on multiple nights with multiple orgasms and it's absolutely incredible, I've never experienced anything like this, so shut up and get back in your cage.

She was getting better at defending herself against herself, she mused. It wasn't her most articulate and faultless logic, but it was effective. She skimmed through the rest of the paper, determinedly ignoring the delicious flashbacks of the night before that kept tapping at her psyche.

She'd forgotten the beauty of a young, athletic body – how the golden skin stretched smoothly over chest muscles as taut as a drum, how soft and sweet the curve of a neck could taste, how powerful and glowing with life a man's upper body could look, pinning her down and towering over her as he pounded...

"Samantha!"

She jerked her unfocussed eyes from the paper to where Ruth stood in the doorway. "Sorry – miles away," she muttered.

"Quick – TV..."

Samantha grabbed her remote control and switched it on. The President was addressing his fellow Conservatives, shaking his head gravely.

"This is a typical example of the morals and values of the liberal party," he drawled regretfully. "Their hottest new candidate isn't best known for her ability to govern, but for her ability to please men sexually. Any candidate who challenges her is exposed as a womanizer himself. That is what the Democrats' political process has come down to: a desperate search for one person with morals, character, and virtues."

Samantha glanced slyly at Ruth. "You think that's the First Lady's cue to denounce her husband?"

"Now *that* would be too much to ask," said Ruth. She clicked her tongue irritably. "That's all virtue means in politics, these days – not getting laid. It doesn't really matter how sound your policies are, or how able to govern you are, the only badge people want these days is not cheating on your spouse. As if fidelity somehow guaranteed the ability to run a country."

"I suppose it does stand for something," said Samantha uncomfortably. "Honesty – integrity…"

"And you're dishonest and lacking integrity?" snapped Ruth, then recovered quickly. "Sorry, Samantha. Sometimes the whole circus just makes me so angry. No one thinks with their heads anymore. Ninety percent of what swings the polls is completely irrelevant to whether or not someone can actually run the country well. Now Daniel – I *know* for a fact that he'd be a bad choice, because I've worked in his office before. He's terrible at delegating, doesn't allow his speechwriters and staff time to research, and gives them either too much or too little responsibility. The man doesn't have a proper notion of how to manage people, either in their work, in a press conference or at a party. He dismisses things as 'just details' that are *important* details – he's impatient and doesn't distinguish between the two. He's too driven by his ego – his own sense of importance dictates what work he'll do or delegate, whether it's glamorous or not, not whose skills are best for the job.

"Speaking of which, *you* need to delegate more, starting with that website of yours…but apart from that minor challenge, you leave him eating your dust. Your overview – your sense of scale – your ability to cut to the chase in every issue… *These* are the things that matter!"

She shook her fist at the television screen, which was innocently offering a new range of smoothies at a major fast-food chain.

Samantha sat quietly, staring at Ruth in surprise. "Thank you," she said at last.

"Sorry. That was a rant."

"No – don't be sorry. It was a good rant. Do I have any space in my calendar this afternoon?"

"You're free at 3:30, after the committee meeting and before the teleconference."

"Good. See if you can schedule a meeting for me with a good web-designer."

Ruth turned to leave.

"And Ruth – thank you."

Samantha sat on the stairs, whey-faced, trembling, and trying not to make a sound as she cried. Halfway up the stairs, she'd lost the impetus to continue, rapidly followed by the impetus to live. Now she sat in limbo between floors. Richard was in the living room and she was afraid of displaying her useless grief. She could no more explain to him why she was crying than she could fly. She couldn't distinguish between the source of her grief and its symptoms. After a certain point, depression feeds upon itself. When something makes one feel very sad for an extended period of time, one tends to find more things to be sad about. This was how she explained it to herself. Her heart broke with longing to have Faith in her arms, the smell of her hair and soft skin burrowing closer. This was the first night in six years that she hadn't put Faith to bed. The pain of separation was, she discovered, harrowing. Samantha took a deep shuddering breath as she tried to sniff quietly. Anything louder would draw Richard's attention to her pathetic state. She thought about phoning her mother and for a moment conducted the conversation in her head.

(The relief of pouring out her feelings) *Mom, I don't even know what to do – I feel so awful and so unhappy, all the time – I feel old, I think. I'm thirty-one this year, and it seems so old, and then it seems maybe it's young, maybe it's okay, and then I just feel old, and I'm so sad all the time, and I can't bear my life, it's so pointless, everything I do, if it weren't for Faith... Faith needs me, I can stay alive for Faith, but apart from her, there's no point – I'm nothing to Richard, I'm an embarrassment or an annoyance in private, in public a housekeeper or an escort would serve better – I'm putting on weight, I look matronly, he said so himself, I'm not svelte like these girls at the office – he never touches me anymore, it's been five months since we had sex and... and then...*

(Would be met with her mother's anticipated reply) *Stop fussing over nothing and pull yourself together. You've made your bed, now lie in it. What are you complaining about?*

If she knew exactly what she was complaining about, it might be easier to complain.

"There might be some mood-swings," the doctor mentioned while Samantha lay in bed, pale and drained. She'd become quiet again after hours spent screaming, crying, hemorrhaging blood and worse. She was so drugged, her concentration ebbed and flowed. Through the fog, as she struggled to comprehend what the doctor was talking about, she watched Richard approach.

"Where's Faith?" she asked her husband.

"With your mother," he said, holding her hand. She knew he'd cancelled a meeting to visit her in hospital, so she shouldn't have cried inconsolably. She should have been more grateful to him.

The little thing she'd been carrying was gone. She couldn't hold it and look after it, she couldn't keep it safe. She'd failed. Her belly, which had successfully nurtured one child to fruition, was now empty.

When Richard left, she looked at the flowers he'd brought her: pink spray roses, pink gerbera daisies, pink snapdragons, and blue delphinium, edged with green ferns, all wrapped in pink tissue paper and tied with a blue ribbon. She pushed down the ungrateful thought that she didn't like pink much, that she hadn't liked it since she was a little girl. He'd brought her flowers, so he must love her. It stood to reason. It was proof, and Samantha desperately needed proof.

"Mood-swings" didn't begin to describe her experience in the days to follow. She lived each day in a black hole of despair and trudged through her weeks across a bleak, gray and featureless landscape. Everything was monochrome when it wasn't busy ripping her heart to shreds. She looked at her hands, noticing how the pores had started to deepen and tiny fine lines appeared from nowhere: her life was passing by in meaningless waves. Not so long ago, a bright seventeen year-old girl stood at the cusp of experience with shining eyes, poised and ready to change the world. In the last thirteen years, the grand total of her achievements were as follows: one university degree; one child. That was it. Apart from that child needing her mother, she could crumble to dust and the world wouldn't notice the difference... and that was *if* the child needed a mother as broken, despairing and needy as she felt right then.

Pull yourself together, snapped her mother's voice in her head. The words were apt: pieces of her lay all over the place, disconnected. She told no one about the brief visions, which seemed so real, even though she knew they were illusory in nature. In closing a door, she saw herself hanging on the back. A glance in the mirror revealed her brain and heart ripped out. Sometimes, for a moment, she saw the baby floating in the air, with its umbilical cord still attached. Suddenly the baby would disappear back inside Samantha's body.

I'm losing my mind... she thought.

Don't be ridiculous. You simply have a vivid imagination. You're aware of what's real and what's not. Besides, anyone who can sit here crying and know that dinner is three minutes from ready still has a grasp on reality.

This being true, she finished climbing the stairs, already feeling foolish for giving in to her emotions like that. In the bathroom, she washed her face and applied concealer under her eyes to disguise the puffy redness. This only made her eyes look yellow, so she hastily smoothed foundation over her whole face. She didn't have time for more makeup and now looked pale. Pale, however, was fashionable, and perhaps looking the way she felt might earn her a little sympathy. Wan was more appealing than blotchy and red-eyed.

Dinner was macaroni and cheese accompanied by a tossed salad: all she had energy for. She opened a bottle of red wine to go with dinner and whisked up some salad dressing as the main dish settled on the side.

"Supper's ready," she called, her voice deliberately strong and cheery. She wished it had wavered just a little, despite her best efforts.

"Where's Faith?" said Richard, settling into his chair opposite hers.

"At Carmel's house – she's having a sleepover, remember?"

"Oh, yes." He grunted.

Every gesture Samantha made seemed stagy, as if she were pretending to be a wife dishing up supper.

Even her orderly movements and calm demeanor struck her as theatrical.

It's because you're thinking about it, she reassured herself. She was deliberately restraining her limbs, so that she didn't throw things, overturn the table, or crumple in a heap. Her face was harder to control. Immobile and morose, it was a carved mask she carried around. She handed Richard his supper and dished up her own plateful. Out of nowhere, a wave of grief smacked her in the middle. Her hand flew to her mouth, her thumb and index finger clamping over her lips to hold in the tears, her face turned to one side. A huge sob was rising like vomit inside her. She sat motionless, pushing it back down. It passed. The wave retreated backwards over the wastelands of her soul. She took a sip of wine and pushed some pasta onto her fork, determined to appear normal. Before she could put it in her mouth, another bout of tearful nausea hit her.

I'm sitting at the opposite side of the table, drowning in despair, and he's just eating, reading the paper, not even noticing that I'm falling apart over here. It's like a nightmare, when you're dying and you can't get anyone's attention to help you, they all just carry on chatting...

"What's with you?"

He did notice! He does love me! The relief made it harder to keep the tears back as she spoke. "I'm – just – feeling a bit down," she said, misting up. "I'm quite... depressed, actually. It's probably still the hormones settling down, after the... after the..." She couldn't bring herself to say the word 'miscarriage'. "After I lost the baby," she finished, the tears escaping her eyes and rolling down her cheeks.

He looked at her glumly. To her, he was infinitely far away; at the distant end of a long tunnel.

"I need..." she said, in a strangled, tiny voice that could have been called a whimper, but couldn't say what she needed.

Richard sighed. "You need to take your mind off things," he said, not unsympathetically. "Come on – drink your wine, that'll cheer you up. And tomorrow morning it might not seem so bad."

"But every day's the same," she said thinly.

He's trying to comfort you and you're just arguing with him.

But day after day, I've thought, tomorrow morning it'll be better, and it's only ever worse, the sun is black...

"I feel like this *every day*," she said. "It doesn't go away, ever." Her mouth stretched and turned down as the despair started to break through. "I don't... know..."

If Richard had stood up and wrapped her in his arms right then, let her cry in the safety of his embrace, the rest of their marriage might have been different. If Richard had mourned the lost baby, Samantha might have been less lost in her sadness.

Richard frowned. "Maybe you should see a doctor," he said. 'That friend of yours – isn't she a doctor?"

"Marilyn?" Samantha sniffed. "She's a psychiatrist. Maybe I should see her." Speaking made her cry more and on the last few words, full-bodied sobs emerged. "I'm sorry," she gasped.

"Make an appointment tomorrow," said Richard. "And maybe now that Faith's at school, you should find yourself something to do – keep busy."

Samantha nodded obediently through her tears.

"Have some wine," encouraged Richard. He obviously wanted her to stop crying.

She took a large sip of wine to please him, and then a forkful of food. It was getting cold and tasted like indigestible glue in her mouth, but she chewed and swallowed determinedly. Richard was right: she should find something to do. She felt purposeless because she had no purpose, but she wasn't useless.

"Can't anyone see that she's *useless*?" fumed Ben, storming up and down his office, fat stogie in his mouth. On the sofa, Cynthia sat with her legs crossed; sipping her coffee while she watched his tirade. *He is a caricature of anger*, she thought to herself, *If he were alone, would he pace back and forth, gesticulating with his horrible little cigar? Surely not. For whom, though, in this office, was he putting on this ridiculous macho display?* She realized it must be for her benefit – or at least, she was the audience that sanctioned it. Ben slammed his hand against the wall and stood, panting, his shoulders sloped and his jaw set, as if giving imaginary cameras a moment to zoom in.

"She's a cheap whore having her fifteen minutes," he proclaimed.

"Oh, stop it," snapped Cynthia irritably. "She's not some pumped-up bimbo famous for fucking a Senator, she's Samantha St. Clair, the congressperson *you* wanted to endorse for president."

"Only to get us some attention," returned Ben. "How was I to know she can't keep her skirts down?"

"And *that*," said Cynthia wearily, "is as much a lie as calling her a whore. Ben – save your speeches for the media, will you? Samantha is Samantha, the same calm hard-working Samantha she's always been, and if you can't get your head around the idea that she had sex, you belong in grade-school, snickering about how your parents *must* have done it because you're the living proof. It's pathetic. Guess what? I've had sex – you've had sex – every single ancestor of every single person on the *entire planet* has had sex, and not all of it was with their legally permissible partners!" She took a deep breath and put her cup down. "Say what you like in public, but don't even attempt to believe your own bullshit."

Deflated, Ben moved over to the coffee pot and poured another cup. "A desperate search for one person with morals..." he muttered. Louder, he added, "He makes out like we're Sodom and Gomorrah, *us*, the Democrats, when the Republicans..."

Don't give me problems, give me solutions, thought Cynthia, but held her tongue. Ben sat down opposite her, stirring his cup, still scowling and shaking his head.

"We've got to find something to attack her on," he said at last.

"Why do we have to keep attacking her? It seems as if every time we do, she gets more popular."

Ben glanced sharply at her. "Because this race is becoming a *joke* with her in it," he said. "The Republicans are laughing at us, and I'm not going to sit back and do nothing!"

Cynthia shrugged. She didn't take it all as personally as Ben did, so Samantha's increasing success didn't feel like such an affront. "So what are you going to attack her on?"

"Her lack of public service," said Ben slowly, feeling the shape of the formal words in his mouth. They were the kind of formula that newspapers would pick up and use, if fed in the right way. "She is too inexperienced to run the country," he went on, thinking the tabloids might prefer that phrasing. "That has to be obvious – what did she do before she came here? Nothing! She was a housewife for Christ's sake, why can't people just see that? She is *not a real candidate!*"

"The fact that Congresswoman St. Clair is becoming a viable candidate is driving the real candidates crazy," Michael Collins told the reporters. His style was 'candid'; he used colloquialisms and leaned over the podium as if he were confiding in them, chatting over a bar table. It gave reporters the sense that at last, *someone* was telling them what was going on.

"All Congresswoman St. Clair is known for is her sexual indiscretions and her choice not to campaign; not to participate in political dialogue." He spread his hands, as if bemused. "Is that what's considered a viable candidate for presidency? The other candidates all have twenty to thirty years of public service under their belts – she's a two-term representative with no other public service whatsoever. All I'm trying to say, people, is…" He huffed in frustration. "Is this someone we should take seriously as a viable presidential candidate? And shouldn't it be obvious to everyone that she's not?" His rueful smile said it all.

"Perfect," muttered Ben to Cynthia, standing on the sidelines.

"She's only a mother and a housewife," added Michael.

"Oh…dammit…" whispered Ben.

"Are you saying that twenty-five years of being a mother and a housewife disqualifies her from being president or that motherhood, congressional lawmaking and voluntary work aren't public service?" The strident voice was already familiar to Ben from Daniel's disastrous press conference. Its owner had been identified as Carol Hart, from the *LA Times*.

A flicker of panic crossed Michael's face as he tried to replay the trichotomy in his head. He paused, choosing his words carefully.

"I would never undervalue the importance of being a good mother," he said. "I see the miracles my wife performs on a daily basis, in raising my children. But that said, it's not a substitute for the experience of traditional public service…"

"*Your* children?" said Carol, raising a scornful eyebrow.

"Our children," he amended hastily. He turned away from her to take a question from another reporter.

"So are you saying that the nurturing, compassion and intuition necessary for motherhood are not the qualities we want in our commander-in-chief?"

He blinked at her, bewildered. What planet were these women living on? Didn't they understand the presidency has *nothing* to do with all this touchy-feely shit, and everything to do with hard-headed common sense, toughness, experience of managing people, and Goddamned *business* sense? Being president wasn't about *looking after* people, for Chrissakes! Nonetheless, he knew he had to choose his words carefully. The women's movement is strong and easily offended – if he told it like it was, he'd be crucified.

"They are excellent qualities," he said confidently, "and of course they are qualities we want – but they alone are still no substitute for the political savvy that only comes with experience. This is a tough town. Experience is the only way to navigate the rough waters effectively enough to get things done."

Ben withdrew deeper into the wings, so that no one could capture his look of dismay as Michael talked himself deeper.

"So are you saying that," came another woman's voice, "being a mother doesn't make you man enough to handle the politics in this city?"

"No, I'm not saying that at all!" Michael snapped.

Ben covered his face with his hands as Cynthia bit down a smile.

"Are you aware of Congresswoman St. Clair's record of volunteer work? And are you also aware of her consistent voting record in Congress?" called the *LA Times* reporter.

"Do you think being president is only a man's job?"

"In your view, is a woman with children automatically disqualified from politics?"

"Mr. Collins, how did you serve the public while you were a trial lawyer?"

"Yes Mr. Collins, can you please tell us what voluntary work *you* have performed?" Carol Hart's voice cut across the others.

"Please! Please!" How the hell was he supposed to answer their stupid questions if they didn't give him a chance? He glanced across the room at Ben, now standing out of the reporter's sightline, who signaled for him to close it down. "All I am saying is," he declared loudly, over the myriad questions, "that Representative St. Clair does not have the necessary experience to be a good president! Thank you very much!"

He left the podium swiftly amid the din of more shouted questions from reporters. Ben looked at Cynthia.

"Maybe we need a peace treaty with St. Clair," he said tiredly.

"Ben – you're fighting a one-sided war, she's not even in this fight. All you have to do is stop the self-inflicted wounds."

"Don't *you* start."

11

Samantha scrolled across the massive spreadsheet of tiny figures, frowning with concentration. She looked back at the Republican's budget statement and took a deep breath to calm her rising fury as she reread the paragraph.

"Our financial statements show how we can work with Congress to achieve a balanced budget by 2018. But, that accomplishment will be short-lived without addressing our longer-term budgetary challenge—the unsustainable growth in Medicare, Medicaid, and Social Security. By 2040, spending on these and other mandatory programs will crowd out all discretionary spending—for defense, homeland security, or education—unless we take steps to reform these programs."

Her anger was two-fold. One part of her saw red at how the other party manipulated the facts. Mandatory spending *is* a problem, true; soon, the tax revenues will no longer cover the government's unavoidable expenses. Their explanation, however, riled her. Defense is more than a quarter of the budget, but not mentioned in the statement as a high expense. It's also thirteen times what the government spends on education, which the Republicans had the nerve to mention in the same breath, as if the two were equally prioritized in the their agenda. She could feel her bile rising.

On the other hand, the Medicare, Medicaid and Social Security spending *was* out of control, which was why she was scanning the figures to see where all the money was going. She looked at the account names whose spending was in the millions. Federal hospital trust funds, prescription drugs, family assistance, child support and foster care... All of them were intensely important, but how could they use so much money and leave so many families and children in need? She thought of how tight a rein she had kept on the finances for the various charities she'd managed, so that administration costs took only a fraction of the money from the cause itself. Judging from the expenditure and results here, these people were spending like they ran a corporation...

"Bingo!" she muttered to herself. Of *course* they were; most of the people in charge were straight out of corporations, accustomed to surfing the creamy tide of their profits, not ordering the cheap stationery, sharing admin assistants, and driving their own cars. Reform was necessary – but it should be focused on the admin costs, not on the actual services delivered.

"We're not even a socialist country, and we spend more on social security than they do, with less results." She said aloud.

"Am I interrupting a private conversation?" Ruth stood by the door.

Samantha shook her head, coming out of her thoughts. "Sorry, analyzing the budget. Math always makes me talk to myself."

"Analyze this," grinned Ruth, waving a sheet of paper in her hand. "You just passed Collins in the polls and are now in fourth place."

"How did I do that? I'm just sitting here staring at numbers!"

Ruth's chuckle was surprisingly evil. "That 'only a mother and housewife' comment did him in. The women are coming to you in droves."

Samantha's eyes lit up and she drummed her heels on the floor in excitement. "This is *great*!" she squealed. "Fourth place! Fourth place! They are going to *listen* to what I say!"

"The polls also state," said Ruth, peering dramatically at the paper in her hand, "that women don't think men understand their issues and needs as well as you do."

"Of course they don't," said Samantha with a smirk. "Men never thought they were worth thinking about."

"We can't run this organization without proper facilities!"

Samantha turned and regarded the speaker coldly. "And this is your minimum requirement for 'proper facilities', is it?" she asked, tapping the sheets of figures in front of her. "Glossy plastic-coated folders instead of the cheap ones, gel pens instead of ballpoints, meetings in restaurants..."

"It doesn't make *that* much difference, it really doesn't." The other woman's voice had precisely the well-bred sound that Samantha tried to cultivate since marrying Richard. Now, instead of making her feel inferior, it made her angry.

"According to my calculations, you could save a thousand dollars a *month*," she said sternly.

The woman wasn't going to back down. "A thousand," she said dismissively.

"Yes!" snapped Samantha. "A thousand! We have volunteers going out there telling people that for *fifteen cents* they can feed a child, and you sit there throwing away thousands? Do you realize that for what you've spent on your pretty stationery and expense account this month, seventy-five starving children could have eaten three square meals a day? Make that a hundred – the breakfasts are usually cheaper."

All around the table, people were shifting uncomfortably in their seats. *This isn't how things are done*, was the collective attitude, *but Mrs. St. Clair just doesn't seem to realize that. Charity – our kind, not the beatnik kind – is run on goodwill, oiled by gracious teas and women with beautiful hairstyles addressing envelopes. It is not conducted in this frankly ferocious manner. Mrs. St. Clair is making a scene.*

"Thanks to your mismanagement," Samantha continued, addressing the entire group now, "a hundred children may have died of starvation this month. Think about that while you have your lunch. We'll meet back here at 2 pm."

She stood up from the table and strode swiftly to the ladies' room. Locked in the stall, she clutched her arms tightly against her body, huffing and shaking with anger. The waste of money upset her, but the killer was their attitudes. They weren't doing this out of genuine compassion; it was just an acceptable hobby for most of them that looked good on their social calendars, along with an opportunity to get out of the house. She grimaced, reflecting that she'd begun in much the same way.

At least you evolved. But don't raise their hackles too much; they might think you're not very nice.

So people think I'm a horrible person and children get to eat – fair trade.

You'll lose your helpers.

Oh, no, I won't. I've cowed and shamed them, now they'll all bitch about me over lunch and feel secretly guilty, and when I give them a dollop of praise in the afternoon, they'll be eating out of my hand.

That's just manipulative.

Call it people skills. They'll like me in the end.

Samantha checked her make-up in the mirror above the basin, avoiding the full-length reflection to her side. She dabbed powder on her shiny nose.

I really am powdering my nose in the ladies' room, she thought, and chuckled.

"*You're* happy," said Joanna spitefully, emerging from the stall behind her. She was the chairperson of Children's Hunger, which Samantha had just finished blasting. Their eyes met in the mirror, hard. It wasn't worth explaining the joke. Samantha snapped her powder shut. Unable to think of anything to say, she gave a tight smile and left.

In the foyer, Tony, their marketing manager, touched her arm. She recoiled as if from an electric shock, feeling the heat and ice wash over her one after the other. Her heart hammering, she gave him a professional smile.

"'What you said in there was good – it was necessary." He was probably her age, but with her eyes accustomed to Richard he looked meltingly young. His fresh skin contrasted charmingly with the early salt-and-pepper of his curly hair. Even in a suit, instead of his usual jeans and tee, he moved like a cat.

"Thank you," she said, her voice hoarse. She didn't dare smile again or look at him for too long.

"I just... wanted to tell you that," he said. "I think the others might be a bit..."

"Mad at me?" completed Samantha swiftly. "Don't worry, I'm used to it, you don't do audits like this and make friends." She gave him a friendly nod and walked on, before her legs gave way or her nostrils flared.

I must be ovulating, she told herself frantically as she stepped out onto the street. She'd find a café for lunch; she needed to be alone for a bit.

In that case, you ovulate every time you see Tony.

She could feel the blood rampaging through her veins, rushing to her groin, as her insides flipped over repeatedly. In the café, the waiter brought her a menu and her eyes slid over his wrist, up the bare muscles of his arm, to meet his face. As her pupils dilated, his smile changed from polite to a spark of interest. Abruptly, she withdrew her glance and stared downwards.

What is with you? You're practically feral!
God, I need it.

She wiggled against the chair, feeling the slippery sensation in her panties. It was definitely ovulation, she decided. She should be locked in a cage until it passed.

This is no way for a married woman to behave!

She ate her sandwich quickly, avoiding the waiter's eye, and went for a vigorous walk to calm down.

That same evening she decided to meet Richard at work. Faith was at summer camp, the air was silky, and the warmth whispered around her arms and legs. They could go to a restaurant for dinner, she thought, and sit outside in the darkening blues and candlelight. Held in the beauty and stillness of a dinner out, they could talk for a while, the way they used to – spend some time together – pretend they were young and free, again. Her mind drifted to later in the evening, having sex with Richard, and a sudden, small strangled noise in the back of her throat made a passer-by glance at her. The blush crept up her cheeks and down her body. Thirty-five was supposed to be some sort of sexual peak, wasn't it? Was that why she couldn't even look at a man without flushing? She and Richard hadn't had sex in so long, she'd given up trying.

You shouldn't give up on your marriage.

I haven't given up on the marriage – it's just humiliating, coming on to him and getting no response...

You shouldn't give up.

Full of resolve and desire, she pushed open the door of Richard's office. He and his secretary, Terry, were standing stock still, about three feet apart, facing the door. She looked from one to the other. Later, she thought of a dozen different things to say, but at the time she just stared at their obvious discomfort.

"I'll get that letter off now," muttered Terry, walking quickly from the office without looking at Samantha. That snapped her out of her trance.

"There's no need to pretend," she said distantly. "It's perfectly obvious." Then, again, she could think of nothing more to say, so she left. Richard ran after her, but she pushed him aside blindly saying, "Not now – let me think – Richard, go away, I need to *think*!"

Eventually, she conceded she had jumped to conclusions. She had unfairly accused him of having an affair.

"I suppose I was in the wrong," she would say to her girl-friends, thinking how grown-up and fair-minded it was, to admit one might have been in the wrong. In the seventies, women blamed men for everything. In the new equal nineties, one acknowledged that it took two to tango. Self-help books explained that she was complicit in her own pain, that by wearing a karmic 'kick-me' note, she persuaded an obliging universe to kick her. In short: it was all her fault, even that which wasn't her fault.

Samantha and her socialite friends met for 'tea' – the kind that came in a 750 ml bottle with a cork – and sat on each other's stylish garden furniture set atop manicured lawns, engaging in self-deprecation. This bonding ritual among women was intended to expose their vulnerabilities. *Look at me, I hurt, I have done this badly, I don't know what clothes are fashionable, I can't get anything right, I feel insecure, look at me, I am small and weak so you can like me, I won't hurt you. Like me.*

They laughed their way through their confessionals. If someone dashed tears from her eyes, they just squeezed her hand and poured some more wine – here, in the world of women, tears were normal and no big deal. They admitted to each other the appalling, painful things they could hardly admit to themselves.

"He said he doesn't love me anymore, but he doesn't want a divorce. He thinks we have a good arrangement." Mere words belied the reality behind them, which was like a poisonous miasma this woman breathed every night when she lay beside her husband in bed, knowing herself unloved; manifested as the sick nausea she felt when he reached for her, having declared his unlove, and she wondered if this penetration was part of the 'good arrangement'.

"I'm not stupid. It's obvious. But just knowing isn't *proof*." This particular friend thought she didn't mind the idea of her husband 'having an affair', when they had ceased to love each other several years back. The idea of him putting his dick inside another woman, though, then bringing it back home to their bed, made her want to cut it off. This violent impulse was not spoken of.

"He treats me as if I'm one of the children. Our daughter throws these ridiculous teenage tantrums; she screams, shouts and throws things. When I yell at her, he says, 'Calm down girls,' and behaves as though we're two teenagers, instead of a bratty little girl and her *mother*."

When one woman spoke about these things, the others would listen, exclaim, grimace, sigh and nod. The one thing they never did was intervene. No one ever said about someone else's husband: "Look – he's a bastard and he's been mistreating you for years. Why are you taking it? Leave him! Today!" Advice towards making a marriage work was plentiful; advice to leave never came. They all believed, to their cores, that it took two to tango, and never saw that perhaps it took two to maintain a marriage, rather than two to wreck it.

Marilyn, of course, broke the code. Samantha had been pouring out her heart: he was dismissive of her charity work and acted like none of it was important; he refused to discuss any aspect of his own life with her; he complained about the money she spent on cosmetics and clothes, but was angry if she didn't look perfectly groomed and dressed at every event; he told her she was overweight and matronly; they hadn't had sex in *two years*. The understanding was that she could say these things to her best friend because nothing negative would come of her complaints. Their usual table in their usual coffee shop was a safe place where all the rage and pain could be expressed and defused. In this understanding, she didn't need to balance all this with the good stuff – which she vaguely thought of as 'the good stuff', without being exactly able to list it.

"Jesus, I am so fucking tired of listening to this *shit,*" said Marilyn, during a particularly harrowing chat date. "Samantha: he's a bastard! He's always been a bastard! You have *never* been happy in your marriage! Just leave him already!"

"*What?*"

"You fawn and scrape around him, you pretend to be ditzy when you're the smartest woman I know, you take his verdict on everything, and you waste your time fretting and worrying all the time about what Richard thinks, what Richard feels, how to make Richard love you more... Snap out of it! He's a selfish prick. Leave!"

"At least I'm making an *effort* with my marriage!" Samantha spat out. Her eyes and nostrils flared with rage. "Maybe if you did the same, your husband wouldn't be screwing the duty nurse!"

Marilyn's face whitened, first with shock and then with dawning realization. When she spoke, it was a whisper.

"So that's how you choose to tell me. I step out of line to tell you what no one else will, though they're all thinking it – I try to do you a Goddamn favor – and you tell me that to *hurt* me. You use this information as a weapon. Jesus Christ, you are sick." She was shoving her stuff in her bag, hurriedly. It always took her a while to gather her possessions. Everywhere she went, she unpacked as though the world were her home. Now she swept it all back in a jumble, muttering through her rising tears, "You think you can trust people, but you can't – you think it's just men that are brutal, but women are the worst – women don't just stab, they twist the knife..."

Marilyn tossed some crumpled bills onto the table and looked up, her eyes shining with tears, her nose and cheeks suddenly red. She never cried gracefully. "I thought we were friends," she said. "I'm sorry we're not."

She left abruptly – to hide her sobs, Samantha knew. She knew the set of Marilyn's shoulders when she cried and how she pulled her frothy hair over her swollen, reddening face. It occurred to her, as she sat numbly in front of the detritus of their coffee date, that she knew Marilyn better than she knew Richard. After a few minutes, she paid the remainder of the check, fixed her eyes where the mascara had bled a little, and stood to leave. She was married to Richard, not Marilyn. Her first loyalties had to lie with him.

Samantha lay on the fold-out couch in her office, a blanket draped across her middle – she was happy to have her legs revealed, she could even cope with her breasts dangling loose, but she didn't like to expose the stretch-marks on her stomach. Thomas lay beside her, hands under his head, staring at the ceiling. Was he bored? She knew she really ought to be cuddling up to him, gazing in his eyes, and purring with sexually satiated contentment, but she really only wanted to watch the news.

"He's stupid for doing this," she muttered.

"Who's stupid for doing what?" asked Thomas, his eyes not leaving the light fixture overhead.

"There are a few women protesting outside his headquarters, so now he wants to put all women in their place!"

Thomas rose up on his elbow and looked at the screen. "Who are we talking about?"

"My husband."

He froze, uncomfortable, and then shifted to sit up next to her, laying a possessive arm around her shoulder. "Okay, babe, get me up to speed here. Who's doing what?"

"Shh! listen!"

"...come forward accusing you of sexual perversions and a need to dominate women. Are you refuting these stories?" asked the interviewer on screen.

Richard was being filmed in a large chair behind his gleaming, broad desk. Samantha shook her head. This display of power was not the way to win back his female customers.

"No, I'm not," said Richard, with a confident smile. She remembered that smile from decades ago, when she had stood on a lawn watching her date throw up, and Richard put an arm around her. Now, through the camera and the TV-screen, it was as if he was smiling directly at her again. *I did love him*, she realized, with surprise. That smile weakened her, still, with its promise of mastery and warmth. *All that trying to make it work – it wasn't for nothing – it was because I did love him, and feeling his love slip away was like bleeding to death inside, where no one could see it and he could pretend nothing was wrong. I knew something was wrong long before he did. It cut me to pieces because I really did* love *him.*

Her eyes welled with tears as her heart went out to the lonely young woman she had been, grieving alone for their dying love, desperately trying to breathe life back into it. *You poor thing. You poor little baby. If only you had known I'd be here, older, wiser, looking back with so much sympathy – I wish I could go back and tell you it'll be okay, even if it would never be the way you wanted. But you wouldn't want to know that, would you? You wouldn't want to know that the love would die, despite your fiercest efforts, and that you would survive it.*

She hoped Thomas wouldn't notice the tears as she blinked steadily, not too fast, keeping them at bay, not drawing attention to herself. All the while, she was also watching and listening to the interview.

"…I'm here to tell it like it is," said the confident smile that brought back the memory of love. "I'm here to make a statement about human nature that everybody knows to be true. That men and women look at sex differently."

"Oh, really?" The interviewer sounded skeptical. "How exactly is that?"

He leaned forward on one arm to speak more intimately to the camera. It was an outdated gesture of confiding trust, and Samantha winced.

"While women look for tenderness and romance and passion in their lovemaking," he explained, "men need to have the excitement of the chase, and raw animalism of conquering their pray, to quench their sexual desire."

"The excitement of the chase?" prompted the interviewer, her voice dangling the words as if from reluctant fingertips.

"A willing naked woman lying in bed next to me is not what gets me, or most men, aroused. What men need to get the full arousal from sex is to see, desire, chase, then conquer their sexual partner. It's the thrill of the chase that makes it exhilarating. It's just the way that men and women are, there's nothing we can do about it, it's a biological fact."

"So there was nothing your wife could have done to turn you on?"

Richard frowned regretfully. "No, nothing," he said, with sadness. "She was an innocent victim of human nature."

"Let me get this straight." The interviewer took a deep breath. "Your defense for your behavior is that you are only being a man, and it's only natural for you to have conquered a large number of women as part of your sexual being."

He half-suppressed a cocky grin. " 'Fraid so" he said. "And I'm not just a man – I'm a man's man. An alpha male. I live to conquer in the boardroom and the bedroom, and that's just my nature. If things are just handed to me, there's no exhilaration – who wants what they can just have? It's striving for things that excites us, satisfies us, makes us want it."

"So women should just accept that men cheat because that's just human nature?"

"If they want men to be real men, they'll have to accept the consequences, yes. We hear a lot of feminist talk about women being their true selves and celebrating their femininity, but when men celebrate their masculinity, people get very upset – but if women are really honest with themselves, it is the masculine men they find attractive. Not the touchy-feely sensitive wimps who share their emotions all the time. In other words, men I like to think of as women with penises." He chuckled at his own joke.

Samantha had been gaping in disbelief. Now she covered her face, peering through her fingers, almost writhing with embarrassment. *It's a train wreck! It can't be true, no one can be this stupid, no one can think it's a good idea to say this stuff – oh God, I can't believe how he's carrying on.*

"Show me a couple who've been married twenty years and still have a passionate sex life. I'm telling you, it doesn't exist, it can't exist, it's not natural."

She couldn't stand it any longer and snapped the television off.

"You know what the problem is?" She looked over at Thomas.

"What?"

"He's got no women to advise him on this stuff. He just hangs out with a bunch of good old boys who think exactly like he does."

"You know," said Thomas thoughtfully, "He's not so far off the mark, though."

Samantha's jaw dropped, but even that wasn't sufficient enough to express her shock. A familiar sense of impotent rage boiled inside her, like bile burning acidic holes through her insides. What was shocking to her was obviously not to him, so how could she shock him into realizing how clearly wrong it was? At times like this, she understood why people resorted to fist fights to settle differences of opinion. Hitting him would be a lot more satisfying than trying to persuade him in an argument, during which she'd have to hear his abhorrent opinions expressed. She breathed deeply, marshalling her thoughts. *Don't jump to conclusions.*

"Which part do you agree with?" she asked cautiously.

"Pretty much all of it, to be honest," he said, puzzled, as if it were a purely theoretical discussion. "I mean, it's what makes our set-up ideal, isn't it?"

"Our 'set-up'?"

"Yes, we're not bogged down by all that relationship stuff – not everything's about one person, we're free to do what we want, see who we want, and have amazing sex together…" His hand reached for her breast as she leapt off the bed, snatching the blanket from him.

"Get out of here," she said shakily. "You faithless shit, get out."

"Honey…" He sat up, looking hurt. "It *is* unnatural for a man to have sex with the same woman for a long period of time."

"Get out of *here now!*" Her voice rose to a roar as she shoved him hard, sending him toppling onto the floor.

"I just need different women at different times – men aren't designed to be monogamous," he pleaded. "It doesn't mean I don't care for you and cherish our time together."

"For *how long*'" yelled Samantha. "What's not a long time – three weeks? Six months? What kind of *shelf-life* do I have as a sexual partner before I'm biologically disposable?"

"I've gone about as long as a year before…"

"Get out!"

He studied her face for a moment. Clearly alarmed by her expression, he struggled into his clothes as fast as possible. She swept his socks, jacket, shirt and tie up in her arms and threw them out into the corridor as he hopped around, pulling his trousers on.

"OUT!" she bellowed. As he fled through the open door, she slammed it behind him. The unused adrenalin of rage, which in some more purely *biological* time might have been used to kill him, made her shake violently. Her gaze fell on his shoes as a tentative knock came at the door. She whisked it open and flung them hard at the opposite wall, to his astonishment. She would have liked to throw them smack in his face, but she wasn't an animal and wouldn't behave like one.

12

Ben glanced around the conference room, surveying the six presidential candidates who weren't Samantha St. Clair with satisfaction. In his own mind, he described them as 'solid', 'strong', or 'convincing' candidates. They were all powerful-looking men, well-dressed in conservative, tailored suits. They looked, to Ben, like presidents tend to look, which he defined as possessing 'an air of authority' and behaving 'statesmanlike' rather than, more accurately, white middle-class middle-aged Anglo-Saxon protestant men in good suits.

"Okay," he was saying, "the first group TV appearance that will include Congresswoman St. Clair is coming up. We need one of you to step up and make her look like the weak-willed woman she is."

The group all glanced at each other expectantly. Nobody volunteered.

"Is there *one* of you who doesn't have some skeleton in the closet?" pressed Ben impatiently. This time, nobody met his eyes.

"For Chrissakes, can't you politicians keep your hands to yourselves?"

The silence continued as Ben put his hand to his forehead, alternately squeezing and smoothing out the deeply wrinkled furrow at the center of his brow with his fingers and thumb.

"Okay," he said eventually. 'If *no one* has an un-checkered past – we'll have to attack her on something else. Ideas, please."

Dallas Clark, the Governor of New York, spoke up. "What does she stand for?"

"Have you read her website?" countered Ben. Dallas shook his head, his lips pursed.

"Then you wouldn't know, now would you." Ben's voice dripped in sarcasm. He hadn't read the website himself – he didn't have time to do his own research – but then he wasn't running against her for president.

The senator from Illinois, Palmer Davis, gestured for his attention. "I've read her website," he offered. He glanced at the group. "It's one big wish-list full of fluff," he explained. "A big government fantasy full of bureaucracy and red tape flowing as far as you can see – not to mention probably unconstitutional, she practically wants to turn us into some kind of socialist commie state."

"Go on," said Ben.

"She lists everything in the world that would make this a better country, but she never says once how she's going to do it, or how she's going to pay for it. It's the kind of unrealistic bullshit that looks pretty on the page, which voters will just lap up, but it will never work in practice."

"Can you attack her on this during the show?" pressed Ben.

Palmer grinned slowly and widely, his teeth never showing, his lips stretching into a huge curve. "It will be my pleasure," he said with satisfaction.

"You will have to break her down, convince the country that she doesn't belong on this stage; that she just hasn't got it what it takes."

"When the show is over," Palmer assured him, "Samantha St. Clair will be toast!"

Hope glanced in the rearview mirror at Samantha, who was staring out the window; hand on her chin, index finger firmly pressed between her lips.

"Are you alright, Ma'am? Is there anything we need to talk about?"

Samantha shook herself out of her reverie and gave a quick unconvincing smile. "No, I'm fine, thanks, Hope," she said.

"Are you sure?"

"Yes, I'll be alright."

Being alright at some future point, reasoned Hope, did not constitute being fine now, but she took the hint and drove in silence. All her other protection jobs had been conducted in this kind of unspeaking stiffness, but after Samantha's usual bright chatter it felt strange.

"Hope – do you ever think men and women just don't belong together in the long run?"

"Yes, I do sometimes. Just about every time I'm dropped off from a date, in fact."

Samantha chuckled. "Really?"

"May I be frank?"

"Of course."

Hope pulled off her sunglasses and glanced at Samantha seriously in the mirror. "If it weren't for sex and procreation, I'd pretty much see men as completely useless." Despite Samantha's obvious shock, she went on. "I know that makes me a pretty militant feminist, and about as sexist as the worst of men, but that's the conclusion I've come to."

"Wow," said Samantha slowly. "You're pretty young to be so bitter... It usually takes twenty years of a failed marriage to reach *that* conclusion."

"Think of my family," said Hope shortly. "That low-life abandoning *shit* of a father of mine... my mom hanging about acting like some notion of a good wife when the husband was long gone... It doesn't have to be your own marriage to make you think like that."

Samantha frowned. "I don't *like* thinking like that..."

"Me neither."

"I guess I'm just some kind of hideously incurable optimist... I spent so many years, just waiting for Richard to change... And then I figured, okay, my husband's a faithless bastard, but that doesn't mean this man's going to be…" She started to cry abruptly and Hope winced in sympathy.

"There're tissues in the compartment in front of you." she said.

La Loma's was crowded, making Samantha feel paradoxically less exposed. The buzzing horde of people around her, all probably more interesting to the press than she, were as much a camouflage as she could wish for. Marilyn ordered second margaritas over Samantha's protests.

"I feel like I haven't seen you for ages, let's have some *fun.*"

"I see you three times a week at the gym," said Samantha defensively.

"Come on, that's not the same as going out together."

Samantha laughed. "That's what I always used to say to Richard. And he could never see the difference."

"Can you?"

"Guess so." She took a mouthful of refried beans, a small blob of sour cream catching on the corner of her mouth. "God," she mumbled, swallowing hard while dabbing at the cream with her napkin. "I am such a pig of an eater sometimes."

"At least you're enjoying your food. I was starting to worry you'd fade away completely with all those salads."

The two women were sharing a *platillos combinados* of enchiladas, taco and tamale, alongside the ubiquitous rice, beans, and guacamole.

"So how's Thomas?" asked Marilyn slyly, drawing out his name.

Samantha's good mood vanished abruptly. "I've no idea. I haven't seen him since I threw him out of the bed in my office, and then his shoes after him." She replied in a hushed tone.

"You kicked *Thomas* out of *bed*? Why would you do that?" She hissed.

"Because he agreed with the prick!" Samantha hissed back, looking around their table to insure privacy. She took a large sip of her margarita and set it down a little too forcefully, sloshing a few drops over the rim. She leaned in across the table. "I mean," she said with forced calm, "he agreed with Richard – that ridiculous press conference Richard held where he said that it's okay for men to sleep with anything that walks and women must just accept it – that that's what it *means* to be a man – he agreed with that."

"Oh. Dear." Marilyn laid her fork down. "Did you think Thomas was being exclusive – with just you?"

"Well, yes, as a matter of fact I did." Somehow, the knowledge that Thomas had been sleeping around made Samantha feel undignified; she straightened her posture in response.

Marilyn leaned in, "Sam? The guy looks like a Greek God, he's hung like a prize salami in the front window of a butcher shop – and you didn't think he was spreading it around?"

Samantha glanced at the table next to them to see if the couple seated there had overheard, but they seemed too absorbed in each other and photographing every stage of their meal.

From her surreptitious perch at the bar, Hope reacted instantly to the camera flash. Snagging a passing waiter, she gestured to Samantha's table. The waiter wandered over to Samantha, blocking the view of the couple next to them, and leaned in close to Samantha's ear.

"Pardon me, Madam, but there is an important message for you at the bar." He jerked his head in Hope's direction and promptly left.

"Excuse me a moment." Samantha dabbed at the corners of her mouth and lifted herself stiffly from her chair. Marilyn watched her move toward Hope, lifted up her margarita glass and took a sip. She noticed the pair at the next table were also watching Samantha.

The waiter soon returned with two white carry-out containers and began assembling the remainder of Marilyn and Samantha's dinner neatly into the boxes. Before Marilyn could respond, Samantha returned and gathered up her things. She leaned in and whispered to her friend, "Let's continue this in private, hon." She caught Marilyn's eye and gestured discreetly toward the curious couple, who suddenly became very interested in their dinner.

Only after the two ladies were safely ensconced in the back of Samantha's car, and Hope had calmly pulled away from the curb, did Samantha turn toward her friend.

"Sorry about that, honey…there was a…what did you call it, Hope?"

"A possible security breach, ma'am." Hope said over her shoulder.

"Right, a possible security breach. Apparently the press just can't get enough of me these days."

Marilyn stared at her friend in astonishment. After a moment, comprehension dawned on her face, "The couple with the camera!"

"Exactly." Samantha replied.

"Wow," leaning forward, Marilyn looked at Hope in the rearview mirror. "Damn, you're good!"

Hope caught Marilyn's eyes in the mirror and nodded.

"So to answer your question about whether I knew that Thomas was seeing other women, no I didn't, actually."

"Why not?"

Samantha sat quietly a moment, staring at the sleek leather posterior of the seat in front of her, puzzling out the answer. Marilyn's words made it seem obvious that Thomas would be sleeping around; but before their fight, Samantha had considered it equally self-evident that it shouldn't be.

"Because… I thought there was more to him than just sex," she said eventually. "I mean – okay, he's a stud, in a way, but that doesn't make him some kind of prize stallion with no purpose – or thoughts – or personality – or *existence* beyond the placement of his...appendage. I was giving him credit as a human being. He acted so sweet, kind and attentive; he *acted* like I was important to him, like I was *uniquely* important to him – it just never occurred to me..."

"He's a *man*, Sam. What did you expect?"

"You're a hypocrite, you know," replied Samantha conversationally, her fingers playing with the folds in her skirt.

"What?"

"You won't let anyone say what women are, how women should be as women, and then you make all these judgments about men."

"It's different."

"How?"

"Because..." Marilyn floundered for a moment, before landing on her argument. "Because women have fought *against* all that shit, while men have fought for it – women try not to just accept their conditioning and men celebrate it!"

"Maybe. It's not important anyway – the generalities, the reasons. He's history." "Good."

"And that's why I'm turning lesbian."

Hope glanced at her a moment in the rearview mirror, before returning her gaze to the road.

"Yeah, right." Marilyn sighed.

"It sure is tempting, though – at least I'd know what the other half is thinking."

Marilyn snorted. "Uh-uh," she said. "Matching bodies doesn't come with mind-reading, you know. And when your PMS falls in synch with each other, your partner has eaten the organic dark chocolate you had stored away for *just that moment*..."

"Are we speaking from experience here?"

"Brief experience. I love women, and I *love* breasts, but I just couldn't cope with the rest."

"Really?"

"Really. It surprised me. I figured if I was fine with my own, I'd be fine with anyone's, but in the event… it just didn't…I mean, it was nice – it was soft – I was *gentle* with a woman, the way I haven't been with a man in years – maybe ever – I even got an idea how men feel with us, sometimes – that – that sense of maybe you'll *crush* something – but in the end…" Marilyn was tongue-tied, describing her experiences with women, as Samantha had never seen her about men. It might not have been what she wanted sexually, but she seemed to feel about it more sincerely than she did about her male lovers. Samantha reached out and gave her friend's hand a squeeze.

"Well, if lesbianism is out of the question, I'm going to become celibate. I did it for fifteen years, I can do it again."

"Uh-uh. No, you can't. Once the dam is broken, the flood gates are gushing. You're going to need sex again at some stage, Samantha, and that some stage will be soon."

Samantha shook her head obstinately.

"Let me tell you – when I left Frank, it had been a *long* time – not fifteen years, but we're still talking years here. *Years*. You weren't around then, but they were double-digit years."

"I remember," said Samantha. "You told me."

"And I thought I'd just stopped needing it, and then suddenly – I just couldn't get enough. I went on a sex-fest, and you will too, just like all the other middle-aged divorcées who've just discovered they don't have to live as sexless matrons for the rest of their lives."

Samantha's mouth was still set in a line, unconvinced. Marilyn felt unpleasantly judged, as if her own need for sex were being sneered at.

"What makes you so different from any other woman?" she said defensibly. "Why do you think you can cope without it?"

"Because I've come to the conclusion that the momentary pleasure it provides is just not worth the emotional flood-damage."

Samantha sat in her designated seat on the set of Meet the Press, replying in measured tones to Tim Russert's questions. Her hands, which she usually rested in her lap, darted through the air in instinctive rhetorical gestures. These would be described later as 'balletic', both positively and negatively. She wore a dove-grey suit and white, collarless blouse, accessorized with brushed platinum earrings and shaped necklace. These would be minutely catalogued to an avid tabloid audience, who would nevertheless be left in doubt about the other candidates' clothes.

"Would anyone like to address Congresswoman St. Clair on her response?" asked Mr. Russert.

Senator Palmer Davis, resplendent in a charcoal Italian suit over a Sea Island cotton shirt, with a woven silk Cheltenham tie in mauve and white, raised his hand, his onyx cufflink gleaming discreetly. "I would like to ask Congresswoman St. Clair a few questions," he said.

"Go ahead, Senator Davis."

"First of all, I would like to personally welcome Congresswoman St. Clair to the show, and also to the Democratic primaries," he said generously, inclining his head.

She allowed her lips to form the hint of a smile.

The arrogance of it! Who's he to welcome me? As if it were his club and I was a guest...

"According to your official website," he continued, shuffling notes in his hand, "in addition to many of the comments you made tonight, you make Lyndon Johnson look like a penny-pincher by saying the government should take care of every less-fortunate person at all costs. Do you really think this is responsible government?"

"Yes, I do. I believe one of the major roles of government is to make sure people are given adequate support in times of difficulty and that in so doing it is acting in the best interests of society, both long-term and short-term. A government must exist solely to serve its citizens."

She had reluctantly conceded the need to use sound-bites. She and Faith had argued the matter over for hours. Faith had insisted that short phrases, which could stick in the memory and be used as headlines, were essential to getting her message across. Samantha thought that any message worth listening to should be given sufficient space and that compressing an important thought into a few stylish words was cheap. The audience didn't need dumbing-down, which was all it usually ever got. Eventually, they had agreed a compromise: Samantha would give her full arguments, but for every one she must add a sound bite. The mother and daughter had spent an increasingly hilarious evening thinking up seven-word summaries for her political platform.

"So what you're saying is," Palmer now said, "that no matter how gravely these poorly-designed public assistance programs are plunging us deeper into our already burgeoning deficit, if you keep throwing enough money at it, things will eventually come up rosy."

Samantha raised an eyebrow. *No more Mr Chivalrous*, she thought.

"I hate to inform you, Congresswoman, it doesn't work that way. We live in the United States, not a dream state, and until you understand the depths of how difficult it is to govern and the complicity of the problems we're facing, your naïve intentions are more dangerous than they are good.

One of her major strengths, reflected Samantha, was that she rarely lost her temper in an argument and so was able to listen and think carefully, without getting distracted by personal attacks.

"Complexity," she said.

"What?"

"The problems are not complicit – although we may be complicit with the problems – they are complex."

Palmer bristled. "Whatever," he muttered dismissively. "The fact remains that you can have whatever idyllic pretty ideas you like, and try to deceive the voters with them, but at the end of the day it *doesn't work like that*."

"Maybe it should."

"Excuse me?"

"Maybe government should be that easy." She transferred her gaze from Palmer to the audience, sweeping her eyes over them. "Maybe if our government envisioned a society where everyone received a living wage, it would happen. Maybe, if our government believed it was possible for every child to go to bed with a full belly, it would be possible. Maybe, if our government officials looked past their own next election and catered to all citizens, not just their big donors, there *would* be health care for everyone, good schools for all, alternative energies that don't pollute and that end our dependency on foreign oil. Senator Davis may dismiss it as naïve, even Pollyanna-ish, but you must be able to envision something is possible before you can make it happen. As long as you believe it is too difficult or too complicated to achieve, it will be. You will never consider how to *make* it possible, unless you think it is. As in life, so in government."

She made a small tick on her list of sound bites. She should have taken a bet with Faith which one the press would like most.

"But, but you can't just *daydream*," stammered Palmer, "and turn around and throw money at it! You can't just say, 'oh I have to believe it's possible' and then pretend that's the same thing as *being* possible – our taxpayers work very hard for their money and they expect their leaders to spend it wisely!"

"Indeed," said Samantha. "Our current spending includes..." She raised a hand to count the items off on her fingers. "Subsidizing *profitable* companies to build refineries, spending a trillion dollars on an Islamic theocracy in the Middle East, building bridges to nowhere, providing obsolete weapons to appease our defense industry lobbyists, and adding yet more nuclear weaponry to an arsenal already capable of decimating the planet many times over. None of this is really particularly clever, or wise. I'd imagine bringing some people above the poverty line, building some decent schools, and giving the less fortunate some health care won't be the worst thing this government ever spent the tax payer's money on."

She gave Palmer a rueful grin but he kept his face averted.

"I am very efficient at cutting waste, Senator Davis," she went on unsmilingly. "If you actually *have* read my website recently, you would have seen exactly how I intend to finance these initiatives with less, not more, national debt than we are currently accruing. If there are any particular steps you'd like to take issue with, please specify them"

Palmer maintained his silence.

"Senator Davis," asked Tim Russert, "do you have anything else to add in response to Congresswoman St. Clair's statement?"

"No, I'm done."

Backstage, Ben's fingers were digging hard into his forehead as Cynthia pressed down a tiny grin.

"You better believe you're done…" he muttered.

13

The next day, Samantha arrived at the office before Ruth and scooped up a fat pile of the day's papers. She flipped through them eagerly, wondering which of her witticisms they might have quoted. The quality papers, as usual, barely mentioned her – either nothing at all, or an inch of who-what-when-where with no detail. Irritated, she turned to the tabloids, where she was usually covered in greater detail.

Nothing... nothing... nothing... What the hell...?

The social pages at the center held the usual array of fault-finding photos of celebrities: who had left a club at dawn, red-eyed and looking like hell; who had more of a tummy today than yesterday; who had kissed who on which beach; and so forth. At the top of the second page of one particularly invasive tabloid were a few carefully arranged photos of Samantha arranged in sequence beneath the heading "Put *this* in your mouth"

All of them were from the same evening – her dinner at La Loma's, with Marilyn – and each were unflattering depictions of her enjoying her meal. Each photograph was accompanied by its own caption; one read, "Open wide…" portraying Samantha's lips parting to take in a forkful of tacos; another chided, "Missed a bit" describing a close-up shot of sour cream adorning the corner of her mouth; "Swallow, spit or gargle?" portrayed her taking a large sip of margarita. A few others were interspersed throughout the article of her chewing, putting food in her mouth, or taking a sip of her drink, suggesting that she'd had a marathon meal and a barrel of alcohol.

The accompanying text reproved, "Congresswoman Samantha St. Clair opened wide for a double-helping at DC's hip Mexican restaurant, *La Loma's* this weekend – the

Democratic presidential candidate just couldn't get enough! No wonder those skirt-suits are starting to look a bit tight..."

"I kick Davis's *butt* in the show last night and this is what they report on? I had a meal out?"

She covered her mouth with her hands, studying the unflattering photos. Hope hadn't reacted soon enough. Faith had warned her about fickle tabloids; if they were on your side today, they'd kick you in the teeth tomorrow. Cruelty sold better.

She heard the clatter of Ruth's arrival in the outer office.

"Sam? You're in early. Coffee?"

"Yes, please," said Samantha glumly.

"What's the matter...?" began Ruth, and then saw the spread of papers. "Bad write-up?" she asked sympathetically.

"*No* write-up. Barely a mention of my appearance on Meet the Press, just a dissection of a meal out that makes me look like Jabba the Hutt."

"I know it's hard to take, but in a way, it is a compliment," said Ruth gently. "They're acknowledging that you're a celebrity, because that's what they do to celebrities. Who else do you recognize on that page?"

"Everyone," said Samantha, glancing through them.

Ruth leaned over to study it. "Take her. Probably the world's most beautiful woman, fantastic actress, UN Goodwill Ambassador – what do they say about her?"

The lovely actor's face was contorted in a momentarily imperfect expression, making it look like she was snarling, and the suggestion of a blemish had been circled in red. "Pregnancy takes its toll" said the headline.

"You've just got to accept it and try not to pay attention," said Ruth. "It's a pretty harsh lesson in how careful you have to be in public. These people sit on the edge of their seats trying to make anything "newsworthy". Besides, how you look in the polls is what really matters."

"Well, the numbers are in and 43% of the viewers said St. Clair out-performed the other candidates on Meet the Press yesterday morning. And she's passed Davis in the polls to be third place." Cynthia hid her smirk as she delivered the news.

Ben scowled, sucking on an unlit stogie. "This can't be *happening*. The Junior Rep. housewife from Michigan is becoming a viable candidate? What's happening to these people's *minds*?"

"It gets even worse," said Cynthia cheerfully. "There are rumors that the Republicans are registering as Democrats all over the country so they can vote for her in the upcoming primaries. They really want her in the general election."

"*Fuck*," spat Ben, dropping his little cigar. "The enemy of my enemy is my friend – they *know* St. Clair is hurting us, she's damaging our reputation…"

"How exactly is she doing that, sir?" The cheer had abruptly vanished from Cynthia's voice.

Ben stared at her and she met his eyes, expressionless. "It's obvious," said Ben. "She's a no-hope candidate…"

"In third place," interjected Cynthia.

'That's just a *fluke*, Goddammit! She's got no real ideas…"

"Hasn't she?"

"Don't give me this bullshit, Cynthia, it's bad enough getting it from my wife without you turning on me as well. She's famous for fellatio and that's *all* she's famous for."

"I'm not sure it's that simple anymore."

Samantha sat curled up under her blue blanket with a box of tissues, watching *Love Actually*. As Emma Thompson fought down tears, waving her hands in front of her face, blotting her eyes with a tissue, straightening the bed, and breathing deeply, Samantha found herself sobbing convulsively. Watching the other woman try not to cry at the discovery of her husband's adultery, while trying to keep up appearances in front of the family, cut at her heart more than a total breakdown would have. She recognized, in that determined normalcy, her own doomed attempts to keep the appearance of a marriage running smoothly, as if the empty façade could last forever. She wept in sympathy for the character, Karen, but also to make up for all the times she'd refused to allow herself to cry over Richard, and now for Thomas too.

"Hey, Mom..." Faith slung an arm around her shoulder and hugged her closer.

"I'm such a flake," sniffed Samantha, half-laughing. Crying over films was easier than crying at real-life events; it was somehow easier to laugh off, and one felt less helpless.

"Don't feel bad, I cry every time I see it and I've seen this film about half a dozen times." Faith wiped her own eyes with a crumpled smile.

When the film ended, Faith switched over to the news channel while Samantha gathered the supper dishes and empty glasses. Halfway to the kitchen she stopped abruptly, turning back to the television.

"As a result of millionaire Richard St. Clair's controversial statement that infidelity in men is both natural and inevitable, many women's groups have organized a nationwide boycott of all St. Clair Industries hair care products. With the majority of the company's market being women, sales are down by over 75% for the week and Wall Street analysts have lowered the estimated public offering price from $56 to $24 a share, with the caveat that it may go even lower if this attack on the company continues. The cost of this move to St. Clair Industries is estimated to be between three hundred and four hundred million dollars."

"Three hundred million dollars," said Samantha distantly, still clutching the dirty dishes.

"Or four hundred million," added Faith.

"All this because of his ego…" Samantha sat down, stunned. "My God, what a price to pay…"

"He got what was coming to him," said his daughter grimly.

"Yes," said Samantha, still sounding far away. "Yes, I know."

"Mom, where's the Mediterranean?" asked Faith, balancing her fork on the back of her knuckles.

Richard set his own fork down with a clatter. "You don't know where the Mediterranean is? What are they teaching you at this school?"

Samantha, equally surprised by her daughter's question, glanced anxiously at Richard.

"I was talking to Mom, not to you!" flared Faith.

"Don't speak like that to your father, Faith," said Samantha automatically, unconvincingly.

"I have the right to answer questions in my own house!" Roared Richard.

"It's *our* house too and we live in it more than you do anyway!" Faith yelled back.

Samantha sat frozen, muscles tensed, eyes filled with worry. Her daughter exhibited a bravery that she never had. Perhaps it was Richard's own temper, come back to haunt him in the form of his twelve year-old daughter.

"I am your *father*," he bellowed back, rising from his chair. Faith was quicker.

"I wish you *weren't* my father," she screeched, leaping up. "I wish you were dead! I hate you!" She fled, wisely, to her room. In the distance, both parents heard the door slam and the faint click of its lock.

Richard, trembling with rage, stood by the table with fists half-clenched at his sides. After a few seconds hesitation, he seized up Faith's abandoned plate of food and flung it across the room. It shattered on the far wall, leaving a smeared stain of spaghetti on the otherwise pristine wainscoting. Samantha said nothing and willed herself invisible. Richard sat down heavily again and began to shovel food in his mouth.

When she judged it safe, Samantha spoke hesitantly, "It's a difficult time for her, Richard – she's going through puberty and very touchy..."

"I don't fucking care *what* her problem is," shot back Richard. "I work damn hard all day and I expect to come home and *not* be disrespected by my own daughter. If you were any kind of mother..."

He left the sentence unfinished, for which Samantha was grateful. After dinner he retired to his study, where he spent most of his evenings in recent days. Samantha had no idea what he did within those four walls - closed off from the world by two heavy, dark doors; but she felt increasingly glad when he withdrew behind them. The entire structure seemed to breathe easier in his absence.

She cleared up the shattered plate and spilled food in silence. With fresh food on a tray, she quietly mounted the stairs to Faith's room. Balancing it on one hand, she knocked softly.

"Go away!"

"Honey, it's me..."

Faith opened the door, her face wet with tears.

"I brought you some supper," said Samantha, walking in and closing the door behind her.

"I'm not hungry."

"Well, I'll just leave it on the dresser in case you change your mind."

Samantha sat down on the bed and held out her arms to her daughter, who hesitated a moment before diving in to her mother's embrace.

"I *hate* him." The words were muffled by Samantha's shoulder.

"You don't hate him, honey, you just feel like you do..."

"Well, that's the same thing, hate's a feeling, so if I feel like I do, then I *do*." In spite of herself, Samantha was impressed with her daughter's logic.

"Why did you have to marry him?"

"If I hadn't, I wouldn't have you," said Samantha lightly, wiggling her daughter's chin.

"You could divorce him. Other people get divorced. Then we wouldn't have to live with him."

"But I love him." Faith could think of no argument for that, so Samantha continued, "And I'd like you to go apologize to him. For me," she added.

"He can apologize first. He called me stupid."

"No, he didn't."

"Yes, he *did*. He *implied* it."

"Oh, Faith..." *Richard's temper and my flare for arguing a case,* she thought wryly. *What are we going to do? And she's still only twelve.*

The next day, Samantha bought two blow-up globe maps of the world. She also bought two wall maps – the Mercator and the Peters projections, which showed the actual size of countries, rather than exaggerating the size of the West – and big sheets of tracing paper.

"I've got a present for you," she said, hands behind her back, on the first day of summer vacation.

Faith's face lit up. She was heartbreakingly easy to please. "What is it?"

"The whole world..."

As Faith frowned, Samantha threw the ball to her and Faith jumped back, catching it.

"And I've got a project for you."

Every summer, Samantha dreamt up a project for Faith, from learning to tie bows to baking to counting in different languages. Each day that Faith completed her set quota of the project, she got a silver star, which added up to different rewards, depending on her age.

"What?"

Samantha pulled out a big piece of tracing paper. "A problem that people have struggled with for centuries and centuries," she said. "How to put *that...*" she gestured to the blow-up globe, "On *this*." She waved the paper.

"That's *easy*," said Faith.

Samantha grinned and raised her eyebrows. "Oh, really? Let's see how you do."

Faith turned to the colorful plastic ball in her hand, examining it. "There's no countries!" she objected. "It's all green and brown – where are all the countries?"

"This is a map of the *world*," said Samantha. "The countries are just something people added. But can you find the United States?"

Over the rest of the summer vacation, Faith tried out various techniques attempting to draw the globe's shapes onto the paper, with Samantha's encouragement and praise urging her on. Gradually, her mother added more information and materials: the two most famous solutions to the problem, in the form of the two wall maps; and a second globe with the countries marked on it. As she learned more, Faith became more creative with her projections and maps. On one particular day, she turned them all upside down.

"You said north isn't necessarily *up*," she said, "so this is just as true to an astronaut, right?" An astronaut Lego-man hung suspended above one of the globes. With Samantha acting as the sun, Faith made the earth rotate and revolve until she was dizzy and fell over, laughing.

When she'd chosen and finished her favorite projection, they began adding information about each country – population levels, languages spoken, what form of currency they used, and so on.

"For an extra-big reward," said Samantha, "I'm going to assign you an extra-hard test."

"What's the reward?"

"We redo your bedroom *completely* – exactly how you want it- now that you're practically a teenager."

Faith glowed with excitement. "And the test?"

"I'm warning you – it's very hard… but then you're very clever."

"What is it?"

"To draw the whole world – from memory."

Faith's eyes widened, then narrowed in determination. "A physical map or a political map?" she asked.

14

Samantha sat in front of her desk, tallying up her workload on a pad of paper. In the early days of her work, she'd estimate how long things would take – and found they usually took two or three times the length she allowed. As a result, she became more realistic with her estimates. With her recent workload, however, she couldn't afford to be realistic or she'd never get home to sleep. Samantha quickly reviewed how long the amount of work would actually take, then how much time she actually had and could afford to allot to each chunk.

"I need more staff," she said to herself.

"Definitely," Ruth replied. "I'm working like a demon all day then I go home and dream about work all night. Why can't I have the *good* dreams, where I'm lying around Hawaii drinking fruity cocktails?"

"Tell me about it!" laughed Samantha. "So what are the other candidates doing – how are they stomping all over the country and still being a member of Congress, or a Senator? What do they know that I don't?"

Her words were part joke and part despair as she contemplated the mountain of paperwork building up in front of her, both actual and virtual.

"They do have a secret, actually," said Ruth, leaning against the desk. "They don't do it all."

"But this stuff is *important*. If this doesn't get done…"

"Of course it's important – to people who care. To people who don't care, or better yet don't even *know* about it because it's buried at the bottom of a tower of paper, it couldn't matter less. Your problem is you're too damn conscientious."

"It may be a problem for me, but it's a damn good thing for my constituents." She looked at the heaps of files again, then wiggled her mouse and looked at the near-infinite scroll of unread emails, all with official subject headings and most with attachments. She pushed her chair back from the desk and folded up, her head in her hands on her knees.

"It's too much, Ruth," she said, muted by her fingers. "I'm delegating everything I can and there's still too much. I wish I could delegate sleeping – or eating…" She sat up again, abruptly. "Okay, get everyone in here. I'm going to have to start giving whole chunks, whole projects to people, or this stuff's not going to get done." She gave a dry laugh. "It's promotion time…"

By the end of the meeting, the only thing she hadn't delegated was sleeping and eating. One or two half-raised objections were met with a warning glare and quickly retreated again into silence.

"We have a lot more on our plate than we used to have," Samantha finished up. "If we succeed, we'll get even more – and a larger staff." That brought a few grateful laughs. "But for now, we've got to bite the bullet hard with what we have. Okay – back to work. Lots to do."

As the small group filed out, she heard the Press Secretary mutter "Someone *seriously* needs to get laid again…"

Her face deadpan, Samantha closed the door behind them and resisted the urge to kick it violently. If a man behaved authoritatively, he was being 'tough' and 'manly'. If a woman did, she was 'sexually frustrated'. The fact that she was *also* sexually frustrated didn't make that double-standard any less irritating.

At nine in the evening, she rang Hope's cell phone. "Elvis is leaving the building," pronounced Samantha.

"Okay – there's someone waiting here who wants a word with you – he says you know him."

Samantha's heart turned to ice with fear. "It's not Richard...?" she whispered

"No, he says his name's James. Don't worry, I frisked him already, he's clean. He's been waiting a while."

"Okay, I'll be out in a sec."

James, James, who do you know called James?

She stood at the door to her outer office, staring at the reflection of her own puzzled face against the glossy finish, trying to place the name. In her mind, she ran through the names of all her acquaintances, people she'd worked with on different committees, members of different charities, people she'd been introduced to at parties...

The problem with being so well-known is everyone knows you better than you know them.

It's late; I just want to go home. Why can't people come at normal hours?

You did say no interruptions all day on pain of death... and you are a servant of the public...

Slave of the public, more like, it feels.

Hope was waiting for her in the outer office, a strange man standing nearby; his back turned as he examined a painting on the wall. With her eyes, Hope indicated that this was the person waiting to see her.

"Hello, I'm Samantha St. Clair." She strode forward, hand outstretched, moving into her super-efficient mode. That usually encouraged people to get straight to the point.

"Samantha!" He spun around. He was tall, pale, with floppy black hair that made his skin even whiter by comparison and his eyes shockingly green; his face illumined with a smile as he shook her hand vigorously and enthusiastically.

"I'm sorry," she said, "You are..."

"It's James," he prompted, in a light English accent.

An Englishman called James...?

"I'm sorry – you don't remember me..." He pushed a lock of hair out of his eyes, a shy gesture. "We used to..."

"James!" She yelped. The face of a beautiful fifteen-year-old, enshrined in her memory with teenage paper hearts all around it, suddenly morphed into the face in front of her. "That James! Oh my God! What are you – but your accent – how..." She reigned herself in. The lovesick thirteen-year-old puppy that had worshipped him was now a fully grown woman with *gravitas* and a presidential candidacy. She tried to return to serious mode, but her smile kept breaking through. "What are you doing here?" she managed to ask, without interrupting herself.

"I'm on holiday," he replied, his plummy vowels running down her spine. "I thought I'd pop in and see you – they do rather keep you in Fort Knox, don't they? Your agent here is positively terrifying!" He cocked his head towards Hope with a grin.

"Are you – what, are you living in England, now?"

"For the last twenty-seven years, yes." He chuckled.

Their mouths moved rapidly through the usual small talk, filling in details, while their faces shone and their eyes remained locked on each other. Occasionally one would break away from his or her gaze and laugh, saying "I can't believe it," and "It's been so long," and other formulaic gap-fillers.

He tracked her down, as it turned out, through a reunion website. "Matthew Johnson told me you were running for president," he said. "I remember you two used to go out, so I asked if he had any news of you."

"And he said..." Samantha was suddenly cautious.

"That you were a presidential candidate for the Democrats – my God, you're impressive. I feel a lot better about losing that debate now! Losing to someone two years younger than me was embarrassing, but losing to a future president? That's an honor!"

Samantha blushed and glanced around. Hope was still sitting patiently on the sofa, leafing through a newspaper.

"Oh, I'm sorry, Hope – I'm keeping you waiting… James, I really want to catch up…"

"Me too!"

"I'm just so busy…"

"Oh, of course." He suddenly withdrew into formality. "I completely understand, you must be absolutely run off your feet. Well, I don't want to keep you…"

"James, that's not what I mean! I won't have another chance all this week, so are you busy now? Have you eaten?"

She took him to La Loma's. Hope perched on a barstool close at hand, as the waitress seated the couple at a table toward the front. Samantha and Hope simultaneously glimpsed a familiar-looking couple at a nearby table, holding cameras. Samantha signaled Hope to stay put.

"Excuse me a moment," she said, standing up. After a quiet word with the *maitre d'*, the two were politely and firmly escorted from the restaurant, protesting loudly about their rights.

"Sorry about that," she said to James, her words belying the faint smirk on her face as she glanced briefly at Hope. "So – what do you want to eat?"

Over dinner, it gradually emerged that James really knew nothing at all about the scandal surrounding her campaign. The British media, it would seem, did not trouble themselves too much about the peccadilloes of American politicians.

You should tell him. It's dishonest not to.

What am I going to say? Oh – by the way – my campaign kicked off with a photo of me giving head? How do I work that *into the conversation?*

He'll find out anyway, you know.

So let him. Just because other people might kick me, doesn't mean I have to join in.

"Did I tell you Marilyn's in DC?"

"Marilyn…?" James began questioningly, and then a spark of recognition flared in his eyes. "Not Marilyn Trent?"

"Marilyn Malone, now. *Doctor* Marilyn Malone, no less. She's divorced, but it's her professional name so…."

James raised his eyebrows briefly. "And you? You're married?"

"Um – sort of." She glanced at her hand uncomfortably.

"Well – you have the ring and the surname…"

She smiled ruefully. "And that's about all I have. That and a beautiful daughter." Her face brightened at the thought of Faith. "We're…" She floundered a moment for a way to describe the nonentity that was her marriage, and realized a word already existed for it. Other people had been in this situation before her. "We're separated. What about you?"

He gave a sad smile and sighed. "I was. That's why I stayed in England – I met this amazing girl…" For a moment, he looked as though he might cry. "She's dead."

"Oh, James – I'm so sorry…"

"It's okay." He blinked rapidly. "It's been a couple of years. It's just strange, telling someone who doesn't already know. Who doesn't – didn't – know her. Tell me about your daughter."

He obviously wanted to change the subject, but Samantha found herself suddenly unable to utter a single word about Faith.

"She's… umm…" Her mind blanked horribly. She wanted to say, *Oh, she's wonderful, she's so smart and talented, she's just beautiful, you should see her, and you'll never guess what she's studying…* but for some reason her throat clogged up and not a single word would come out. The food arrived, sparing her the embarrassment of continued silence.

"So, what do you do?" she asked instead, lifting a spicy chicken wing.

"I'm an environmental consultant."

"Really?" she said, surprised, then with more excitement, *"Really?* My God James…that is *just* what I need. James, you *have* to help me… oh, damn, you're on vacation aren't you – I'm sorry, I just don't switch off…"

"Relax," he laughed. "What is it?"

"It's just, my campaign – I don't actually have an environmental consultant, and I do need one, it's an aspect that's important – it's not really part of my platform yet, I'm unrolling things gradually – the whole campaigning process takes a long time you see, and I do think it's important for things to develop – to have proper research before you just say *this* is what I'm going to do. I'm sorry, I'm talking too much."

He was sitting with his hands steepled, chin resting on them, smiling at her. "That's okay, I'm enjoying it. God, it's good to see you again. You know you haven't changed a bit."

She tossed her head a little. "Don't be silly…" At his words, her body seemed to melt and reshape itself into youthful freshness. Her face felt beautiful as she laughed away her embarrassment.

"Really, I mean it."

"Then either you're a liar or I look thirteen."

His eyes crinkled with amusement. "Taking you for dinner is probably illegal, then."

She made a gesture as if to swat him and sent his margarita flying into his lap. He leapt up, grabbed a napkin, and she flinched, raising one arm defensively. He stood, margarita running down his pants, staring at her as she slowly lowered her arm.

"I was reaching for the napkin," he said, appalled.

"Yes – of course."

"Samantha." He sat down again and very slowly, reached over and took her hands in his. "Did you think I was going to hit you?"

"Of course not," she said uncomfortably.

"But you backed off – you raised your arm."

"Instinct," she said lightly.

He shook his head gravely, his eyes never leaving her. "I'm not a violent man," he said softly, "but right now I think I could hunt your husband down and kill him. Because I think he is. I think he hurt you."

"Don't be ridiculous, of course he didn't. He had a temper, but he didn't *hurt* me."

She never took Richard's temper seriously. "It's just his way," she would say, or "He doesn't mean to upset anyone." Taking it seriously would have put everything in a different category – it would have made an angry shove into 'domestic violence', which was just an absurd exaggeration. He simply had a bit of a temper that was all. He was under a lot of stress. *It's normal*, she told herself, and learned how to live around it, to avoid provoking it, and to pacify it.

When Faith was fifteen, she came in half an hour late from a date. Sheer bad luck had it that as she closed the door softly behind her, Richard was walking from the kitchen to his study with more ice for his whiskey.

"What the hell is this?' he demanded, staring at his daughter. Samantha, who sat in the living room, closed her eyes for a moment in dread. She'd told Richard Faith was already home and tucked in.

"What the hell is what?" countered Faith. Samantha winced. Despite her fear, she stood and moved towards the hallway.

"Don't you speak to me like that, young lady," Richard habitually engaged in fatherhood-by-cliché; throwing out appropriate lines at selected intervals but otherwise relatively absent from her life. "Your curfew is eleven o'clock!"

"So it's eleven-thirty. There was traffic. Hi, Mom."

"Hi, baby." Samantha stood in the doorway, throwing a tight smile towards her daughter before glancing anxiously back at Richard.

"You lied to me!" he said, turning on his wife.

"I just didn't want you to worry..."

"It was a goddamned *lie!*" He approached her and she shrank back. *Don't show fear, don't show fear*, she reminded herself, even as she retreated. Faith followed them into the living room, stomping and confident.

"She's home now, it's fine." Samantha tried her hardest to sound normal. "Everything's okay, isn't it, honey?"

"Yeah," said Faith, unconvinced. "Just fine."

"Where were you?" Richard looked hard from his daughter to his wife.

"At the movies." Defiantly, Faith flipped back her long straight hair and jutted out her chin. Samantha's eyes darted to the purple love bite on the girl's neck and quickly away again, but not before Richard had seen her glance.

"What's that?" His voice was low and menacing.

"What's what?"

"Honey... Richard..."

"I will *not* be undermined, Samantha! I am the authority in this house!"

"You're the *money* in this house!" snapped Faith.

"Faith!" cried Samantha, terrified.

"You little slut..." Richard's voice was rising as he bore down on his daughter. Moving faster than she thought possible for herself, Samantha bounded across the room to stand in front of Faith. Her eyes filled with pure hatred as she spoke.

"Don't you *dare* lay a single *finger* on my daughter." Her voice was low and quavering, but venomous.

"I won't," said Richard, his anger needle-sharp. "Because it's not our daughter's fault, is it? Who taught her to be a disrespectful little slut, huh?" His hand grabbed Samantha's throat. "Huh?" He shook her, clattering her teeth together.

"Dad, *stop it!*" screeched Faith.

"Shut up!" With his other hand, he shoved Faith's shoulder, sending her tumbling backwards onto the sofa.

"Faith, honey, just get to your room," said Samantha, her hands tugging at her throat to pry away Richard's fingers. "Your father and I need to talk."

"You're not *talking;* he's *hurting* you," wailed Faith, almost in tears.

"Faith, *get out!*" screeched Samantha. Her only concern, while Faith was in the room, was that Richard's desire to hurt someone stayed focused on her, the mother; as long as he was trying to throttle her, Faith was safe. If the girl would only get herself behind a locked door, Samantha could risk fighting back. Part of her stood separate, withdrawn, making notes on her reactions, surprised at the force of her maternal care and amazed at the scene that was taking place. The threat of violence had always crept around the outskirts of their marriage. She'd been physically afraid, many times. He shoved her on occasion, or clenched his half-raised fists, but never actually *hurt* her like this.

Samantha realized she was struggling to breathe. Faith was still vacillating in the doorway, tears streaming down her face, while Richard's expression turned more and more thunderous, his skin pulsing and red. She managed to fight down a deep shuddering breath through her nostrils, and the remote part of her mind said *Whisky – he's drunk*, as she forced out the single instruction, "*GO...*"

Faith ran. Samantha kicked up with her knee. Richard howled, doubling over, yelling "You *bitch*, you *bitch*..."

Samantha wavered, unsure what to do. If she ran after Faith, Richard might still chase her, and then her daughter would be back in harm's way. The other side of the house had no doors she could lock. Her body seemed to be running in two directions at once. Before she could make a decision, Richard slapped her across the jaw, jerking her head violently to one side and knocking her off balance. She let herself fall, because it seemed easier than attempting to stop it. At least, it *felt* like she was letting herself fall, as if she could have caught herself if she'd only tried. Something about the whole absurd scene seemed *put- on*, despite the pain, despite the fear. She bounced off the side of the armchair, hurting her ribs, and landed on the pale deep-pile carpet. She didn't notice her head hitting the living room table as she went down; the impact impairing her before the nerves could report any damage. She now lay on the floor, her head twisted to one side, staring at the carpet. Disconnected thoughts meandered through her mind.

I remember choosing this carpet, she thought.

You have chosen your carpet, now lie on it.

If I get up, he will hit me again.

I could get up, if I wanted to – it's not that I'm incapable, it's not that bad, and I'm not that hurt. I'm just pretending.

She could hear his breath, hoarse and uncertain. She thought, *It's quite nice, just lying here. I think I'll stay here for a bit.*

Why am I lying on the floor?

She heard a knock at the door, then the doorbell. Stillness blanketed the household. The knock came again, with a shout. "Police! Open up!"

The sound of a door opening, then Richard's voice: "Evening, officer. Is everything alright?"

The police took statements. Faith's and Samantha's differed slightly: Faith, crouched on the stairs, had seen and heard her mother's head smash against the wooden table, before she called the police on her cell phone; Samantha had no memory of it. Their descriptions of the fight were confused. Samantha was taken to hospital, where a concussion was confirmed, but "no lasting damage has been done," she was assured. Richard stood mute. This was a time when domestic violence wasn't necessarily criminal, not if it was against your wife, at any rate. Samantha was asked if she wanted to press charges and she stared at the police officer, bewildered. "Against my husband?" she said numbly.

"Yes, ma'am," said the police officer, a young Caucasian woman who crouched down to speak to her; radiating sympathy. "He has committed violence against you, Mrs. St. Clair, but we cannot prosecute him unless you state you would like to press charges."

Samantha shook her head in disbelief. She was still disoriented and struggled to process all the information.

"We can protect you if you are afraid of retaliation," urged the officer. "In this day and age, this kind of behavior is completely unacceptable."

Samantha's confused eyes settled on the young woman. "This day and age?" she said distantly. "*Was* there a time, then, when it was acceptable?" The moment of clarity, like a blue butterfly that had briefly settled, moved on. "No," she said, her eyes faraway. "He didn't mean it. He won't do it again."

The officer compressed her lips. "If you change your mind... You can change your mind, you know." In her experience, the women who said "he won't do it again" were the ones she saw again, with more severe injuries, sometimes fighting for their lives. Sometimes it was too late.

"He won't do it again."

"I won't do it again – oh God, Samantha, I'm so sorry." Richard was a powerful man, unaccustomed to making apologies. He sounded urgent instead of ashamed. "I don't know what came over me."

She knew she was expected to say something, but couldn't find any suitable words. Even in her addled state, the truth: "Whisky, a propensity for violence, and the need for absolute authority: that's what came over you." In her floaty faraway state, she found she could think more clearly about her marriage than she ever had. Some self-preserving instinct held her back from fully expressing her thoughts, however, so she took refuge in the injury he'd provoked.

"I'm just so tired," she murmured. "I just need to sleep..."

He never did do it again. The shoving, clenching of fists, slamming of tables, throwing of crockery, all that went on, but he never *hurt* her again. She grew so accustomed to the sour smell of fear that she barely noticed it anymore. It faded and she even forgot why she avoided doing or saying certain things.

"They're all pretty mad at me," panted Samantha, "apart from Ruth – obviously. But they'll get over it."

"Good for you!" gasped Marilyn.

Their legs pumped up and down in unison, cycling up imaginary hills represented by little graphics on the electric screens of their cycling machines. Above them, the gym's in-house television played music videos.

"And you know what? I don't even care! Because I know that ultimately it's going to be to their advantage…"

"No…" Marilyn wailed, pounding her head against the padded handlebar. "Have I taught you nothing?" She let her pedals spin free and took a large swig of water from her bottle before handing it to Samantha.

"Thanks," her friend gasped.

"The whole point," Marilyn resumed, "Is not to let all your behavior be decided by what's *nice*. How many times have we been through this? Self-actualization 101! It's okay not to be nice!"

Samantha grinned and with a flick of her wrist, splashed Marilyn with condensation from the bottle.

"Hey!" Marilyn barked, then stopped herself. "Okay – point made – well done. That wasn't being nice."

"Actually… I thought you looked kinda hot and could use some cooling down…"

Samantha laughed as Marilyn groaned.

They carried on pedaling in silence as Samantha drifted into the imagery of a *Tristan and Isolde* music video above them. Fragments of the film were interrupted by the lead singer, woolen cap on his head and wrapped in winter clothes, trudging down an urban street at night. She wished they would show more of the actual story. The young Isolde's creamy beauty as she flipped through the pages of a book, lying on the sand, lit up Samantha's heart. Images of dolphins and slow-motion running across the beach were probably a bit over the top, she mused, but as the camera settled on Tristan for the first time, she smiled.

"That reminds me!" she exclaimed abruptly. "You'll never guess who I met up with!"

"What reminds you?" said Marilyn, bewildered.

Samantha jerked her head up to the screen, just as Tristan's pleading beauty was replaced by the scowling singer. "Someone we both know," she prompted. "Someone quite – um – yummy, and fifteen years old… Well, he *used* to be fifteen years old."

"So did everyone! Who the hell are you talking about?"

"James!"

Marilyn stared at her, eyes widening. "James Franco? You met James *Franco*? Of all the lucky…"

"Who's James Franco?"

"That is." She pointed at the video, which showed him sailing the Irish Sea.

"Huh? Oh, no, that just reminded me. I'm talking about James *Laughton*."

Marilyn still looked blank.

"Oh, come on! You used to date him."

"Oh, yeah… that James…" said Marilyn vaguely. "I remember now. We weren't ever that serious, though, it was just a fling. So what's he up to?"

Samantha gave her a brief synopsis, fuming inwardly that the boy she'd adored had meant so little to her more fortunate friend.

"I still don't get what the video had to do with it," said Marilyn when she'd finished.

"Never mind," said Samantha shortly. "I just thought they looked similar. That's all."

Samantha and James sat close together, their heads bent towards each other. In front of them lay a colorful photo album which Samantha was flipping through, smiling with pleasure, while James pointed to particular pictures and gave a running commentary.

"I had no *idea* it was so pretty!" she exclaimed at last, sitting back and picking up her coffee again. "I mean from the name, it just sounds… well, muddy."

"That's what most people think. But it's beautiful, isn't it?" James lingered over one of the photos, his finger running over it. "Look at those colors. That rich purple maroon – it's almost like wine – and then that scattering of green, just enough to set it off. And there are so many different kinds."

"And you say peat bogs are more important than rainforests?"

"No, no, *no*," exclaimed James quickly, turning from the photos back to Samantha. "We need everything we can get, the rainforests are crucial, everything is. Peat bogs, though – all of them, put together – store *three times* the amount of carbon, compared to the rainforests. So they're a major help to us. But, the reverse is also true – digging them up is *worse*. Most people think that with plants, it's just a question of whether or not they're there to absorb the carbon. What they don't realize is that all these plants are *storing* the carbon, not destroying it. So when we kill the plants, we're doing two things: we're knocking out one of our precious carbon sponges *and* we're releasing a whole lot of carbon. Double-whammy, you see?"

"Yeah... There's so much I don't know," she sighed, looking up. Around them, the cafeteria was filling up.

"You're not supposed to know everything – that's why people have consultants." James grinned and Samantha's face brightened a little.

"I don't want to encroach too much on your vacation, though..."

"Sam, it's fine, I promise. I will tell you if I mind – I haven't become *that* English. But I love this stuff – I love being able to explain it to people who are in a position to actually do something – and I really...enjoy spending time with you again. Anyway, I'm only half on holiday – I'm also here to look into moving back to the States. Jobs and such. So helping you might just help me, as well."

Samantha picked up the other file on the table and flipped through the summaries and graphs of his presentation again. "Be careful what you offer," she said mildly, "It might be accepted..." She closed the file and checked her watch.

"Have you got to dash?"

"No – I've got another five minutes. So what are you doing for Christmas?" She only meant to make conversation and abruptly realized how tactless a question that was, to a widowed man. "Seeing your parents?" she added quickly, trying to soften it.

He shook his head. "I'll pop in to my mum's. She's in a care-home. She doesn't recognize any of us anymore, so it'll really be just to make an appearance. And my dad's dead. My sister's invited me over, but I don't know... we don't really get on, you see – she hated Emma. So, what about you?" A quick slight widening of his eyes showed that he realized the question was equally awkward for Samantha. "Sorry. I suppose it's – painful. Being separated from your husband and your daughter and all."

"I haven't even thought about it. The campaign's been taking my every waking moment. There's no way I'll be seeing Richard.

"And your daughter?" he asked.

"Faith? Umm – oh... I..." Samantha frowned, swamped by a wash of grey sadness. She stared at the table, trying hard to marshal her thoughts, but her mind was abruptly empty.

"I'm sorry," said James, putting his hand over hers. "I didn't mean to upset you."

"It's okay," whispered Samantha, her eyes filling with tears. "Um – I don't... know..." Trying to think about it was like wading through mud.

"If she's not going to be around," said James cautiously, "do you want to do dinner together?"

Samantha nodded wordlessly. She couldn't work out why she wouldn't see Faith on Christmas. Perhaps there were some plans or something she'd forgotten about. She looked at her watch again and suddenly snapped back into the present.

"I've got to run – James, I'll call you, okay? And I definitely want to hear more about this." She gestured at his presentation. Seizing her bag, she dashed off to her next meeting.

15

What little daylight January had to offer was blotted out by persistent, gusty sleet. Wind chased people into their buildings and by the time they left work in the evenings, they met darkness and rain. In contrast, Samantha's office glowed with warmth, light, and order. She snapped another file closed, added it to the growing out-pile, and checked her email again. With the new staff she'd taken on and the reshuffle of responsibilities, she no longer needed to do this task herself. Nevertheless, she scanned the list of names looking for James Laughton, assuring herself that she only wanted his input on her environmental stance. Her mouth twitched and she double-clicked her mouse.

"Hi Sam," she read. "Yes – can give you lots of useful links for your website, interactive pages, etc. that can bring home to people what's actually happening. Check doc attached. Re: your point about fuel – *do not be sucked into the idea that 'science will fix this'!!* Everyone says, oh don't worry the scientists will sort it out, but won't listen when the scientists say this is damn serious and we need to act NOW to sort this out. Sorry. This bit makes me very angry. WE ARE THE SCIENTISTS AND WE SAY WE'RE ALL GOING TO DIE AT THIS RATE (graph attached). Okay, rant over. Fuel – has to be a mix of solutions, no one answer is "the answer", and HAS TO include using less. We *cannot* support consumption levels and will never find a way out if we continue to consume the same amount of resources – the 1st solution is to use less. Unpopular, I know. But in my experience, people are very willing to change their lifestyles to help; it's only the politicians who say the public will never accept that. Yourself excepted, of course! Ok, enough chattering – the docs you need are attached. Hope your busy schedule can squeeze in a coffee sometime soon. Would love to see you. James.

She smirked at the last two lines and glanced at the clock. Time was tight, but she could just manage a quick reply.

"Thanks for docs" she typed rapidly, "Can't wait to read them though am hidden behind giant towering pile of paperwork and may never see daylight again." She stopped and frowned. That made it sound as if his research were an unwelcome addition to an already heavy workload. She changed it to, "Can't wait to read them! Sorry about comment re: science – obviously this is why I need a consultant!" She scowled at her words. Perhaps it would be better if she only replied when she had read the papers and had something to say. Then again, his friendly comment at the end deserved a response. She started again.

'Thanks for docs – can't wait to read them! Feels like my calendar is full till eternity but how about..."

She stared at the screen, thinking. She no longer managed her own calendar and was not entirely sure when she was free. She had a meeting right now, however. She deleted the half-written email and closed the window. Impulsively, she hit reply again and as fast as possible typed "Thanks for docs – can't wait to read – coffee sounds lovely, no idea when free but will ask assistant."

She shook her head. She should ask her assistant *first*, then email him. She hit close. "Save changes?" asked the computer optimistically.

Samantha and James had just spent Christmas together. Somehow, even though both of them had done all the normal and proper things in life, both were ending up in middle age alone. Death, estrangement, and senility had made short work of all the family ties that ten years ago had seemed so multiple and demanding. To avoid attracting the press's attention, which would likely revolve around her spending such a 'family-oriented' day with a strange man, she'd

invited him to her apartment for dinner.   Aside from
Marilyn's quick visits, James was her first real guest. With
her Christmas decorations stored in Michigan, the rooms he
walked into were Spartan, yet candlelit.

"Sorry it's so bland," she said apologetically. "I meant to
get a tree, at least…"

He raised his eyebrow. "That I would not have
forgiven."

"Oh. Of course!" She burst out laughing. "And I guess
not getting any decorations or anything…"

"…is entirely responsible and I'm impressed by your
environmental commitment," he finished smoothly, winking.
From behind his back, he drew out a crimson potted
poinsettia. "I don't buy cut flowers," he said quietly, "or I
would've brought you roses."

Flustered, she retreated into hostess mode, offering to
take his coat and replace it with a drink. She rushed off to
the kitchen to get ice for the gin and tonic he requested and
stood in the center of the neon-lit room, fanning her cheeks
with her hands. She hugged herself, trying not to giggle.
Once again, she wanted to travel back in time to her younger
self who was crying her eyes out over James with Marilyn
and say *just wait, just you wait, it's going to be fine…*

*What would you tell her? Don't worry, when you're
forty-seven you'll have him over for Christmas dinner?*

She chuckled to herself.

"Having a good time in there?" called James.

She stepped back into the living room to find him
meandering around its edges, studying her pictures and
books. Her other home – the smart mansion in Michigan –
was geared up towards this kind of inspection and presented
as seamless a façade as her entire life, until recently, had
done. This apartment did not showcase her in the same way.
These things don't say anything about me, she wanted to
explain, *It's just the stuff I like having around me*. Before
she could speak, she realized that her current environment

signified a raw honesty far beyond any tasteful display of classic literature and muted décor. She sipped her drink and enjoyed watching him as he scanned the shelves, his hands deep in his pockets, and his head tilted to one side. She'd laughed at him when he said she hadn't changed, but now she could see, exactly, the fifteen year-old she'd worshipped so helplessly. His lanky frame and floppy hair had the same effect now as they did then, and when he glanced over his shoulder and gave her a silly grin, her knees nearly folded.

"Sorry," he said. "Terribly invasive of me."

"It's fine. I've got nothing to…" As she spoke, Samantha's eyes fell on a row of four matching books – two from Marilyn and two she'd bought herself. She blanched. His eyes followed her stare and lingered on the spines. When he turned back into the room, his expression was unreadable. He sat down without speaking and reached for the drink she'd set on the table.

"I – I hope I haven't shocked you."

He shook his head. "No – not in that way, at any rate. Just, déjà vu. Umm. Emma used to buy those. I used to tease her." He took a gulp of his drink. "Shit. Trust me to ruin the atmosphere."

He hadn't, though. If anything, it softened and became more relaxed. She stopped feeling the need to impress him by having four vegetables ready simultaneously or by having each course appear without any apparent effort. He stopped being a good guest and instead donned an apron over his suit, made the gravy, whipped the cream, and helped her dish up.

"It's funny," she said, as they lingered at the front door saying goodbye. "Hanging out with you like this feels like…" She bit back the words 'coming home' just in time, saying instead "…family. It's just so comfortable."

"Brother James, eh?" he said with the ghost of a smile, raising one eyebrow.

She glanced in his eyes shyly and shifted her weight from one foot to another. "Kind of. Yeah."

"Are you *sure* you don't want me to sort out the dishes?"

"Really – it's fine. I don't think I've ever worked a guest so hard, as it is!"

"Right, then. I'll say goodbye." Through the usual ritual phrases of salutation, he kissed each of her cheeks and gripped her hands warmly, then left.

After her meeting, Samantha checked her calendar with her assistant and rattled off a reply. "Thanks for docs, can't wait to read! Coffee sounds great. How's Thurs 9 pm? Hope you can make it!"

She studied it, wondering if two exclamation marks was excessive and if so which one to delete. It could seem warm and friendly, or it could be taken as hysterical. Something blurred in front of her face and she screamed in fright.

"Sorry, sorry," said Ruth, whose hand had been waving in front of Samantha's nose. "I did say your name a few times…"

Samantha held one hand over her solar plexus, breathing heavily to calm herself. "Sorry – concentrating…" she gasped, and then laughed. "You scared the shit out of me!" She hit 'send' on the email before she could change her mind again and turned to Ruth.

"Latest analytics from the site," Ruth slid a report onto the desk. "Summary's on the front – you're doing well. And your own site now comes up on Google way before those pictures do – in fact, you've pushed them onto the second page."

Samantha picked up the report and scanned swiftly through it. "Good. Now if only the press would start taking me equally as seriously… Oh, for God's sake!" She slammed the report down, dislodging a tower of files that Ruth caught mid-slide. "Most popular page – about me. Second most popular page – photo album. *Photo album!* They'd rather look at my photo album than read my policies? Maybe I have overestimated people."

"Easy, tiger..." said Ruth. "Don't let the press hear you say that."

"What would it matter?" snapped Samantha. "They don't report what I say anyway, they'd just tell people what color my hair is today. As if it changes. Only *apparently* it does, *apparently*, according to People magazine, I'm experimenting with different tints and tones!"

"Okay, okay." Ruth pulled up a chair opposite her. "What's got your goat?"

"Meeting with PR," Samantha said tiredly. "I was just fast-forwarded through last month's press coverage and it wasn't pretty. It wasn't all cruel, it was just – fluff. In the eyes of the press, I'm fluff. And then this." She smacked the report with her knuckles. "Give people the opportunity to find out some real facts, some real policies, and what do they hone in on? The fluff. I really, *really* believed you could run a campaign without the entire media circus, but..."

She drifted into silence, chewing her lip as she stared down at the traitorous figures.

"I'm getting you coffee and a doughnut," said Ruth, decisively. "You're tired and your blood sugar's low."

"Not a doughnut, I'm on diet," replied Samantha automatically.

"Okay, a piece of fruit then. And you're not giving up. Don't you *dare* give up just because people are interested in who you are, you hear me?"

Samantha looked up with a rueful smile.

"You'll find a way to make them listen to what you stand for as well, I know you will," Ruth went on. "Now you just cheer up and look on the bright side. Be the Pollyanna that Palmer said you were on that program."

"Right before I smashed his argument into smithereens," said Samantha, with a reminiscent smile.

"That's the spirit. Backbone! Stamina! The Iowa caucus is four days away and you are on the rise."

When Ruth left, Samantha looked at the report again, feeling gloomy despite Ruth's encouragement. Restlessly, she turned back to her email and scanned over it quickly. 'James Laughton' was in bold, unread, at the top. She double-clicked.

"Today's Thursday" it said. "You mean today or next week? I can do either. Or both? Why not? (Thursdays. Never could get the hang of them.) . – James"

She blinked and checked her calendar.

You're losing it. You're losing track of time.

And I'm not surprised, I'm exhausted.

She hit reply. "Really? I definitely need some time off then! Yes, today's great. See you soon."

"Samantha? Samantha!"

"Marilyn!" Impulsively, Samantha flung her arms around her friend in a hug, before quickly pulling away to stare at her. "You look great – what are you doing here?"

"I live here – we moved to DC a couple of years ago. What about you?"

"We're living in Grosse Pointe. We moved about – Faith was eleven and she's sixteen now, so... five years, my goodness."

"Faith is *sixteen*?"

"I know – I know, it's so hard to believe."

The two women were standing in the main street of Adams Morgan, under a flashing neon outline of a martini glass. Around them, the fading light was turning the buildings rosy and russet, the lights of the shops and restaurants sparkling while the sky still held traces of blue.

"But what are you doing here?" said Marilyn.

"I'm representing a charity – well, a group of charities. I'm only here for the weekend, I leave tomorrow."

"Come on, then, let's get a drink." With the familiarity of their old friendship, Marilyn seized her hand to lead her into the bar, before remembering that they were not the close friends they once were. "If you can – are you free? Would you like to?"

"Of course I would," said Samantha. "Oh, Marilyn, it is so good to see you!" She wrapped her arms around her friend again, this time both of them held on tightly, saying with their embrace what was more difficult to put into words. When they pulled apart, Samantha's eyes were moist.

"God, I'm sorry," she laughed shakily, fanning her face with her hand. "I'm such a complete cry-baby."

In the bar, they unraveled their stories of the last six years. In the initial shock of seeing each other, they reverted straight back to the natural ease they had always shared. Now, in speaking of the time that had passed, they were careful not to mention the fight that separated them. Clumsily, they gave each other the press-release versions of their lives.

Frank was now in plastic surgery and Marilyn had her own psychiatry practice; they loved being in Washington and found it vibrant and challenging; they were happily childless; they'd recently returned from a vacation in Europe.

Richard's business was extremely successful; Faith was doing well at school and filled the house with Britney Spears, which really wasn't the worst thing that could happen.

"No doubt she inherited her mother's taste," interjected Marilyn.

She herself, Samantha went on, was doing a lot of voluntary work and finding it very satisfying. The hollow words did not express the real enjoyment she got from the work; she sounded false and she knew it.

Marilyn ordered more drinks and the sudden silence became stiff.

"So, two perfect lives," said Marilyn after a few minutes.

Samantha gave a faint laugh and vague smile.

"Can I ask you..." said Marilyn, all in a rush, then suddenly pausing. "When did you two last have sex? No, no," she held up her hand to forestall the expression emerging on Samantha's face. "I'm not saying anything about your marriage – it's just..." She fiddled with the table in silence as their drinks arrived. When the waitress left, she blurted out, "Frank hasn't touched me in years. And I don't actually have any other girlfriends I can ask this stuff. All our friends are – *our* friends, both of ours – I can't confide in them about things like this."

Samantha propped her cheek on her hand and stared sadly at Marilyn. "I don't know," she said simply.

"Weeks? Months?"

"Years. I don't know how many, exactly." She thought for a bit. "I know I stopped taking the pill in 1997. I ran out and just didn't get anymore. So that's five years. And then before that it had been... let me think..." She scratched her head, trying to puzzle it out, then gave up. "Well, long enough," she finished ruefully.

"So it's not just me," said Marilyn. "I don't know – I mean I've tried to talk to Frank about it, if it's erectile dysfunction there's nothing to be ashamed of, it's usually treatable..."

"Do you think that's the problem?" said Samantha, with a flicker of envy. "That it's just not working?"

"Who knows?" Her face darkened. "I'm not sure I like the alternative hypotheses much."

Samantha looked down at her drink. She'd never considered that Richard may have been struggling to get it up.

That's because you know he's getting it up nice and regular, just not for you.

I don't know that for sure. I can't just assume.

Oh, don't be so blind. He just doesn't find you sexy and frankly, are you surprised?

"Sometimes I can't sleep I'm so frustrated," she whispered.

Her friend nodded glumly.

"I've tried everything," Samantha went on, her eyes welling. "But now – when I want it – I don't even bother trying, I know he's never interested. He's so not-interested that I can't even fantasize about him anymore. So I just lie there next to him thinking about other men. And that feels so wrong."

Marilyn was animated with angry recognition. "It gets to the point where he just leaves you stone cold. When someone never finds you sexy, never shows any interest, never wants to touch you..."

"Then one day out of the blue he suddenly rolls over with a hard-on and expects to be allowed to poke it in..."

"As if you're some kind of Goddamn blow-up doll, that can just be left in a cupboard for years then pulled out and taken."

"How did we get to this point?" asked Samantha. "What happened to that idea of sex as something romantic, something special – something about *love*? When did it become a war?"

"I think maybe it always was, since the dawn of time," replied Marilyn bitterly. "Whoever stuffed that bright shiny pink idea of love 'n roses in our heads should be shot. You spend your whole life waiting for it to come true and then the rest of your life trying to recapture it and I don't think it even happened in between."

They fell silent again, sipping their drinks and looking around the darkened bar. The lights were dimmed since they walked in, turning the faux-leather vinyl seats to rich mahogany, and reflecting the red glow. Pink lighting surrounded the bottles behind the bar in a halo. The mirror behind them showed an old-fashioned clock of the kind one would find in British railway stations during the nineteenth century. She smiled vaguely as she watched the ornate minute hand jerk forward a step. It was twenty-seven past eight.

"Hey," she said, breaking out of her trance. "Don't you need to phone Frank to let him know where you are?"

Marilyn stared at her. "You really are the world's most unliberated woman," she said in amazement. "No, I don't need to phone Frank. He's working tonight. Our working hours are now on almost opposite sides of the clock, and I sometimes think that's the only thing that's keeping our marriage ticking. Hell, it's not even a marriage. It's a time-share arrangement on an apartment."

To Samantha's shock, Marilyn burst into tears.

"And I haven't been able to tell anyone," she sobbed, "And I think I'm going to leave him because I can't carry on living like this and I'm so *scared* of being alone, I don't want to be a... a *divorced woman in her forties.*"

Samantha lay on the carpet of her living room, her chin on her palms and her elbows sticking out in front of her. The joy of living alone, she reflected, was that one didn't have to mold to other people's standards of behavior all the time. Sprawled on the floor, she felt youthful again. Living with Richard, she'd been expected to behave like a proper grown-up and what happened? He stayed late at the office with his teenage girlfriends.

The main reason she was on the floor was to practice stomach crunches and realign her back. She'd switched the TV on for company while she exercised, but rolled over when two pundits started critiquing the Democratic race.

"With Clark taking Delaware, Missouri, North Dakota and South Carolina, and Thompson taking Arizona, New Mexico and Oklahoma," one of them said, "I believe the Democrats have the horse race they're looking for."

"Yes, it's a horse race, but it still seems lethargic with low voter turn-out and no real stimulation to the voting public," added the other.

The first one grinned hugely at what was obviously his cue. "Speaking of *stimulation*, St. Clair did surprisingly well yesterday, collecting a hundred and twenty-two electoral votes. It seems the side joke of this campaign continues to amuse."

"The bastards," whispered Samantha venomously. "I came in third in four of those states, and fourth in the other three – and they still don't take me seriously?"

"Try the E-channel, Mom," said Faith from her customary place on the sofa. "They take you seriously there."

Samantha stretched out for the remote and punched the buttons.

"There's a very hot rumor going around Hollywood," the anchorman was saying, "that George Clooney is not only supporting the St. Clair candidacy for president, but also dating the sexy politician on the side. Clooney's spokesperson states that George is in DC only for the filming of *Bushwacked* and claims there is no romance between the two sexy and politically charged liberals. But as you know, *Hollywood Now* doesn't believe in coincidences... We believe that Clooney may be in DC to whack a *couple* of bushes."

Samantha was staring open-mouthed at the screen. "Me and George Clooney. *Me* and George Clooney. In my dreams! I've never even met him!" She sat up and spun around to face her daughter. Even through her outrage, she was pleased with her suppleness as she leaned over, grasping her toes for balance. "All they're going on is that we're in the same *city!* There must be...what, three hundred thousand men in DC? More? Am I doing *all* of them?"

"The mainstream media still sees you as a joke," said Faith, "and the tabloids think you're their queen."

"I *know* that," said Samantha, frustrated, "but what am I supposed to do about it? I can't just stand up and say look, for heaven's sake, can we leave my hair out of it and talk about my policies and while we're at it my love life is none of your business."

"Why not?" Faith said, turning back to her book.

"Why *not?*"

"Yeah." The girl closed her book and sat up, crossing her legs. "You stopped playing by their rules ages ago, right? So why not?"

16

Samantha strode out onto the platform, her heels thumping audibly on the thin carpeting, and came to an abrupt halt by the podium. Instead of standing behind it and smiling for silence as usual, she stood at its side and stared out at the crowd of photographers and journalists. The cameras were already flashing wildly.

You shouldn't be doing this while you've got PMS...

I can't think of a better time to tell people off, frankly.

But you've got to be nice *about it!*

Uh-uh. I'm through with nice. I've had it up to here *with nice. Anyway, nice is giving them cookies and coffee, and I've already done that.*

After a while, an expectant silence fell, although a few flash bulbs continued to go off like the last explosions of an amateur firework show. As Samantha remained quiet, the journalists started glancing at each other uncomfortably.

"Is there anything you'd like to say?" one of them called eventually.

Samantha swung the microphone closer to her mouth.

"I wasn't aware that was necessary," she said. "As you only ever report on my outfit and my hair, I thought I'd dispense with the speech this time."

A ripple of laughter ran around the room.

"This is not a laughing matter," she said, her eyes narrowing. "I would like the press to start taking me seriously as a candidate or not write about me at all. I no longer see the point of conducting press conferences when all you write about is the details of my wardrobe."

She heard the slow, low whistles of people taking in breath through pursed lips. She remembered James doing the same thing, when she'd ranted to him about this, and how he'd then muttered teasingly "Strict nanny." For a moment, her straight face twitched, threatening a smile, but she brought it back in line.

"It's not us who don't take you seriously," a reporter near the front said belligerently. "It's the public who doesn't take you seriously, we just report their opinions."

"You report people's *opinions*?" said Samantha scathingly. "What are you, a mind-reader?"

She could feel the mood turning angry and sour. For a moment, her determination wavered, but the ferocity of her PMS symptoms came to the rescue. *Stick with it, dammit, they deserve it. You've done this successfully before; making people dislike you and reeling them back in. You'll survive a few waves of resentment.*

"They don't take me seriously as a candidate, because you don't *write* about me seriously as a candidate," she went on, her voice harsh with scorn. "You write about my hair, my weight, my clothes, and who I am supposedly dating, you write about what I had for *dinner*, but you don't cover my place in the race – and you think this is good journalism?"

"You don't even campaign!" retaliated one of the journalists. "You don't campaign, you don't do commercials, you don't even take campaign contributions – how are we expected to take you seriously as a candidate?"

As usual, Samantha waited for the hubbub to quiet down before she spoke. She'd been brought up not to talk over people and reasoned that if they were here to listen to her, they'd shut up eventually.

"I've surpassed five candidates in a race that you take very seriously," she said into the silence, at last, "and I'm currently in third place in that race. I think that's serious enough to be mentioned."

"So what you are saying," a voice called sarcastically, "is if we can't say anything nice don't say anything at all?"

Samantha chuckled and shook her head good-humouredly, deflecting the barb. "Of course not. You can criticize my policies all you like. But I'm a serious political candidate in a serious political race and my hair is not a political issue. I'm calling for some journalistic responsibility."

One of the older reporters lifted his ballpoint pen for her attention.

"This is all very well and good," he said in a rich, gravelly voice, "but you're ignoring the main reason we don't take you seriously as a candidate."

He paused and Samantha continued to watch him expectantly.

"You came onto the national scene because of a picture of you in a, shall we say, *compromising* position," the old man went on. "Six out of ten people associate you more with Monica Lewinsky than a serious candidate." Samantha raised her eyebrows at that statistic, but didn't interrupt to contest it. She wondered, sometimes, how on earth these polls were conducted and how people were able to delude themselves that numbers equaled scientific fact. What did they ask – "Do you associate St. Clair with Lewinsky?" and then the passer-by scratches their chin and says, "Um, yeah, now that you mention it, yes I do"? The reporter was still talking, his voice stern as a father giving his daughter a good telling-off. "And *that's* why we don't consider you a viable candidate, and it's why we see you as an interesting pop-culture icon that sells tabloids to housewives at the checkout counter."

A few people laughed uncomfortably. No-one knew where this press-conference was going. St. Clair didn't play the game properly – you weren't supposed to stand up at a podium and argue with the press.

As Samantha was reviewing the reporter's logic, her brow creased. The photos led to the association which led to being tabloid material; the link was his questionable statistics.

"Okay, let's address that subject," she said with a heavy sigh. "Any men here who have never experienced a woman in a 'compromising position', please raise your hands now." She looked around expectantly as the journalist's eyes widened and arms twitched. "Okay, women, if you've never been in a 'compromising position', please raise your hand."

Only the *LA Times* reporter lifted her arm. With a wry smirk she said, "I'm a lesbian" and winked at Samantha. The rest of the room simply stared at the presidential candidate in shocked silence.

"Okay, great," said Samantha. "And how many of you feel that having engaged in fellatio, you should be disqualified from being taken seriously as a journalist?" Deliberately, she worded her statement in a way that left them unsure whether to reply 'Yes' or 'No'. While a few still had puzzled looks as they tried to work it out, she went on. "Right. So please extend me the same courtesy as a candidate that I extend to you as journalists. Now if we've finished on the subjects of my hair, clothes and sex life, does anyone have any questions on my policies?"

Carol Hart raised her hand again. "In your discussion of child and family support, you talk exclusively about the nuclear family. What about single-parent families, other family members who look after children, lesbian and gay partnerships? Or do you only value children from nuclear families?"

"Absolutely not," replied Samantha, her face stern and focused as she began to explain her policies. Inwardly, she was rejoicing. *This is more like it!*

"Hair Today, Gone Tomorrow" said the Wall Street Journal's column heading. Underneath, a sub-heading added "Girl power hits St. Clair where it counts" and below that "Public offering a disaster".

"Oh, my God..." murmured Samantha, her eyes scanning rapidly down the text for the opening stock price. She found it: $0.58. "Holy shit!" she whispered.

"What's up?" said Ruth.

"I think my husband may have just bankrupted himself... they're probably exaggerating, but this is not good, this is so not good."

"What are you talking about?"

"Listen to this." Samantha read aloud. "The public offering for St. Clair Industries opened disastrously yesterday, caused in large part to its owner-founder Richard St. Clair's negative image with women..." blah, blah, blah – then, they say, "this may be the fastest move from public offering to bankruptcy in the history of Wall Street."

Ruth looked worried. "Will this affect you? Will you lose your home?"

Samantha shook her head. "I should be fine. I've hardly touched his money since I've been in DC – we might lose the Michigan house, but..." She shrugged. "I've got my apartment, and I can let another apartment back home to maintain my residency status. Oh my, oh my..." Her eyes returned in awe and horror to the article in front of her. "I am so glad I'm not living with him right now – oh my word, I am so *glad* I don't have to see him tonight!"

While Samantha was still staring at the *Wall Street Journal*, Ben was smacking the *New York Times* for emphasis. The *Washington Post* already lay crumpled in a heap on the floor of his office where he'd flung it.

"This is ridiculous!" he was saying. "She calls the press out on blow jobs and she not only moves *up* in the polls, the press is treating her like the Virgin Mary all of a sudden!"

"People like the fact that she's honest," explained Cynthia from behind the *LA Times*, which she was holding up to hide the persistent grin she couldn't entirely erase.

"People aren't so stupid, you know. They recognize spin, they hate it, and she's giving them the exact opposite."

"I don't see how telling the press what they can and can't write about is the opposite of *spin*," retorted Ben, rustling the pages loudly.

And that, thought Cynthia, *is why she's beating your boys hands down, because you* don't *see.* "We have even bigger problems coming up," she said.

"What's that?" Ben put his paper down and scowled at the window where the freezing sleet of February was spattering against the glass.

"The next primary's Michigan, her home state. If she wins that, there might be a paradigm shift among voters that she is a legitimate contender, after all."

Ben leaned back, holding his coffee between both hands. "Do you think she's a legitimate contender?"

"Honestly? Yes, I do. I've thought so for a long time."

He exhaled slowly. "Yeah, I figured that. But you see – I don't. It's nothing personal, I've got nothing against St. Clair herself – but she's *not* president material, she hasn't got a snowball's chance in hell of running this country. I've been in this business a long time and she's no Margaret Thatcher, I promise you that. So her candidacy can only weaken the party and *that* makes me angry."

"Maybe the times, they are a-changin'?" suggested Cynthia lightly. "Maybe she doesn't have to be an iron lady with balls of steel to be presidential material. Maybe people are ready for a more... *caring* face."

Ben snorted. "This country? They aren't ready to sign up for equal pay, they're certainly not going to vote in Miss Congeniality for president."

Cynthia shook her head sadly, suspecting that he was, after all, right. As long as even so-called liberals like him were dismissive and sexist without even noticing, what hope was there?

"So what's the next plan in 'Operation Bring Down St. Clair'?" she asked caustically.

"I don't know. But I'll think of something. We've got to make people see she's just wasting everyone's time; that she's put herself up for a job she'll never get and can't do." He drummed his fingers rapidly on the desk.

"Don't forget whose idea this was in the first place."

"Fine, fine, rub it in. I'm Frankenstein. Now will you help me catch my monster?"

"Do I keep my job if I say no?" asked Cynthia pointedly.

"No."

"Fine." She stood up and folded her arms. "In that case, I do have one or two ideas that might work."

Dusty morning light, warmer and more golden than usual at this time of year, slanted down the street as Samantha packed the car. She concentrated on the Tetris-puzzle of slotting everything into the trunk, in an effort to avoid thinking about what this meant. Her throat felt painfully obstructed and every time she opened her mouth to speak, tears threatened. Two large suitcases, a duvet, a bedside and desk lamp, a bicycle, a box of lovingly wrapped ornaments marked 'fragile' and a box of books... She leaned on her straightened arms, feeling the tears begin to fall. Between her feet, she could see the sleek cherry-reds and lemon-yellows of fallen ash leaves.

"Mom?" called Faith from the front door.

Samantha turned, frantically blinking, a bright smile at the ready. The sight of her daughter standing on the front step, weight on one hip, lithe and glowing with energy, tore at her heart.

"Yeah, honey?" she called back casually, her voice only cracking on the last syllable.

"Do you know where my tennis racket is? I can't find it!"

"It's here, I've already packed it."

"Great!" Faith came bouncing down the steps and peered in the trunk. "Nice work, Mom, very impressive. Maybe we could squeeze an ant in somewhere, but not much else!" She laughed then, looking up, saw her mother's watery eyes. "Ah... Mom... don't look like that, I'm not going away forever, you know."

"I know." Samantha sniffed. How could she explain to her daughter that a cord of love tied them together and that every step away Faith took ripped her mother open? Did all mothers feel like this? Had hers when she left for college? She suspected it was universal. Mothers all over the world were holding back tears, smiling determinedly, saying, "go on, you have a good time" while their hearts broke, hoping that this was the best way to make sure they came back.

"I'll be back every vacation." Faith's hands were on Samantha's shoulders, the taller daughter bending to look into her mother's downcast eyes. Samantha put her hand over her daughter's and clutched it.

"Of course... It's always a shock for the mother-bird," she said, making light of it. "You go on in and make me some coffee, I'll finish up here."

Over the last of the packing and the freshly brewed coffee, Samantha managed to get her emotions in check.

"You want to pick out some CDs for the drive?" she suggested. "How about that Britney Spears..."

"Mo-om!" Faith rolled her eyes. "I do *not* listen to Britney Spears anymore!"

"Sorry..." Samantha laughed and they were back to normal until it came to stepping out of the house.

In the quiet purring cocoon of the car, gliding down the highway, Faith said, "I don't like to think of you stuck with Dad on your own."

Samantha glanced in her rearview mirror, switched on her turn signal, and swung smoothly into the next lane. Driving meant she didn't have to look Faith in the eye.

"He's horrible to you. I don't know why you're with him! I don't think I've *once* seen him do anything nice for you..."

"Oh, baby," said Samantha. "You're so angry with him."

"Of course I am! He's a bastard..."

Samantha held up her hand and Faith fell silent, but sullenly.

"You know the ironic thing?" said her mother, after a pause. "I've mostly stayed with him for your sake."

"Well, I wish you hadn't."

Samantha nodded. She geared down to overtake the van in front. It was carrying a lot of timber, which was precariously rattling in its ropes. "Shouldn't be allowed on the road," she muttered as she drove past it and swung in front. "Okay, I'll tell you a secret, baby. I've been waiting – I didn't want to upset you during your exams or anything – and then I didn't want to disrupt your vacation, but now that you're off to college..." She glanced at her daughter warily. "I think I'm going to leave him."

"Really?" Faith's eyes were saucers.

"Really."

"But for real? You're not going to back down or anything?"

Samantha shook her head. "I thought maybe I could go stay with my friend Marilyn – I haven't spoken to her about it yet, but she wouldn't mind, I'm sure – just for a bit..."

"Yes!" Faith punched the air as much as was possible within the limited confines of the car.

"Hey, you!" Samantha laughed, shocked. "Don't sound so damn pleased! You're about to become the child of a broken home!"

"About time, too! I couldn't bear the thought of you having to live on your own with him glowering around the place like a black thundercloud. It's like living with a time bomb."

Samantha shook her head in wonder. "I had no idea..." she started saying, then glanced out the window in irritation. The van with the timber was roaring alongside her. As she glanced at the driver, he gave her a sneering grin and a wink, before accelerating to cut in front of her again.

"Male ego," she snapped irritably. "Just can't stand being overtaken. Now look!" She gestured at the speedometer. "He cuts in front and then he forces me to slow down!"

"It's okay, we'll get there," said Faith peaceably. "So you're really going to leave Dad? What are you going to do?"

Samantha eyed the shaking pile of timber warily and considered overtaking again. That would only start a game of tag with the irresponsible driver, though, so she just clicked her tongue in annoyance and stayed where she was.

"Oh – I don't know... Really, I've got no idea. I can't think about it. I feel that as long as I'm in that house, under his thumb, I can't even think about what else I might do. Look, baby, are you sure you're not upset?"

"Mom, I'm *thrilled*," said Faith. "Cross my heart and hope to die."

Samantha leaned back in her chair and stretched lazily. Her head hurt, she had black circles under her eyes, she'd barely slept, and she felt terrific. Ruth walked in, a sheaf of papers under her arm, two coffees in her hands.

"You're like some kind of divine coffee-bearing angel in my life, you know that?" said Samantha dreamily. "It's like your mission on this earth is to simply supply my caffeine needs…"

"And you sound like you're still drunk," said Ruth, amused.

"Uh-uh." Samantha shook her head, then groaned and held it with both hands. "I can't feel this bad and be drunk. It's champagne, it always makes my head hurt the next day."

"This should help." Ruth set the open *New York Times* in front of her with an aspirin carefully placed on top.

"Thanks…" Samantha threw it in her mouth and swallowed the aspirin with a swig from her water bottle.

"You're supposed to read what was underneath it," said Ruth, disappointed.

Samantha leaned forward and scanned the article, a smile breaking out on her face. "They don't call me sexy *once*! They even refer to me as a member of Congress!"

She leaned back, savoring her triumph once more as Ruth left. The previous night, she and her team stayed up late, waiting for the Michigan results to be counted. The champagne was chilled and waiting - whether for celebration or commiseration - when the news came in that she'd won her home state. Since that moment, she'd been floating on air. Every time her mood threatened to return to normal, she hugged herself and whispered "I won Michigan". The thought carried her back into the air like a warm updraft lifting a flying bird. The sound of raised voices outside her office broke her trance.

"I don't give a *fuck*," a voice was bellowing, "I am going to see my wife!"

Samantha whitened. That exact belligerent mood was something she'd spent twenty-odd years learning to sidestep and deflect. Now it was in full throttle and bursting into her office.

"Look what you did to me!" roared Richard, as the door bounced against the wall. His face was red, his eyes bloodshot.

Samantha stood up, her eyes wary, her voice forcedly calm as she said, "Richard, I think you ought to leave."

"You ruined me, you bitch!"

Her body told her to back away. Her mind told her not to show fear and to keep the desk between them. Richard was striding through the room, around the narrow space of wood, towards her chair. Despite herself, she stepped backwards, circling the desk, away from him. Now that he was closer, she could smell the alcohol on his skin. He couldn't be reasoned with when he was drunk; she just had to keep him calm. His fingers were curling into fists.

"I need Hope, and call security." she called to Ruth.

"She just ducked into the bathroom...I'll run get her!" Ruth said, lifting the receiver and dialing security.

"Fucking right you need hope," scoffed Richard. "But you know what? You haven't got any. You deserve to be beaten to a *pulp* for what you've done to me – you've *ruined* me!" His voice was rising again. "My *company* is going down the *tubes* because of my *stupid fucking bitch of a wife*!"

"Richard," said Samantha in the careful tone she'd developed over years of managing his behavior, "I know you're angry, but this is a mistake. You need to leave. You shouldn't be here."

"Don't tell me where I should be, you fucking slut!"

She breathed steadily, still circling around the desk. He was still talking, at least.

"Richard," she repeated, "you need to leave, just leave."

"My life was *perfect*," he said. A small fleck of saliva flew from his mouth. "My company was fine, everything was great, until you stuck that guy's *dick* in your filthy mouth!" He lunged across the desk. She leapt back just in time.

He must've been drinking all the way from Michigan to DC, she thought wildly. Somewhere beneath that rage and liquor was a rational being. She had to make him hear her.

"Richard – you don't want to do this…"

"Don't tell me what I fucking want!" He lunged to move around the desk, bumped into the rolling chair, and shoved it out of his path. It shot across the office, smashing into the glass shelves. One cracked, and with a groaning screech the two pieces of glass twisted apart and the books tumbled down, smacking and fluttering on the floor.

"I'm still your husband," he said through gritted teeth. "You show me some respect." He smashed his fist on her desk, knocking her coffee onto her files. Watching the havoc he was wreaking on her office, a flame of pure cold anger leapt up.

"I'll give you respect when you earn it," she shot back.

"Oh, you want me to earn it?" He started moving around the desk again and she circled opposite him until, once more, she stood behind it. "Okay, have it your way," he was saying. "I'll come over there and earn it the old fashioned way."

In a bound, he leapt over the desk, kicking her files and stationery to the floor as he did. Samantha had already backed away into the corner as he landed.

"Stay away from me, Richard!" Her voice was shrill with panic, now. It was a sound that always fed his fury, she knew, but she could no longer control it. "I'm never letting you hit me again!"

"Oh yeah? What are you going to do about it?" His arm whirled around, his outstretched hand smashing against the elbow she'd instinctively raised to protect her face.

"You're getting what's coming to you, you whore!" he yelled, his hands moving faster as he tried to hit her across the face. The slaps rained down over her arms, hard across the side of her ear with surprising pain, on her cheeks when she wasn't fast enough. She was cowering, enraged at her

218

helplessness and terrified, her body crouched down. She dropped to the floor, curling into the fetus position, wrapping her arms entirely around her head, whimpering. A shockingly hard blow came to her thigh – he'd kicked her. She found she was sobbing and pleading. He gave a roar of pain and Samantha heard a cracking sound of bone against wood. She flinched, drawing herself into a tighter ball, but no more punches came. She looked up cautiously. The diminutive Hope had Richard in an arm lock and was smashing him hard against the desk. His face showed the strain as he fought back with all his strength, and then suddenly crumpled as she brought a swift knee up between his thighs. As he howled in pain, she smashed him down face-first onto the desk. She was cuffing his hands behind his back when security came dashing into the room.

Samantha sat where she was, folded up in the corner of the room, trembling violently, looking at the swollen face of the man she'd married. His eyes met hers.

"Why?" she said, her voice a shrill wail. "Why did you come here, why did you hit me? Why was it so important to see me in pain?" She sounded hysterical.

"Because I can't stand to watch you win," snarled Richard.

"Win what? Richard?" Security was dragging him away. "Win *what*?"

"Take him to emergency," said Hope curtly to the security guards. "I'm pretty sure I broke a few things. I'll be down in a bit."

She turned back to Samantha who was crying uncontrollably, rocking back and forth in her corner. She dropped to her knees and took the congresswoman in her arms.

"Are you alright? I am so sorry, ma'am...I was only gone for a few minutes." Hope pleaded.

"Thank you," whispered Samantha. "Thank you, thank you, thank you..."

17

The plain, functional furniture was dimly lit – not by a selection of candles or tasteful arrangements of lighting, just darkness and the streetlamp reflecting onto the ceiling. Samantha sat on her sofa, her knees tucked under her chin, her blanket wrapped around her. On the table stood a bottle of wine, from which she occasionally topped off the glass cradled in her hands. Her eyes swam with tears as she sang along to her Shirley Bassey CD.

He doesn't act as though he cares, but deep inside I know he cares... As long as he needs me... and you never treat me like you should, so what's the good of loving as I do ... impossible to live with you, but I know I could never live without you. When a tear brimmed over the edge and rolled down her cheek, the salt stung the broken skin under her left eye. Singing to the music, she could take her pain and wrap it up in these soothing sounds and turn it into something magnificent and epic. The plaintive lament to Natalie, *send him back to me*, the haunting plea that *I understand him – he's all I have*, made the woman spurned seem noble, not pathetic.

"This – is – fucking – ridiculous."

She looked up. Faith stood in the middle of the room, arms folded tightly across her chest. Despite the dark, rage was clearly etched across her face.

"Darling…" she whispered pitifully, extending her hand.

Faith shook her head, her face wet. "No, Mom. It's enough, now. Enough of this pity, enough of thinking you're a better person for taking this shit." She pressed eject on the CD player, and Bassey's voice cut off mid-croon. Fumbling in the drawers, Faith's hands closed on a pair of scissors and cut the CD into pieces.

"What are you doing – Faith!" Samantha sat up, alarmed, slopping her wine on the taupe micro-fiber cushion.

"What you should have done *years* ago," said Faith. She grabbed the bottle of wine from the table, the glass from Samantha's hand, and marched into the kitchen. Throwing the pieces of shattered CD into the sink, she poured the wine over them.

"You're not going back to that. You're not going to sit around anymore getting drunk and listening to sad music, he's not dragging you back to that, you gotta have some spine now! You promised me, you *promised* me, you said you would leave him…"

"But baby," said Samantha helplessly, standing with the blanket trailing around her, "what can I do?"

The wine glass sailed across the room and shattered on the tiles, leaving red threads of wine like blood among the broken glass.

"Don't *say* that!" screeched Faith. "You're a presidential candidate, Mom! You can be president, you can change the world, *that's* what you can do! But you can't spend another minute of your life martyring yourself to that bastard, do you hear me?" She was gripping her mother's upper arms tightly, almost shaking her.

"You always did have his temper," said Samantha softly.

Faith's shoulders slumped. "Maybe you should borrow my temper for a bit," she said sourly. "Anger can be kind of useful, you know – it's a way of drawing the line in the sand that says *no more*."

Samantha looked down at the floor.

It's not ladylike to lose your temper.

But maybe Faith is right – maybe it's useful, helpful even.

Is that what you want for your daughter? To be a shrew? A fishwife?

She knows her worth. That's something.

"Would you like some coffee, baby?" She moved towards the cupboards, avoiding her daughter's eyes.

"Don't do this, Mom," said Faith ominously. "Don't just keep pretending and brushing stuff under the carpet…"

Samantha stood, her hand on the cupboard handle, her back turned. She stared intently at the plain white gloss of the cheap unit. "I'm not. But I need to think about it. I'm thinking about it. That's all."

With her face washed, the living room and kitchen tidied, the lamps on, and a mug of coffee in her hands, Samantha felt less mired down. She and Faith sat on opposite ends of the sofa, both cross-legged. Studying her daughter's face, Samantha could see traces of herself flickering through the features, the expressions, the gestures. For a few moments, she had the eerie sensation that she was looking at and talking to her younger self, not her daughter at all – that Faith wasn't even there, just an impressionable young Samantha in her place, or a mirror that not only swapped left/right, backwards/forwards, but also old/young. She blinked rapidly, returning herself to the present.

"Don't ever be a proper lady, Faith," she said eventually. "And don't listen to anyone who tells you that you should be."

Faith nodded. After a pause, she prompted her mother, "Go on."

"My mother taught me to be a proper lady – to be ladylike – and now I look back at how those ideas damaged her own life, and I think, how *dared* she, how *could* she teach me to make all the same mistakes? Being a proper lady means never saying no – so then no one knows that you didn't like this, don't want to do that. It means never losing your temper, so no one ever knows where your boundaries are. It means smiling graciously, never crying in public, never making a scene, so no one knows when you're hurting so badly that you're falling over the edge and crumbling to little bits behind that nice no-fuss smile. All that shit about sticking with your man, so you just think it's your duty to

222

ignore affairs, gloss over mistreatment, pretend to your friends that everything's fine – all of that is being *ladylike* and it's the most self-destructive behavior I've ever heard of. It's like sticking a giant kick-me sign on your back and then thanking people when they do.

"You know – I didn't make Richard into the selfish bastard he is. I can't take responsibility for that, I'm not going to think that everything's my fault. I was loyal and faithful and eager to please and did whatever he wanted – he could have responded in kind and it's his own fault that he didn't. But I certainly didn't stop him from treating me the way he did. If he walked all over me, I was the one who painted 'welcome' on my back. It was his choice to be a shit, but it was my choice to put up with it. And you know why I did?"

"You thought you were being ladylike?"

"Exactly. You hear so many stories about women being miserable in their marriages, being cheated on, and so on, that eventually you think that's what being a woman *means*, and then, when it happens to you…"

"It'll never happen to me," said Faith, very quietly. She leaned back, studying her mother. Under her daughter's speculative gaze, Samantha raised her hand and traced the outlines and swell of the puffy bruise beneath her eye. "You want not to be ladylike?' said Faith softly. "When you're in public – don't you dare disguise that bruise. Brandish it. He hit you, so don't you cover up for him. You say being ladylike is pretending you're not in pain – so don't pretend. *You hear me?*" Her voice was fierce.

Samantha smiled gently. "When did you become such a lioness, my darling?"

"Promise me! If you won't stand up for yourself, I'm here to stand up for you."

"Okay, baby…"

She glanced at the clock – it was getting late. Whatever dramas and bruises, her work still needed doing and she still needed sleep. She stood slowly, folded the blanket, and tidied the living room, switching out lamps as she went. In the kitchen, she washed up the coffee mug and studied her bruise in the window's ghostly reflection. She lay in bed, on her right side instead of her left to protect the tender skin, and thought about how she'd always feared being middle-aged and alone. On the whole, she reflected as she drifted to sleep, it was better than a sock in the jaw.

"And Richard St. Clair hit her?" said Ben, disbelievingly.

"Yes, he did." Cynthia was tight-lipped. "Multiple times, I believe. I understand he gave her a black eye and a swollen lip. From what Ruth said, there's no permanent damage but it's still pretty severe."

"Jesus Christ," he muttered. In an abrupt flare of anger, he smacked his desk with his palm. "Women are going to flock to her more than ever before. Is her luck never gonna run out?"

"Luck?" Cynthia's voice rose almost to a screech. Her knuckles tightened over the pile of documents she was holding. "A husband hits his wife, and you call it *luck*?"

"When it's politically brilliant I do," muttered Ben. He pushed some paper around his desk aimlessly. "I mean – for her position in the polls, in public opinion – right now – she couldn't have planned it better herself."

Cynthia's voice was tight. "There is no way this could have been staged. Richard St. Clair ended up in the hospital when Hope – her Secret Service agent – pulled him off Samantha. Apparently she gave him quite a beating."

"I didn't mean she plan… Hold on, Hope? A female agent?"

Cynthia nodded, impatient. "You've met Hope – at the TV shows…"

Ben, however, was no longer listening. Flung back in his chair, he was berating the ceiling. "God, this is a feminist's wet dream! A self-proclaimed macho husband hits his wife and some *female* beats him up and puts him in the hospital!"

"I think you'll find *feminists* don't have *wet dreams*," said Cynthia flatly. *You misogynist fossil of unrestrained prejudice*, she added to herself.

"You know what I mean." He flapped his hand. "So – what's the damage to us?"

Cynthia pinched the bridge of her nose. "She's pulled ahead in the polls in the next four primary states."

The bar shone with muted expense, from the leather padding to the sparkling curves of the designer glasses. Along the bar top, gold pools of light gleamed on the polished surface, cast by the recessed bulbs above. Samantha sat to the right of one such light shaft, sipping her wine from something she would usually have assumed was a small vase. Despite the shadows, she could still see her ugly bruise in the mirror opposite and tugged her hair forward, half over her face, to hide it. In the far corner of the reflection, she saw James approaching her and her stomach contracted.

"Don't pretend." The words came as clearly as if Faith had spoken next to her. When James reached her, she turned her face up, smiling, and let her hair fall back. His smile evaporated.

"What the hell…?"

"You should see the other guy." She'd always liked that line and this was surely the only time in her life she'd be able to use it.

"Who the hell…?" He breathed the words more than spoke them. His hand gently traced the skin around the purple and black mess. "What happened? Who did this?"

"My husband. Or as I like to call him now, my ex-husband."

"Jesus!" James turned abruptly to the bar, his fingers curling into fists. His face tightened as he took another look at the damage to Samantha. "Your beautiful, beautiful…"

He couldn't finish the sentence and breathed in and out steadily, struggling for restraint.

"I'll kill him," he said eventually, trembling with rage.

"James…"

"I'll rip him limb from limb for this."

"James! Look at me." Her voice was sharp. She pinned him with her eyes. "I have already been attacked by a violent man – the last thing I feel like dealing with is another man getting all violent about it. Got it?"

"But…"

"No but. I don't believe in revenge, just in defense. Although I think my agent's defense may have strayed a little into vengeance…" She smiled, despite herself. "Like I said, you really *should* see the other guy…"

James sat on the stool next to her, the light above him threading his dark hair with gold and dusting his skin with warmth. Just looking at him made Samantha want to purr with contentment. They spent half an hour talking shop, mostly out of a sense of propriety, before the conversation wound back to more personal matters.

"I know I should feel like I'm saying goodbye to twenty-six years of marriage," Samantha was saying, "But I don't – in a way, I'm not. I feel like we haven't been married for years. How do you define marriage, anyway?"

"You mean apart from two signatures on the same piece of paper?" James looked into the glistening depths of his gin and tonic. Samantha studied his profile, the swell of his high cheeks and the curve of his lips. He looked like a statue of a mourning angel. The conversation was probably harder for him than for her, she realized – he'd lost something he genuinely valued.

"The only thing I can think of is a stupid metaphor," he said. "It's being in the same boat. Whatever else happens, there's the two of you and then there's the rest of the world – even if you fight sometimes, or live in different places sometimes, or…"

"Or stop having sex for years," contributed Samantha, unthinking.

He looked up sharply. With the oblique light cast into them, his eyes were as green as grass. He raised his eyebrows. "That would... matter to me."

"Yeah, it mattered to me too," she said sardonically.

Shut up! The alcohol is speaking...

So what if it is? I'm not still *trying to protect Richard's reputation.*

Trying to recuperate the situation, she went on with forced casualness. "But that's everyone, isn't it? I mean – after a few years, nobody's got the hots for their spouse anymore, it's just a fact of life."

"Not for everyone," he said forcefully. "I *never* stopped wanting Emma. Okay, you don't necessarily get a raging hard-on *every* time you see your wife undress, but..."

The vision created by James's words completely derailed Samantha's train of thought.

"I hate it the way one generation does that to the next," he went on. "Our parents have a shitty time of it so then they teach us that life is shit and that's just the way it has to be – or their marriage ends up stale, so they teach their children that all marriages do – well, they don't. And it seriously pisses me off when people preach a cult of disappointment like that. You don't always fall out of love with someone. You don't necessarily get bored. You don't lose interest in their bodies. You can live with the same woman every day for twenty-five years and still catch your breath when she takes off her bra!"

"Wow..." Samantha said softly. "Emma was a very lucky woman."

"She was a very special woman," said James glumly.

They both stared at the bar top then up at each other, aware of how much both had exposed themselves.

"So are you, you know," he added after a pause.

She jerked her head, as if to say "Whatever". She didn't want him to feel obligated to flatter her.

"Really, I mean it. That's why it kills me to see you hurt like that, that someone can be lucky enough to be married to you and then *hit* you? It just defies comprehension."

"Yeah, well, it happens. And I'm not really anything so amazing." Uncomfortable, she twisted her wine glass, rolling it around on the edge of its base.

"Oh, come off it," laughed James. "You're great! You've got this thin veneer of being proper and respectable and grown-up, but it's barely skin-deep – and underneath you're passionate, sincere, you're completely committed to what you believe in, you're outspoken and spontaneous… Oh, and you're not bad-looking, either."

Samantha lost hold of the glass, which smacked on its side, shattering and throwing wine into the bar area.

"And clumsy," James added. "Major selling-point. All my best friends are clumsy."

In the fuss over apologizing for the glass, the broken pieces being removed, and her drink replaced, she replayed his words in her head. For a moment, under that onslaught of compliments, she'd wondered if maybe – just maybe – he might be interested in her. Then came the damnation with faint praise: 'not bad-looking.' *Ouch.* The comment about 'friends' only confirmed it.

Half a loaf is better than no bread.

The evening after Samantha won the District of Columbia and Nevada, Ben Morehouse came to find her in her office. She was sitting in a small pool of light, her face tilted to look down her nose through her bifocals. Her expression as she concentrated was as stern as any avenging angel. With his stomach sinking, he rapped sharply on the open door. Samantha glanced up.

"Ben." The ghost of a polite smile darted across her face.

"Can I come in?"

"Certainly." She took off her reading glasses and sat back as he paced up and down her office. "Would you like to sit?" she asked pointedly after a few minutes.

"No, I think I'll pace this conversation standing, if you don't mind," he said distractedly.

"Actually, I do. Please have a seat." Her tone was as gracious as ever.

Surprised, he obeyed and sat on the edge of the chair opposite her.

"Samantha…" He leaned his elbow on the desk. "Will you drop out of the race?"

"Drop out of the race…" she repeated slowly. "Ben – what sort of question is that? Why would I do that?"

"For the party. For the sake of the party."

Samantha sat in silence, too angry to speak, considering his words and the wealth of assumptions that underlay them.

"Samantha…" Ben was wretched. "You're beating all the guys who have a fighting chance in the general."

"They're knocking themselves out, one by one. I am *literally* not campaigning. I defend myself when I'm attacked. You really can't blame me if they shoot themselves in the foot every time they attempt to fire at me."

Ben shook his head, moved to stand, and thought the better of it. "I know, I know. And…" He met her eyes. "I'm guilty of loading their guns."

She sat impassively, breathing in through her nose and out through her mouth. "So, Ben. Tell me. Why should I drop out?"

"Because the Conservative party is *praying* you win this thing, so they can cruise to an easy victory in November."

"I see. And do they think they can win that easily, if I take the Democratic party?"

Ben breathed more easily. It seemed she would listen to reason, after all. "Yes. They see you as a big-government type – to be honest, a kind of femi-nazi adulteress, someone who'll energize their base like nothing they've ever seen before – the perfect enemy to scare their voters with."

Samantha nodded. Off-handedly, she said, "You know, I'm developing a base of my own." Her words sounded almost plaintive.

"Not much of one," he said gently. "A bunch of lonely housewives and disappointed women?"

She shrugged, as if in agreement, and Ben grimaced sympathetically.

"You know…" she began. Ben held his breath, waiting for her reluctant agreement to step aside. "I'm starting to believe that these people are a hidden majority in the Democrat's base, and a base I can relate to. You see, I've been working with facts and numbers, Ben, which none of the other candidates really seem to do. They think – pah, miserable women, weak. I think – women, the majority of voters, strong. A lonely housewife, as you say, might be weak in the economic sphere, but in politics her vote carries equal weight, and you forget that at your peril. I see, in the midst of our base, a mass of wounded women, trying to find their place in a man's world, who get down on their knees every night and pray to be healed and pray to be heard. And once these hearts are healed, and their voices heard, we will see an explosion of feminine compassion that will not only change the political landscape in this country, it will change the country's entire ideology and philosophy. That's what I think."

Ben's head was in his hands. She thought she heard the words "Fucking idealism," before he lifted his face and looked at her, strained.

"That'd be nice, Sam, that'd be real nice," he said tiredly. "But I can't count on a bunch of heartbroken housewives to beat a political machine that steamrolls the weak for sport."

She raised her eyebrow. These men all had the same knee-jerk reaction. Say "women", and they think 'housewife'; say 'housewife' and they think 'weak'.

"I understand your concern, but I think it's misplaced and I assure you I won't be stepping aside." She stood up to see him to the door. He took the hint, walking with slumped shoulders and anxious face. In the doorway, he stopped and barked an abrupt laugh.

"You realize," he said, "I'm going to have to pull the Conservative play book out, and attack you on being weak on security and defense, exploit you for all the assumed weakness of being a woman."

"As you see fit," she said. *And thanks for the warning. You really should stop underestimating me.*

When she arrived at the gym the next morning, a half-naked Marilyn glanced at her then turned her nose dramatically in the air.

"She doesn't write, she doesn't phone, she doesn't email…" she soliloquized.

"Marilyn, please, I'm not in the mood." Samantha undressed swiftly.

Marilyn was still gazing skywards. "She doesn't come to gym, she doesn't come to lunch… I'm beginning to think she doesn't love me!" She gave an exaggerated sniff.

"I've been busy. I'm damn well running for president, okay?"

At Samantha's irritable tone, Marilyn turned around. She dropped her hairbrush as she saw her friend's cheek.

"Oh, yeah – and being beat up," added Samantha bitterly. She ran through the details fast, before Marilyn could ask any questions. While she agreed with Faith that she shouldn't feel ashamed of what someone else had done to her, it was still tedious to recite the order of events at every meeting. She wished she could hide it under make-up, but the swelling and discoloration were still too severe. "Anyway, didn't you see it in the papers?" she finished.

"I've been a bit – busy for the papers," said Marilyn awkwardly.

Indifferently, Samantha tossed her towel over her shoulder, and headed out of the changing rooms.

"What's got your goat?" asked Marilyn as she caught up.

"Apart from being beat up and stressed out? Ben Morehouse. The party chairman." She flung her towel down next to the first machine. "I'm doing wonders for our party and he still thinks I'm the enemy. He basically said he's going to attack me for being a woman."

The timer beeped and Samantha lifted the weights, her biceps flexing. Marilyn stood waiting her turn to join, shaking her head reprovingly.

"So what's he going to say?" she asked at last. "Don't vote for her, she's got breasts?"

"Just about. They're going to target all the things women are considered to be bad at on the two TV appearances he's scheduled for the democratic candidates…sort of like unofficial point/counter-point sessions…"

"So, what are they going to focus on – farting competitions? Mid-life crises?"

Samantha spluttered with laughter. "More like war – national debt… It's fine, I've got time to research, it's just annoying."

After showering, Samantha blow-dried her hair in record speed and began slapping on her make-up. Marilyn stood next to her by the mirrors, combing her own hair haphazardly and shifting from foot to foot.

"Sam… I need to tell you something."

"What?" Samantha had her eyes half-closed to keep the powder from getting in them as she swished the brush across her face. She snapped the case shut and swept on her eye shadow. As she was applying her eyeliner, she caught Marilyn's eye in the reflection. "What?" she asked again.

"I'm seeing someone – I thought you ought to know who. Well – seeing – sleeping with, to be honest."

Samantha screwed the lid onto her eyeliner. Her stomach was ice-cold. "Who?"

"Thomas."

Not James. She brushed mascara over her eyelashes and pulled out her blusher. After the first relief, she needed a moment to adjust.

"I know he upset you, but it's not like it's a relationship – it's just sex… Samantha?"

"What do you want me to say?" She put on her lipstick, protracting the silence.

"I just wanted to make sure you heard it from me, not from someone else – DC's a small town in its own way, gossip gets around."

Samantha dumped her cosmetics back in the bag and zipped it up. Leaning against the basin, she folded her arms and looked at Marilyn.

"It matters," she said simply.

"What?"

"It matters. It's not okay. I mind."

"What are you saying?"

"Well, what you want me to say is 'it doesn't matter, it's okay, I don't mind.' But that's not true, I'm actually quite hurt. Obviously I can't stop you and it's not my business, but I'm not going to lie about my feelings to make you feel better." She combed out her hair.

"I can't believe you're being such a bitch!" Marilyn was outraged.

"I'm not being a bitch," insisted Samantha. "You asked, I said." She walked over to the bench to pack her bag.

"Yeah, but you don't have to be so… so… I mean you could be nicer…"

Samantha looked up at her. "Oh, really? You spend years telling me I shouldn't be so nice, and then when you start fucking the man who nearly ruined my career and then screwed around behind my back, I should be *nice* about it?"

"That's not what I meant…"

"I know exactly what you meant!" She stuffed her gym clothes in the bag and slung it over her shoulder. "You mean the same thing that everyone means, which is – 'stand up for yourself, except to me.'"

Seeing Marilyn's confused mix of anger and hurt, Samantha sighed heavily and folded her arms.

"Marilyn – it's not the end of the world, it's not the end of our friendship, but if you're asking for my blessing, I can't give it. That's all."

Marilyn sat down. "I'm not used to you getting mad at me," she said in a small voice.

Samantha laughed humorlessly. "You think this is mad? You ain't seen nothin' yet. But I promise I won't throw your shoes at you."

"That was *true*?"

"Yup. So – screw him if you want, but don't ask me to like it and don't expect me to speak to him. I've got to get to work. And stop looking so woebegone, the world doesn't end because I'm not nice, you know."

"It's still a bit of a shock to the system… but I guess I should be proud of you." She gave Samantha a rueful smile and a thumbs up. "Good for you, girl."

Ben was true to his word. In the final television appearance before the Democratic primaries, This Week with George Stephanopoulos, the other two remaining candidates – Senator Edward Thompson and Governor Dallas Clark – had clearly been groomed to attack her on defense, to the exclusion of all other topics. Dallas's every question was on the situation in the Middle East.

"By withdrawing our troops from the region," he argued, "aren't you basically saying to the terrorists – here you are…you win?"

A murmur ran through the audience. Samantha surveyed the crowd in their plush red seats, gauging their mood and giving the camera time to focus on her calm, certain expression.

"It is absolutely crucial that we don't look as if we're winning or losing, but that we're doing the right thing in the Middle East," she said.

"I disagree with Congresswoman St. Clair's assessment. I believe it's *all* about winning or losing. I believe pulling out is telling the terrorists they win and I believe the American people do not want this defeatist attitude in the White House!" He looked out at the audience, waiting for signs of their approval. Again, his words were greeted with a faint murmur.

Samantha turned her head to meet Dallas's eyes. "Can you honestly look me in the eye and say we are winning under the current conditions? That we are giving the region more long-term stability, more economic strength? That for what we've achieved, the cost in money and in lives is acceptable?"

"I can," he said grimly, "But I don't expect you to understand the cost of war, the sacrifices our men have to make."

He hadn't quite spelled it out, but his implication was clear. Samantha discreetly slid a color-coded card out of her pile of notes she held in her lap as she turned back toward the camera and responded.

"Men like to assume women know nothing about war," she told them. "I've never been in the armed forces – true. Neither have either of these men." She gestured at her two sparring partners. "The difference is, I don't *assume* I know about the military – I find out. I have five questions for you, Governor Clark. What is our annual defense budget? How much have we spent to date on the war in Iraq? How many US troops have died? How many Iraqi civilians – not soldiers – have we killed? And what is the nation's average threat level since the war in Iraq began?"

"What is this, Quiz Bowl?" he snapped.

"Can you answer the questions, Governor Clark?"

He ground his teeth. "I don't have the exact figures to hand…"

"Well, then," said Samantha. She shuffled her notes to indicate that particular line of discussion was over.

Edward Thompson stepped in. "Whatever the statistics," he said, "This country goes to war when it is in clear and present danger. Are you suggesting that 9/11 did not show a clear and present danger?"

"For the benefit of the television and studio audience," replied Samantha, "Could you spell out the connections between 9/11 and Iraq?"

"The *connection* is *terrorism*," said Edward.

"I'm sorry; perhaps I didn't make myself clear." Samantha smiled brightly. "I meant how the Iraqi administration or Iraqi citizens were involved in 9/11."

Edward stood in mulish silence. Samantha watched him expectantly. She knew he knew there was no involvement whatsoever. She'd done her background checks on Edward and knew he was personally opposed to the war – one of those who had argued most vociferously against suppressing the events of 9/11 and the war in Iraq. In essence, by trying to shoot her argument down, he'd stumbled into arguing against his own beliefs.

"Senator Thompson?" George Stephanopoulos urged him to answer.

"We have a duty to root out terrorism wherever we may find it…" the Senator began.

"So who's next? Ireland? Florida? The UK?" she interrupted. Before he could object, she went on, "Pardon me – you were saying – we have a duty?"

"Yes, we do."

"Senator Thompson, you have a senior in high school and two children in college, correct?"

He nodded.

"Have you stressed the importance to them of enlisting in our armed forces and protecting us from this clear and present danger?"

He didn't answer.

"So are you saying that they are cowards or unpatriotic? Or maybe both?"

Stung, he retorted, "They are both brave *and* patriotic, and I resent that question!"

"Then obviously, they don't see the clear and present danger you do, or recognize the duty you speak of, otherwise they would be the first ones to enlist if they did, I'm sure."

She turned on Dallas. "Governor Clark, when Vietnam was seen as fighting the spread of Communism, when our presence there was interpreted as reinforcing the security of the nation, how many deferments did you apply for in order to avoid serving our country in that conflict?"

"I refuse to answer that," he snarled.

"This is not meant to be a character assassination." Samantha looked from one to the other and deliberately softened her voice. "I can understand not wanting to fight in the Vietnam War, and not wanting your children to fight in the Middle East. My point is this: it's easy to talk about the duty of war; it's easy to say the cost of war is worth it – it's easy to say we need to win at all costs. But the words "win at all costs" are empty, when the costs are not your own."

Her voice turned more strident and ringing as she faced the audience again. "As Commander in Chief," she declared, "I will treat our brave soldiers as if they were my own sons and daughters. Not as disposable items that can be sacrificed on inaccurate intelligence and unknown circumstances. I will conduct my foreign policy based on what's right for the stability of this country and the world. I will not be drawn into wars of ego, afraid that people might think I've lost my nerve if I withdraw. If the cost is too high, I will not let the deaths of our children pay it.

The audience burst into spontaneous applause and she resisted the urge to smirk. Neither Thompson nor Clark had seen what she saw in the audience: more women than men.

"Virginia, Maine and Tennessee," said James, raising his mug. "Not bad!"

"Not *bad*?" Samantha was indignant. "That's three of the…"

"No – no, not bad means good," he explained hastily. "It means fantastic, brilliant, amazing. In British speak."

"So why not just say fantastic?"

"That wouldn't be British."

"You need to get back to your American roots, boy." Samantha grinned. She smacked her mug confidently against his, slopping her coffee on the table. "Shit – I mean Christ, sorry – oh God." She stopped, looked at the coffee, looked at him, and chuckled. "Sorry for spilling *and* using bad language," she said with exaggerated grace.

"Don't mention it," he replied smoothly, pulling out a tissue to mop it up. His mouth twitched. "You'll probably only swear again if you do." He winked. Samantha grew suddenly hot.

Clumsiness and hot flushes? You're getting menopausal. When did you last have a period?

It doesn't have to be menopause. It could just be – oh, no, no I can't still…Not at this age!

She snuck another look at him and her cheeks heated. She prayed her foundation hid her heightened color as she said, too briskly, "Well, to work then!"

"Of course." He promptly pulled out his laptop. "I've been looking at your other policies, to make sure they're compatible with your green policy – obviously, we're talking very broad strokes here, but there are a few slight changes you might want to consider…"

They leaned inwards over the screen. One person, at least, had read her platform in minute detail and she swelled with pleasure, as if her mind were opening out into the sunshine. Just knowing that someone was listening properly to her thoughts made it easier to think. At the same time, her body was moving steadily between hot blushes and cold sweats, her stomach keeping rhythm by diving as if she were on a rollercoaster. She even began to enjoy the sensation and found if she snuck a sidelong glance at James, or flared her nostrils to catch the smell of his skin, it intensified.

Supper time came and went as they worked. Around them, the café's stream of customers moved through and the waitress periodically topped up their coffee. When they finished the policy review, he started showing her various websites she could link to, with useful graphics or quick interactive games, and gradually they drifted into playing.

"Here's another one," he said excitedly, "This is nothing to do with the environment – it's just hilarious…" He quickly typed the address in and brought up a short animation. He was already chuckling before it started playing and Samantha found herself laughing more at his reaction than the lame cartoon.

"Sorry," he said, when it finished. "I'm the original geek – I was a geek before they even invented geeks… Well, you know what a nerd I was at school."

"No, I – what? But… but you – I don't…" She stared at him, stymied. As far as she knew, he'd been in the highest echelons of social standing at school, way up in the stratosphere, while she'd crawled along the river bed with the other bottom feeders. "But you were so good at debate," she finished.

"Exactly my point," he said wryly. Seeing her bewilderment, he laughed. "Come off it, Samantha – you really think the jocks let me get away with that? Plus, I couldn't catch a ball to save my life. It didn't hurt my career, not being able to catch, but…"

"Amazing." She laughed and leaned back, studying him while trying to fit this new information into her perception of him. "It's funny," she went on, thoughtfully. "When you're an adult, it's all about getting to know somebody – what are their politics, what's their background, their history – and when you're a kid, you don't think about any of that, really. You can have the wildest crush on someone without actually knowing the first thing about them." Too late, she realized what she was saying; too abruptly, she stopped speaking.

It was James's turn to stare. "You didn't…" he breathed. "You had a crush on *me*?"

An inch of make-up could not have hidden her blush. "For years."

"Damn. *Damn!* Damn it all, why didn't you *say*? I was so hot for you! I thought you didn't know I existed, you just looked right through me."

"But I stared at you all the time – when you weren't looking, obviously, I tried to hide it…"

He raised his eyebrows and she laughed in embarrassment.

"I guess I managed, then. But I didn't think you'd ever like me, I was too fat."

"What?"

"I was – you know. I was pudgy. I was the fat kid."

He was shaking his head in absolute disbelief. "You were never fat," he said simply. He swung back to his laptop and keyed in the address to her website. "Here," he said, clicking through to the photo album. "Look at your own photographs. You weren't fat."

Samantha looked at them, at him, and back at the screen. She leaned her forehead against her fingertips. She wanted to go back in time with a list of instructions for that kid: "1. James likes you. 2. You're not fat. 3. Don't listen to your mother. 4. Don't marry Richard." She didn't know whether to laugh in wonder or break down in tears of inconsolable regret for the previous thirty years of her life.

"Do you think we can get a drink here?" she said weakly. "I mean – while we're rewriting my life story…"

"In here, Congresswoman," said the nurse, indicating the door. "And may I just say – I *loved* your speech the other night!"

"'Thanks." Samantha gave a quick grin. She peeped through the small window and winced. Richard's face was pulped and swollen on one side, his right arm in a sling.

"We gave him painkillers because we had to," the nurse said grimly. "But around here, we don't take too kindly to wife beaters. Let's just say he's not Mr. Popular."

"I'll wait out here," said Hope.

As Samantha stepped through the door, she heard the agent saying to the nurse, "I'm afraid I'm to blame for his condition." Somehow, she didn't sound contrite.

Richard's head turned towards her and away again.

"Richard, I'm not here to win. I'm not here to gloat. I'm not here to beat you. I didn't even know we were in a competition. I'm here to get a divorce."

She removed the papers from her bag and put them on his nightstand next to his newspaper. The headlines proclaimed her victory in Hawaii, Idaho and Utah. Samantha looked at him sadly. They'd lived together for over twenty years and he couldn't even bring himself to congratulate her. He refused to look at her or speak.

"When you're physically able, please sign the papers and get them back to me."

He ignored her.

"You'll be happy to know that I don't want your money – well, if you have any money left – or the houses or anything else as a matter of fact. All I want now is my freedom and to be away from you."

He gave a curt nod. Anger surged at his refusal to acknowledge her as a person, as a success, as anything other than a prop in his own life. Impulsively, she blurted out what she knew she shouldn't say. "And you can forget about trying to win Faith over in all this. She's already on my side."

At that, he turned and looked at her, his face incredulous. "What the hell are you talking about?"

"Don't expect Faith to back you up in any way – as far as she's concerned, she thinks you got what's coming to you." Saying the words felt terribly wrong, but she forced them out anyway. Perhaps standard wisdom said not to involve the children, but in this case Richard had forfeited all right to consideration. Riding roughshod over the intense sensation that she shouldn't say it, she went on: "I've spoken to her, and she supports me."

Richard stared at her. "Oh, my God," he mouthed. "You've lost it." He seemed genuinely appalled.

"What?" His strange expression sent chills up her spine.

"Faith has been dead for over five years, and if she's supporting you, she's doing it from the grave."

Samantha stepped back from the bed, her skin crawling. "What are you talking about?" she whispered. "Faith is totally fine. I speak with her almost every night." Her own voice sounded tinny in her head.

"Jesus Christ, this explains everything. You're delirious. Sam – she died five years ago, in a car crash. You were driving her to college. Don't you *remember*?"

Samantha flattened her back against the wall, her eyes wide, her mouth twisted. "No," she whimpered, "She's not – she's…" Hysteria rose in her, making her gulp for air with every word she tried to speak. "No!" The word came out in a thin scream.

The door flung open. As Hope dashed into the room, Samantha barreled past her, running blindly. Hope stopped in midstride, her head twisting as she tried to work out whether to confront Richard or race after Samantha.

"What did you say to her?" she demanded.

"Nothing," said Richard defensively, flinching.

"Why is she so upset?"

"Because the crazy bitch thinks our daughter is still alive."

18

Before the impact, there were distinct moments when it hadn't happened yet, when there were still options. In one such moment, she saw the van's brake lights, checked her own rearview mirror, and thought about veering around into the next lane. Instead, she braked. In another moment, with her head slammed back against the chair and her eyes flaring with fear, she saw the ends of the heavy slabs of timber shooting towards them, like an overdone 3D film, and she waited for the net – or rope – or *something* – to stop them. They kept coming closer, but there was still a moment when nothing had happened yet and so everything could be avoided. Faith started to scream for a split second, before the smash of the wood against the windshield drowned out the sound. A few moments must have blanked out, after that. Her next memory was of looking down a wooden tunnel – a heavy plank lay on either side of her head. Her eyes shifted down – her lap was thick with rounded fragments of glass. Her neck didn't want to move; her body felt beaten. She glanced to the side, to where Faith was hidden by the plank between them.

"Faith?" she whispered.

Outside, she could hear screams, screeching brakes, traffic whizzing, and a man's voice repeating, "Oh my God, oh my God, oh my God..." She wished he would shut up so she could hear Faith. She could feel, but not see, her daughter's hand, damp with sweat. She held it, squeezed it gently.

"It's okay, baby, I'm here," she said shakily. "It's okay, they'll get us out."

The man was still shouting as sirens came closer. Someone must have taken him away and tried to calm him down, because his voice receded. Samantha became aware of a warm, ticklish sensation running down her jaw and over her neck. She realized it must be blood dripping down – so she wasn't unhurt. More sirens approached – different ones – everyone must be coming, the police, ambulance, fire department... She was embarrassed to be the center of such a fuss when they were quite alright. Still, the fire department would be helpful in getting them out of the car.

For a long time, they seemed to do nothing. The plank on her right shifted – they were pulling it out. Her head wouldn't budge but she lay against her seat with her eyes twisted as far to the side as they would go.

"It's okay, baby..." she said. Her voice was as thin as a wisp of smoke.

She waited for Faith's face to appear, but it didn't. She couldn't take it in. She could see her daughter's body, her torso, the slope of her breasts in her t-shirt, her shoulders... nothing more. Only when she saw the blood on the huge wooden sleeper that was withdrawing from the front window did she register. Someone began to scream: a weird, unearthly howl that bore no relation to human speech. Who would've believed a person could even make that sound? She was above the car, looking down into it despite its roof, at the headless body on the right and, in the driver's seat, a figure with a head, its face distorted and white, frozen in a rictus of terror. Although the scream went on, it had faded to a tiny distant sound.

She shifted between being inside the body looking at the headless girl, and outside, above, removed from the sounds and smells of the world. The emergency personnel were in a flurry, shouting instructions, running this way and that. Back in her body, she lay and stared and screamed and disbelieved while they took away the planks, cut the car open, and finally carried her out, her eyes still glued to the car and her mouth still open, letting out the horrible sound she couldn't stop making. People's hands were on her, trying to turn her away and shield her from what she'd already seen. Her hands reached back, clutching empty air, trying to gather her daughter back into her arms. Someone wrenched her away, slapping her wrist, and she saw behind the car. A twisted desk lamp had shattered its cover on the pavement. The two boxes lay tumbled out. One of the suitcases had burst open, scattering clothes down the highway. A long spray of blood ran behind the car, ending abruptly in a puddle. Despite the protective cocoon of shock, despite the veil of disbelief that shielded her senses, she saw and understood. Her body went slack. Someone put a needle in her arm.

When she woke, her body flung itself back, rigid; her foot stamped for the brake and her eyes flew up to the rearview mirror. The sheet constricted all her movements. Her body was still taut, her mind still panicking, as she realized she was not in the car. Above her was a ceiling of white squares and a rectangle of metal from which hung a blue and green floral curtain. The next thing that entered her mind was the false memory, the horror she'd imagined but not seen: Faith's beautiful face frozen in shock, her long hair whipping, and her head bounding and tumbling down the road. When she thought of what she actually had seen – the headless body – she was devoid of any response.

The curtain opened quickly and a nurse appeared with a hypodermic needle.

"It's okay, keep calm," she was saying, holding Samantha back down. "Quiet, now, try to keep quiet..."

Samantha stared at her, puzzled.

"You're okay, Mrs. St. Clair, just try to stop screaming..."

Samantha closed her mouth, sealing off her throat. Abruptly, she threw up, spattering her arm and the nurse's hands.

"I'm sorry," she said, appalled. "I'm so sorry – your hands..."

"It doesn't matter, really – don't worry." The nurse's eyes shone with tears for a moment as she gave a brisk, tight smile and turned away to clean up.

Samantha lay back, numb. Her body knew what had happened. Her mind knew what had happened. Somewhere between the two was the real her, unable to respond, hiding behind the shelter of senselessness.

"I know what happened," she said. Her mouth twisted hideously. The nurse – Jane MacCullum, said her name tag – was wiping down her arm. The words stuck in her throat, but she had to get them out. "Her head bounced." She retched violently again. Nothing remained in her stomach and it occurred to her that what she had already thrown up was the coffee Faith had made for her. It seemed so cruelly ungrateful to vomit out that last gift from her daughter, and she began to cry, still dry-heaving, then screaming, all at the same time in a mess of tears and sick and noise. The nurse was hurting her wrist.

She slammed back as the planks shot towards her, a scream of fright caught in her throat. Her hands found only the firmness of the mattress. Her eyes saw, not wood smashing in her skull, but the white ceiling from earlier. The curtains were open. A sound, *heunhhh,* of sharply indrawn breath, lingered in her ears. She waited for her pounding pulse to slow. The blood hammered in her neck. She turned her head and saw Richard standing by the window. His face was very red. Their eyes met, but she couldn't think of a word to say. She tried to sit up a little, but could only lean forward a few inches.

"I'll sue them," he said at last, "I'll sue the bastards for everything they're worth, I'll crush them into the fucking *ground*." His body hummed with tension. She couldn't respond. His anger hurt her, like burrs on raw flesh. Any reaction or words were pointless, because they wouldn't restore Faith, whole and alive, to this moment.

"I'll make them pay for this," said Richard.

"What price for your daughter?" Samantha's voice croaked.

Richard stared at her, shaking, and rushed out of the room. She slumped back onto the pillow as a nurse hurried in.

"Mrs. St. Clair, are you okay?" she asked gently.

Samantha didn't answer.

"Would you like another sedative?"

She shook her head.

"Would you like to speak to someone?" This last enquiry came very tenderly.

Samantha turned her head away.

"Mrs. St. Clair – you've been through a terrible shock," the nurse persisted softly. You're still in shock. It might help you to speak to someone. We have a counselor who can come visit you – or if you prefer someone you know, is there any friend or family you'd like to speak to?'

"Yes, there is. My daughter."

Faith was in the middle of the living room of the apartment, her arms wrapped around herself, looking thin and lost.

"Hello," she said in a small voice.

Samantha walked past her into the bathroom. She saw her daughter's reflection in the mirror and for a moment their eyes met. Samantha's face twisted. It broke her heart to do this to her daughter and it broke her heart to acknowledge that her daughter wasn't there. The two contradictory feelings, instead of canceling each other out, doubled her pain. She opened the cabinet door with a fierce smack, replacing Faith's image with rows of bottles and jars. A corner of her mind marveled that a hallucination's reflection still needed a mirror. If she was imagining it, surely Faith's face should still hover in view, superimposed over her medicines?

"You're not going to talk to me now?" said Faith.

"I would if you were real, but since you're not, I'll pass," said Samantha. *This is not your daughter you're hurting,* she told herself determinedly.

"What do you mean, I'm not real?" Faith sounded scared. "You're talking to me now, aren't you?"

Samantha was rooting through the plastic and cardboard containers, creating from them a frantic mess.

"I'm delusional right now, so I'm not sure I'm qualified to make that judgment," replied Samantha coldly. Hurting even the illusion of Faith caused her actual physical pain, she realized. Her stomach knotted and the side of her neck throbbed with tension.

"You don't believe I'm real?" Her voice was so small and pitiful.

"Goddammit!" Samantha slammed the door shut, saw Faith's face, and covered her eyes with her hands. "Where are my *pills*?" she yelled into her palms.

"Mom, answer me!" Faith tried to turn her around and Samantha resisted. How was this happening? How could she see, hear and feel her daughter while knowing the truth? "How can you say I'm not real, Mom? Mommy?"

"Stop it!" screeched Samantha, unshed tears burning in her eyes. Her shoulders heaved. "I killed you in the car accident! I was driving you to college, I remember it, you've never been to college, you're *dead*!" With the back of her hands, she wiped her tears away as fast as they fell.

Faith's face was wet. "Did your love for me die when I died?" she pleaded.

"Of course not – baby, no…"

"Then I'm as real as the day I was born. Mommy – please…" She held out her arms but Samantha backed away.

"What are you saying – you stay alive because I love you? I know that's not true, Faith…"

"I *am* your love for me."

Samantha turned and left the room. "I need my pills. I need my pills…" In her bedroom, she opened and slammed shut her wardrobe and drawers.

Faith trailed after her, entreating, "I'm not just your love for *me*, Mom – I'm the love and compassion you have for all children, and the elderly, and the poor, and for the planet – and I'm the love and compassion you have for yourself. I told you! I said I was here to stand up for you and help you and mother you…"

Samantha strode from the bedroom to the kitchen where she ransacked the cupboards.

"Mom… what I'm trying to say is, you manifested me because you were able to love others, and yourself, *unconditionally* – do you know how rare that is? Truly unconditional love?"

"You're dead," Samantha spun around. "You're dead and I'm delusional. Anything you say is only me speaking and I'm obviously crazy." She looked at her daughter's despairing, tear-stained face and her own eyes spilled over again, leaving trails of moisture down her cheeks. She turned her back again, unable to bear it.

"You're able to open your heart *so wide* that you transcended a level of consciousness! You're able to turn physical love into a metaphysical form! And you chose to see that love in what you love most in the world. Me."

Samantha wiped her face with her arm, her eyes and nose a torrent now.

"That's great, Faith," she muttered, stepping around her towards the front door. "But your insane mother needs to go find some help, right now."

Behind her, she heard Faith yell, "Mom – you don't get it! You're not insane! You're *divine!*"

As she ran out of the apartment block, she collided with Hope, who caught her around the waist.

"What do you think you're doing?" exclaimed Hope.

"It's none of your business." Samantha tried to sidestep her, keeping her tear-wrecked face averted.

Hope grabbed her by the arms with surprising force. "It is my business. I'm assigned to protect you and you just bolted out on me…"

Samantha tried to pull free, but Hope's grip was firm. "For God's sake, Hope…"

"We're not going to make a scene out here," said Hope grimly, forcing her back into the building.

"How *dare* you manhandle me!" Samantha spat out, as Hope released her in the lobby.

"I'm sorry for the use of force," said Hope stiffly. "I don't think you want any photographers snapping us wrestling on the pavement. And I don't want you to run off again."

"I can do what I want," said Samantha rebelliously.

"It's my duty to protect you, even from yourself. You're a presidential candidate."

"I'll tell you what I am! Fucking *insane* is what I am!" She made a bolt for the door and Hope caught her, swinging her back around.

"So what are you going to do? Throw yourself out into oncoming traffic?"

"Get *off* me!" She tried to push away the arms around her, but Hope folded her into a tight hug. "Hope – let go…"

"Tell me where you're going and I'll take you there."

"I'm going to see a psychiatrist, happy? I'm not a presidential candidate, I'm a lunatic. Richard was right."

Hope held her closer still. "It's okay…" she whispered repeatedly as Samantha sobbed.

When Samantha was calmer, Hope released her and handed her a tissue from the pocket of her suit.

"You're not insane, ma'am – you're the most amazing woman I've ever met."

"You don't understand." Samantha blew her nose heavily and Hope passed her another tissue.

"Your husband blurted out that you've been talking to your dead daughter. Is that it?"

Surprised, Samantha nodded.

"Well – it's unusual, I grant you…"

"It's a sign of madness," insisted Samantha.

Hope looked unconvinced. "Shouldn't you leave that diagnosis to a professional? I don't think you're insane, personally… Grief-stricken, yes. But insane? I certainly can't see it."

"Hope, I talk to my dead daughter!"

Hope shrugged. "I talk to my dead mom. She's the voice in my head."

"Does the voice in *your* head sit on your sofa and drink wine with you?"

"My mom's more of a gin-and-tonic drinker…" she said, her mouth twitching. "Listen ma'am, and it's certainly up to you, but – are you sure you want to see a psychiatrist? Can you trust one to be discreet?"

"I know one I'd trust with my life. Not with my husband, but…" For a moment, Samantha almost smiled.

"Come on, then."

As Samantha began to cry again, Hope pulled out the remaining clump of tissues from her pocket and handed them to her.

"Sam, what are you doing here this time of day?" Marilyn leapt up from her desk, her broad smile faltering almost instantly. "Jesus, what's happened?"

Unsteadily, Samantha walked forward and sat in the client chair on the other side of the desk. "I need a new prescription," she said dully.

"Sam, look at me." Marilyn reached over, lifted her friend's chin, and studied her bloodshot eyes. "Have you taken something already?" she asked. "Have you been drinking? Has something… Has Richard…?"

Samantha was shaking her head, her lips compressed. "I need a new prescription," she repeated.

Marilyn sat back, frowning. "What happened to the pills you had? You shouldn't have run out yet."

"I've lost them. I haven't been taking them. I don't know what I did with them." She was desperately trying to cling on to some semblance of normalcy; it was important that Marilyn understood this was a rational and sane request.

"How long have you been off them?"

"Not sure – a few months, at least."

"And you've been fine, suddenly you want more. Why? Sam, look at me!"

Reluctantly, Samantha raised her gaze from her folding and unfolding hands, afraid that the grief in her eyes might blast her friend to pieces.

"I've been talking to Faith," she whispered. "I've been seeing her. I didn't know she was dead. But I did know. I must've forgotten."

Marilyn's expression became stoic with professionalism as Samantha's confession trickled out. When she'd finished, Marilyn wrote out a prescription. As Samantha held out her hand, Marilyn held it back a moment.

"You know I've never agreed with this line of treatment for you, Sam."

Samantha nodded.

"I do not think you are psychotic, depressive or delusional – no, hear me out, *whatever* the circumstances. I've told you this time and time again. So I will give you this prescription on one condition: you find yourself someone to speak to. It doesn't have to be a psychologist, a counselor is fine. I can refer you to someone discreet and good. Promise me that this time you'll get help."

"I thought that's what I was doing," said Samantha tiredly.

Marilyn shook her head, smiling sadly. "I'm giving you this now because you're under a lot of pressure, and this a tense time for you, but long-term – I'm not the help you need. This isn't." She shook the paper. "Not long-term."

"Okay." Samantha's eyes hurt from crying and in the aftermath of her grief, she was deeply tired. She'd agree to anything Marilyn said, if it would just make the pain go away. Marilyn slid the paper over to her. "Thanks."

Ben and Cynthia sat on opposite sides of Ben's desk, staring at the same set of numbers on individual documents. Cynthia's fingernails clattered rhythmically on the wood as she studied them. The tapping rose to a quick crescendo and reached a finalé as her hand smacked down on the desk.

"There's no way around it," she declared, releasing her document and letting it float softly onto the shiny wooden surface. "If she takes Super Tuesday, that's it."

"Over for our guys," said Ben, scrutinizing her sharply. In his opinion, Cynthia didn't look suitably downcast. He pushed the papers away, leaning back in his chair. "I don't get it… How can a woman who is so non-political be so politically savvy? In thirty years in politics, I've never seen anything like it."

"Neither have I," said Cynthia calmly, thinking to herself that such honesty as Samantha has shown was truly rare.

"It's like all the rules have changed," Ben continued, waving his arms grandly. "How can I fight a war when I don't know the rules?"

"Maybe you should just drop the fight altogether."

"Give up? Never!" He hit the desk emphatically.

"No – I'm actually thinking we should start backing Samantha St. Clair."

Ben stared at her, then shook his head. "That's crazy. The Republicans are licking their chops for a St. Clair match-up and I'm not going to sit back and give it to them."

"But look how many people have voted in the last five primaries!" Cynthia moved behind Ben's chair. With her fingernail, she pointed out the figure on Ben's sheet. He glanced at it and looked away.

"With us fighting her every step of the way," Cynthia went on, "I think Samantha St. Clair has singlehandedly united and re-energized our party!"

"That can't be true."

"Can't be? Or you don't want it to be?" Cynthia folded her arms, giving him a steely-eyed stare. "We are seeing voter turn-out like we have never seen in Democratic primaries before."

"There's a picture of her sucking a man's cock on the internet and she re-energizes our party," he said, as much to himself as to Cynthia. "How does that *happen*?"

"Because she is smart. Because she's compassionate, articulate, and has no political agenda other than helping the less fortunate and it's been a *long* time since our voters had someone like that to vote for!"

Ben pushed his fingers deep into his hair, tugging it from the roots. "Which is great news," he said despairingly, "But if she wins she would still get crushed in the general!"

"That may be true," said Cynthia calmly, "but at least she'd lose with the same philosophy as the party's base.

We've been throwing them candidates they don't like for a long time, and they've been ignoring them accordingly. Now at least we've got a candidate that people are prepared to go to a ballot box for."

Ben's shoulders slumped and he massaged his forehead. "I guess you're right," he said. "I can't believe I'm saying this, but... We need to back St. Clair."

19

After two nights in her office, the capsule wardrobe
Samantha kept at work had run out and she was forced to
confront her apartment again. When she opened the door,
she half expected to see Faith still standing in the corridor.
She wasn't there.

"Hello?" The silent apartment mocked her greeting. She
walked to the kitchen, switched on the light, and looked
around - no one was there. The living room was equally
empty. In the bedroom and the bathroom, she checked
behind the doors. She stood between the rooms, her arms
around herself, feeling very alone.

"Hello?" she said again, without conviction. She began
another circuit of the apartment, like a child checking for
monsters, or a jilted lover hoping to catch a glimpse of her
beloved against all likelihood. The rooms remained
decidedly empty. She sat on the sofa and looked at the other
end, where Faith usually sat reading her book. *Faith never
sat there*, she thought. This sofa and this apartment were
bought after Faith's death.

She stood again to lower the blinds and close the curtains.
At the window, she hovered, peering outside, expecting to
see her daughter standing on the wet cement under the
streetlamp. No one was there. Shaking her head at her own
stupidity, she shut the curtains and resisted the temptation to
look again.

Returning to the sofa, Samantha switched on the
television and numbly sat through a summary of her various
victories on CNN.

"…and is now considered the number one candidate for
the Democratic party." finished the presenter. Apart from
saying she'd 'rocketed to fame after an internet scandal';

they made no mention of her sexuality. Without Faith's devilish grin and words of encouragement, the triumph felt hollow.

Leaving the television blaring, Samantha wandered into the kitchen and stared at the contents in the fridge. The lettuce had gone brown and soggy. She tossed it in the garbage, followed by some lemons with white and green mold, a loaf of green-spotted bread, and some wilted herbs. When she lifted up a cucumber, her fingers went right through it. She considered the remaining tomato while she ate a piece of cheese. Popping another piece of cheese in her mouth, she stared at the contents in the cupboards while she chewed. *Perhaps a glass of wine*, she thought, and remembered Faith pouring the bottle down the drain. Was the wine real? Had she poured it away herself?

"You're not going to sit around anymore getting drunk and listening to sad music!" Faith told her. Had she told herself? Her head spun. Either way, it was good advice. She switched the kettle on and wandered into the bathroom, eating a dry bagel. For a while, she watched her reflection chewing in the cabinet mirror. She realized she has absolutely no idea what to do with herself for the next three or four hours before bedtime.

Samantha returned to the kitchen and ate another biscuit, contemplated opening a bottle of wine, then pulled out her cell phone.

"James? It's Sam here – yes… Not too great, actually… I could use some company, if you're free…"

"I don't want you to think I'm crazy," Samantha began. She and James sat at a dark booth in a cellar bar. She twisted her wedding ring around her finger as she spoke, then played with her wrists, squeezing them tightly. "I don't know how you cannot think I'm insane, because – well, the thing is – I sort of am."

"Okay," said James cautiously. His smile held traces of amusement as he waited for her to go on.

"I told you about my daughter?"

"Yes – Faith, wasn't it?"

"She's dead," she said flatly.

"Oh my God, Sam…" Shocked, James shot his hand across the table to cover hers. "I'm so sorry! When? What happened…?"

Samantha pulled her hands away, cupping her elbows defensively. "It was five years ago."

James sat there, jaw slackened a moment. "But…"

"So I'm back on my medication," she said casually. "Something went – funny – in my head for a while, but it's fixed now." She took a sip of her drink and carefully set it back down.

James covered his mouth with his hand. "I don't know what to say," he said eventually. "Samantha…I really am so sorry – it's a terrible thing to lose someone, I know…"

"Do you know what it's like to be a lunatic?" cut in Samantha. "No - don't answer that. Anyway, I'm not really crazy – well, obviously I *am,* because I've been hanging out with my dead daughter, but Marilyn's given me a prescription. I told you she's a psychiatrist, didn't I?"

"Yes, you did. Sam…"

"Doctor Malone, no less."

"Yes, you told me. Sam, I know you say you've got a prescription now, but – surely there's more to it than just medicine? I mean, it's okay to grieve, and grief does very strange things…"

"She's kept her married name even though she's divorced, because that's the name she used when she became a psychiatrist… Samantha went on speaking over him, her voice careless and hushed.

"Sam…"

"I think I might do that, too. I mean, I'll have to, won't I? Did I tell you I'm getting a divorce? Of course the difference is purely legal as we're already separated…"

James stopped trying to get her attention and sat in silence as she rattled through the various things that might, or might not, be affected by her divorce. When she was silent at last, he said, "Grief does strange things. I know. And it's okay to still be grieving after five years."

Samantha gave a gracious smile. "James, it's very sweet of you to be concerned, but really I'm fine. Now, here I am prattling on about me, and I haven't asked a thing about your house-hunt. How's it going? Seen anything you like?"

He sighed and signaled the waiter. "A double whiskey and a tonic & lime, please." He turned back to Samantha. "Is that alright? I assume it's a bad idea to consume alcohol with your medication."

"Sure. I don't get… *drunk*," said Samantha stiffly. "It's not ladylike."

He shook his head in disbelief. "Is this the medication doing this?" he asked. "You're behaving like one of the Stepford Wives."

Ignoring his comment, she went on, "Anyway, I don't drink whisky."

The waiter, arriving with the drinks, looked quizzically at James, who shook his head minutely as if to say, *Don't worry about it.* The two glasses were set on the table and he pushed the tonic water towards her.

"Bottoms up," he said cheerfully, taking a gulp of his drink. James watched as Samantha sat motionless, drink untouched. "You know, it seems we have two choices here. We can have a nice conversation, or you can just start crying right now and save yourself some time."

Samantha tensed like a cornered animal gripping her purse on her lap. Her shoulders were rigid. "I'd really rather not…"

"Feel anything, I know," cut in James. "I've been attending group support for bereavement for the last two years. I *do know*."

"Faith said I shouldn't get drunk!" burst out Samantha, then slapped her hand over her mouth in horror.

James nodded gently. "Why did she say that?" he prompted.

"She said I shouldn't just sit around crying and getting drunk, I should do something about it – I should leave Richard. Divorce him."

"And you're doing that now?"

Samantha nodded.

"So it was good advice?"

Again, she bobbed her head. "But it was – me." Her mouth tensed for a moment. "She couldn't have said that because she's dead." She sounded like a child patiently repeating a lesson.

"You know," said James slowly, "It's not so unusual, when people die, to still feel them near you. Even see them, sometimes. I'm not really religious, I've never believed in souls exactly, but when Emma died – sometimes, afterwards, she was *with* me. That's the only way I can explain. And other people have had the same happen to them."

"Except other people know the person's dead and I didn't," she objected wearily.

"And when did you find that out?"

"Umm – a couple of days ago maybe…" Samantha absently picked up her tonic water and took a gulp of it.

"And did you cry?"

Samantha took another large sip. "I suppose so. A bit." She considered vaguely that she might like to cry now, but the thought was far away and her heart was numb.

"And when she died five years ago? Did you grieve?"

She snapped out of her semi-trance. "I really don't care to discuss this," she said in her most officious voice. She downed the tonic water and put her purse on the table as she stood to leave. "I'm sorry to have to leave so suddenly, I'm sure we'll catch up soon," she said, expressionless. She sensed movement and looked up to see James standing next to her. At such close quarters, he towered over her. Wrapping his arms around her, he pulled her in, hiding her face against his chest. Her stiff demeanor faltered as she leaned into his embrace.

"Don't run away," he whispered against the top of her head. "I'm sorry if I pushed too hard – but don't run away."

Her cheek rubbed against the smooth starchiness of his shirt. He held her tighter.

"I just hate seeing you like this."

"Like how?" Her voice was subdued, muffled by the hug.

"All – stiff, false and pretending…" His gentle squeeze softened his words. Pulling away to look her in the eye, he said teasingly, "I'd rather you threw your drink at me than turned all polite on me. 'Cause that's more real, Samantha."

"I'm just so numb, James…" she admitted. "But I don't want to bore you, talking about it…"

He helped her back into her seat, sliding in alongside her. With her hands in his, he said, "Sam – you could read me the phonebook, and I would not find it boring."

Marilyn and Samantha sat on opposite sides of the living room, each with a glass of wine.

"Of course, with the new line being launched, Richard's extremely busy at work…" Samantha was saying.

Marilyn thought that if she heard one more word in that stilted, polite tone she would scream. She surreptitiously studied the room. It'd been redecorated since she last saw it, after the funeral – the quiet dusky pinks had been replaced with equally subdued shades of pale green. A formal row of orchids replaced the photographs that used to line the sideboard. Nothing gave any clue about the inhabitants – except that they

were wealthy and paid for good taste. Facing each other
over this distance, both with their ankles neatly crossed,
made relaxed conversation between the two women
impossible. Marilyn missed the familiarity they used to
enjoy.

"Can we sit outside?" She suddenly interrupted
Samantha.

"Yes, of course."

"It's a beautiful day," added Marilyn, apologetically.
"It seems a shame to miss it." Out on the patio, Marilyn
was at least able to lean her elbows on the table and
feign relaxation. The conversation faltered, and was
rescued by the summer flowers: the roses were doing
well, the wisteria was disappointing this year, and the
lawn was very dry...

Samantha suppressed a yawn behind her hand. "I'm
sorry – it's the antidepressants – they make me so
tired..."

"Why are you taking antidepressants?" said Marilyn,
surprised. Inwardly, she berated herself for not having
spotted the signs earlier.

Samantha stared at her as if she'd said something
unforgivable. A moment later, her expression was
resolutely polite once more.

"I've been – finding things a little difficult. The
doctor said this might help me to manage my emotions
better."

"What are you taking?"

Samantha told her the brand name and Marilyn
swore.

"No wonder you're a zombie! What kind of clown is
this guy?"

Offended, Samantha stiffened. "I've actually found
them very helpful. I was very badly depressed..."

"Your daughter died nine months ago," said Marilyn bluntly. "It's normal to be depressed in those circumstances."

"Yes, well, life has to go on and I was not managing to..." She floundered.

"Not managing to what? Get up in the morning? Keep the tears back? Stop thinking about Faith?"

Samantha flinched as if she'd been slapped. "I was in a very bad state..."

"Of course you were!" wailed Marilyn. 'Your daughter *died*! That's what grief does to you! Jeez, that doctor should be stripped of his license – but they all do it, all of them just *medicate* the problem away... You need to *cry*, not pop pills!" She swore under her breath again. Samantha sat very tight, her face rigid.

"I cried too much." Her voice shook with anger. "I was out of control, I couldn't function, and I needed help. There's normal grief and then there's hysteria."

"Was it Richard's idea?" said Marilyn suspiciously.

Samantha didn't reply.

"Richard put you up to this, didn't he? He decided your terrible grief was inconveniencing him and he'd sooner have you drugged than..."

"I'd rather you didn't speak about my husband like that." Samantha stood, her face hard. "I'd like you to leave now."

"Okay – okay – not another word. Don't throw me out. Sam, for God's sake, sit down, *please*. I'll be good."

Reluctantly, Samantha resumed her seat.

"But do you know those pills of yours are incredibly strong? You must have noticed the side-effects – I mean, I can see you've gained weight." Samantha bristled and Marilyn held up her hands apologetically. "It's not your fault, it's the pills. Is your vision blurring? Dizzy spells? Shakes?" Samantha was assenting unwillingly. "You've already said you're getting tired a lot – what about your libido?"

Samantha shrugged.

"Have you thought about sex in the last – month, say?"

She shook her head.

"Still getting your periods?"

A quick nod.

"So it's not early menopause, but your libido's gone. That'll be your pills as well then."

"I'm not stopping them," said Samantha mulishly. "I can't cope without them... I can't bear..." She stopped, unable to finish her sentence.

Marilyn's eyes softened. She took her friend's hands in her own and held them up to her cheek. "You are my best friend in the whole world; you know that, don't you Sam?"

"Yes," said Samantha quietly.

"Then please, honey – at least let me prescribe you something milder than what you are on. It'll make life easier; you'll get your own mind back. You'll be able to carry on living your life. Okay?"

"Okay."

Ben looked up from his desk to see Samantha silhouetted in the doorway, one hand raised to knock.

"Samantha!" He leapt up, hurrying forward with his hand outstretched. "What a coincidence, you are exactly the person I would like to see!" As he shook her hand vigorously, he guided her into the room by her elbow. "Come in, sit down, please..."

"What did you want to see me about?" Samantha was too taken aback to resist as he steered her into a seat and sat opposite her, beaming.

"We surrender!" he announced happily, throwing his hands in the air. "You win. The DNC is going to back you."

"Excuse me?"

"Yep – we're one hundred percent behind you."

Her eyes narrowed. "What's caused this sudden change of heart?"

"Look Samantha, I know we've had our differences. I thought that picture would ruin your chances and I just didn't want to hurt the party, that's all – but I was wrong, you were right. Touché! The voter turnout for you has been just incredible and it's about time we started backing the winning horse!"

He leaned back happily, waiting for her effusions of delight. Instead, she folded her hands and looked down at her lap.

"Samantha? What's wrong? I thought you'd be happy with the news. I'd understand if you have a few hard feelings, but…"

"No, it's not that." She hesitated, morose. "I'm sorry, Ben. I came here today to tell you I'm getting out of the race."

He stared at her sad, determined face. "But…" he began, dumbfounded.

"You win. I'm quitting."

"Why would you do such a thing?"

"Personal reasons."

"But what *kind* of personal reasons?"

"Personal, as in too personal to tell people." Her expression allowed no argument.

Ben's shoulders drooped and he scratched his forehead. "This is the worst news I could possibly have imagined…"

"I don't see why," said Samantha acidly. "You've wanted me out of the race ever since those pictures hit the internet – now you get your wish."

Ben was shaking his head. "It doesn't work like that – every liberal out there that passionately loves you will blame us, we'll never get them back on our side in time for the general election!"

"Well, that's easily solved. I'll back whoever you want me to when I make my farewell speech." She stood to leave.

"It won't matter! They'll still blame us!" He leapt to his feet.

"I'm sorry, Ben." Her tone was final. "I really thought I was bringing you good news."

As she headed for the door, he scurried over and grabbed her arm. "Samantha…"

She looked pointedly at his hand, which he withdrew, and then at him. "Yes?"

He'd been planning to beg her to change her mind, but looking at that icy gaze his courage faltered.

"Please," he said instead, "At least explain. After the scandalous pictures, and your husband making an ass of himself in front of the whole country – what personal reason could be so great to get you to drop out of the race after all that?"

She deliberated for a moment and then tilted her head in reluctant concession. "Okay. No further than this office."

"Understood."

"I've been interacting with my daughter ever since I decided to run for president and she's been basically acting as my campaign manager and guiding me along the way."

He blinked, bemused. "But isn't your daughter dead?"

"Exactly my point. I'd like to see you spin that one to the media."

Dumbfounded, he watched her leave and stood staring at the wooden back of his door after she closed it. On impulse, he yanked it open again and called after her. She turned back to find him giving her a wry half smile.

"She did a hell of a job on your campaign. I wish I could hire her."

"Yes," said Samantha ruefully. "She did."

20

"Hi," said Samantha, smiling wanly as she walked towards the car. Expressionless, Hope opened the door. As she slid into her seat, Samantha glanced nervously in the rearview mirror at her reflection, but Hope kept her eyes firmly forward.

"Okay…" said Samantha slowly. "I'm getting the silent treatment?"

"No, ma'am." Hope started the car and backed out the parking space.

"Hope?"

Hope didn't reply. Samantha leaned forward and laid a hand on her shoulder.

'Talk to me – tell me what's on your mind. What have I done to upset you?"

Hope hit the brake and looked over her shoulder at her. "You're withdrawing from the race, aren't you?"

"Yes, I am."

"Why?"

"Because I have to."

"That's no answer."

"No, it's not. But it's the only answer I have. I'm sorry."

Hope slid the car back into gear and pulled away. In silence, she spun them smoothly around corners and onto the familiar route back to Samantha's apartment. After a few minutes of silence, she spoke again.

"May I say something, ma'am?"

"Of course you can, Hope. What is it?"

"You can't withdraw from this race." Her eyes were fixed on the road, but her chin jutted out with mutinous determination.

"Why not?"

Hope was quiet for so long that Samantha thought she wasn't going to reply. Finally, she blurted out, "Because I believe in you more than anyone else in my life!"

Samantha's face stilled.

"You are intelligent, kind, and generous-hearted – your vision of the country is pure, and that is the candidate I want to vote for…"

Samantha closed her eyes, feeling a spasm of sadness course through her features. She hadn't let go of her dream to be president, because that had never really been her dream. Until Ben and Cynthia had approached her with the idea, she hadn't imagined it possible. Her hopes had all centered on finding a vehicle for her ideas, her conviction that she could see what was going wrong and how to fix it. In discovering – or remembering – Faith's death, all she could think was that she was unfit for the job and needed to get out of the public eye as fast as possible, before anyone uncovered her terrible secret. She'd briefly forgotten that fierce hope of helping people.

"You're the only candidate I want to vote for," repeated Hope. "And… will gladly take a bullet for."

Samantha glanced at her. The sadness rose so fast that she had to blink it down. "I really appreciate that, Hope," she said with forced steadiness, "But I'm withdrawing from the race because I'm not fit to lead this country."

"Bullshit!" burst out Hope, hitting the steering wheel. "I'm sorry, but who told you that? What happened to your belief in yourself? What's happened to *you*? Don't tell me you started buying their shit after everything you've fought for… Ms. St. Clair, I don't care *how* you've been handling your grief over your daughter's death, I look at what you've achieved and I think you can do anything! And the fact that you did all of that, in that state, only confirms what I believe. You know you're still capable of doing your work because you've *been* doing your work! The only thing different about you are those damn pills you're doping yourself up with!"

Samantha looked out the window, curiously divided. Inside, she still had all the same emotional responses. She wanted to weep with disappointment, to rant about Ben's sudden about-face and fair-weather friendship, to flare up with anger and fight back against Hope's accusations. All that tumult of feelings seemed to be contained within a nice plastic globe inside her, where she could observe them indifferently.

Hope was still going at it. "I don't see you driven by ego like the other candidates I've protected. I see you driven by love, and compassion – we *need* you, ma'am! The country needs you, because some day love will have to lead us, not the fear-based mind manipulation of all these white male lawyers! No one believes in governing through fear anymore, except in politics, where it's all about scare-mongering and who can build the biggest boogieman to scare the electorate into voting, and you don't do that – you show people something beautiful they can build, be a part of and be *proud* of – not proud of bombing the shit out of some other country, not proud like a bully, proud of what we *are*… Don't you *get* that?"

Samantha's soft laugh sounded almost like tears.

"What's so funny?"

"Those are the exact words my daughter would use if she was here right now." Somewhere inside the plastic globe, a woman screamed her grief, hammered her fists, and wept out her inconsolable loss. Samantha gave a small, wry smile.

"Well, it's settled then," said Hope. "You can't withdraw."

"And why's that?"

"How can two people who love you so much be wrong?"

Samantha's heart almost stopped. The warm golden glow of those words began to trickle into her heart, but she couldn't let it in. If she softened now, she would break completely.

"Agent Seward, you're out of line."

Looking as though she might cry, Hope ripped off a salute. "Yes, Ma'am."

As her apartment door came into view, Samantha saw a silhouetted figure standing nearby. For a wild moment, her heart soared – Faith had come back to her, after all! The next second, she realized the person was too broad and at least a foot too tall. Samantha drew back momentarily, and Hope blocked her path before they both recognized the figure was James. He had a backpack slung over his shoulder and slouched against the wall.

"There you are." He smiled at her, glancing at Hope. "Hi Hope. Samantha, I've been waiting for hours."

"Were we supposed to meet?" She still stood a few feet away, uncertainly.

"Nope." He offered no further explanation for his presence, so she walked past him and unlocked the door.

"Thank you, Hope. Have a good night, hon." Hope gave a quick nod before retreating back into the shadows. She'd wait until Samantha was safely ensconced behind closed doors before departing.

James followed Samantha through the doorway, setting his bag down next to the sofa.

"What is this?" she said.

"A one-man intervention." He smiled ruefully. "I heard you're planning on withdrawing."

"What – but I only told Ben this morning!"

"It's a small town, I guess…"

"Well, it's none of your business." She walked around the room, trying to do the things she would normally do if she were alone. Having drawn the curtains and switched on a few lights, however, she was left with no more activity.

'That's why I'm calling it an intervention. It sounds nicer than 'nosy meddlesome bastard.' "

She folded her arms, staring hard at him. "James, I like you. You know that. I couldn't be happier that we've met up after all these years." She sounded anything but happy. "Nevertheless – my decision is my decision."

"But you see, that's why I'm here." He sat on the sofa, legs crossed, leaning his chin on one hand. "I don't think it is your decision."

"If you're trying to suggest that I don't have the right to make up my own mind... If you think you can just waltz in here telling me what to do…" Her voice rose in volume and pitch, until she was almost yelling. Getting angry was almost a relief.

"That's exactly what I *don't* mean," he said earnestly. "I absolutely think it should be your decision – but at the moment, I think, your medication's making your decisions for you. Because the Sam I knew before this one appeared would never have given up."

"Yes, and she would also be spending cozy evenings in with her dead daughter!" argued Samantha.

"So *what*? I told you, grief does strange things, it doesn't mean you're insane…"

"Who died and made you such an expert on grief?" she spat. It was just a figure of speech. When he flinched at her words, she realized what she'd said and slapped her hand over her mouth. "James…Sorry…"

"Emma did," he replied, his face hard with pain. "Emma died and made me an expert on grief. I spent years in groups and therapy because I couldn't cope on my own, so I'm talking from my own experience. I'm also talking from what I've seen other people go through, from people who've counseled me and people I've counseled."

"So sorry…" she said again, sinking down cautiously on the edge of the sofa. "I didn't mean…"

"The thing about losing someone like that is," James went on, his eyes shining, "The person who would usually help you through something like this is the exact person whose loss is tearing you apart. And it really does feel like you're just going to blow apart with the pain of it all – it's as if once you let yourself feel it, you'll never stop screaming – so you begin to deny it…"

"So you're here to shake me out of my denial?" charged Samantha.

He shook his head vehemently. "Absolutely not! Your mind knows what it's doing, Sam." He took her hands in his, twisting around to face her directly. "When it feels like the pain is too much to bear, it probably is. Your mind protects itself – it knows you can't cope with everything at once. People who try to shake you out of that denial risk doing enormous damage."

Samantha's eyes widened.

"Gradually, little by little, one thing at a time, you start facing the loss – you feel it a bit, you retreat a bit – it's like a spiral, you gradually work your way in, round and round. The thing is – you can't do that on medication. It blocks everything; all emotion. Not just the stuff that's just too much to bear, but the healthy emotions as well."

"What business is it of yours?" She heard herself speak from inside that hard bubble at her center, her feelings churning in response to his words. On the outside, she remained stoic.

"I guess none on the personal level, really." He squeezed her hands, clasping them together. "But I was really hoping to vote for you in the national elections and I don't want to see you drop out. And I – well…you're important to me. If you stop taking your pills, you *will* feel pain, and I figured, well, I couldn't cope with it on my own, perhaps you can't, either. I just thought…"

"What?"

The asperity in her voice felt like a slap in the face. He studied her hands, biting his lip.

"Maybe it was a mistake coming here. I wanted to help, but…" He stood, feeling suddenly awkward. "I'm sorry – God, I feel such a fool."

She glanced up to see him nervously push his hair out of his eyes, then trip on the side of the sofa as he made his way to the door.

"James, wait… I'm sorry." Her face was as bland as ever. "Really, I am. I just…I can't feel anything. I am so numb. It's like being a robot. And I know this is the medication and that actually there are emotions about all this stuff somewhere. I just can't feel them. But I'm afraid that if I stop taking the pills, there will be a tsunami inside me…destroying everything."

His face was compassionate. "That's why I'm here if you need catching; if you don't want to go through it alone."

"Marilyn keeps saying I shouldn't be on these things, and I should listen to her professional opinion – but she doesn't have the slightest idea how this feels. She has *no clue* how much pain is waiting for me."

James moved closer, crouching next to her, taking her hands again in his and capturing her eyes. "I know."

Samantha met his eyes, while her slack grip seemed to respond slightly. "It does feel like a kind of madness; this much pain…" She went on, tonelessly.

"I know. But it's normal, if you felt that much love for her in the first place."

She met his gaze at last, her eyes hollow. "So you think I should stop them? You see, I can listen to you…you're someone who knows – what's there…"

"Yes. Yes, I know what's there. Yes, I think you should stop them. Because as long as you're taking them, they're robbing you of your spark – your inner glow – that pure loving energy that makes you so vibrant…so compelling."

"But I still can't run for president. To do so…in this emotional state… it would just be irresponsible."

"You've got to decide for yourself about that. But don't allow pills to decide for you."

"And without them…? When the wave hits?" Her voice was small.

"I'll be here."

The withdrawal worked quickly. Over the next two days, the mist began to peel back, exposing the terrain of her soul once more. The calm before the storm still held. She lay in bed at night, sleepless, feeling her eyes swim with tears, but a peculiar sweetness lingered in even that. She found herself wondering how long she'd been sleepwalking through her life.

"Faith will come back..." she whispered in the moonlight. Talking to herself felt strange and silly. She imagined walking in, any day now, to find Faith back on the sofa, reading her textbooks...the only difference being that she'd know she wasn't real this time. Did it matter? If the illusion was complete, why was it important? She could have her daughter back, to hold and talk to. The fantasy was like velvety quicksand, tugging her in, an alternative storyline that could play behind her eyes in tune with this one. *After all*, she reasoned, *what's the difference between memory and imagination? Both are intangible, inaccessible, existing only in our heads...*

She got up and walked around the house. She switched on all the lights and checked every room. She looked in the bath, under the tables, behind the sofa, and even in the fridge. For the first time, she actually felt mad, because she knew beyond certainty that Faith was not in the house, that no comforting illusion was in the next room, and yet she couldn't stop looking.

She pressed her knuckles hard against her mouth. *But I stopped taking the pills*, she thought. *Why isn't she back? Where's my baby? I miss her so much... I want her back...*

She began to rock back and forth as the tears descended. Blindly groping in her purse, she found her cell phone. It was three in the morning. He'd said any time. She really shouldn't phone now; it was far too late. She dialed anyway.

"James?" she said, her voice barely intelligible through her sobs. "James, I miss her so much… Oh, God, James, I don't know what to do, it hurts so much… The pain… The pain…"

"It's okay, just cry – just cry."

"But it *hurts!*"

"I know… I know… I'm on my way. I've got you on hands-free now, keep talking, I'll be there soon."

She couldn't talk, because the tears had taken over her vocal cords. Sobs, not words, were shaping her mouth. She could hear him murmuring comfort in her ear, while in the background the sounds of his car coming closer. She heard him pulling up outside her apartment, and the slam of his car door. When he arrived at the apartment door, she was standing there, looking truly dreadful – her hair tangled where she'd pulled at it, her eyes swollen and red, puffy cheeks, runny nose.

"Hey," he said tenderly, with a gentle smile. As he wrapped his arms around her, she suddenly realized that crying was the sanest thing she could do, and letting herself cry was the bravest thing she'd ever done.

The cheering roar seemed to wash up and down the arena. Banners and placards, made tiny by distance, showed Samantha's name and face. With such a crowd, individual people seemed to melt into the texture of an impressionistic painting. She breathed deeply, stilling her nerves. She reminded herself that every brush stroke out there was a person who had left their home, given up their evening, driven or caught the bus or the train, walked up the stairs to their seat… It was important for her to keep a sense of them as individuals, despite their collective chanting.

To the people on the far side of the arena, she was only a brightly colored pinprick of light. The cameras, however, zoomed in and superimposed her face onto the giant screen. The audience would observe her face more intimately than if she were addressing a group of twenty. She stood at the podium, waiting for silence to fall. Feeding off each other's frenzy, the crowd kept roaring and yelling, back and forth, until at last, she had to hold her hands up for quiet.

"Thank you." The microphone relayed her voice to speakers several times her own size around the arena. "With such an extremely warm welcome, this will be very tough for me to say."

The crowd's hush became a vacuum of silence, frozen, waiting for her next words. Samantha's eyes scanned the faces.

"I know there have been a lot of rumors flying around over the last couple of days," she said. Her next words stuck in her throat as her eyes fastened on a cluster of people sitting near the front - Faith stared back at her, fierce and compelling. Unable to look away, Samantha continued her speech from memory. "I'm here to announce that I'm not running for President of the United States because I'm pretty sure I'm not capable of doing everything a man can do."

The sound of thousands of people moaning softly in the backs of their throats was a symphony of woe. Faith's eyes blazed. Samantha swallowed, glanced down at her speech, and back up. She took a breath and let it out. Just as she'd known when she was fourteen, she knew now that the audience was hers; the elastic pause stretching out for effect. She looked at Faith again with a faint smile.

"I am, however" she continued, "running for President of the United States because I know, absolutely, what a woman is capable of doing...and I *am* capable of doing that."

The crowd exploded, waving their banners and whistling on their fingers.

"I don't want to be a man," she said. "I think even the men are tired of having to be men. For so long, we have been so hard, so brutal, so tough-skinned, so determined to repress any flicker of anything softer, that we can't feel anything anymore. We think 'soft' is a dirty word.

"But exactly what defines 'soft'? I believe that it's in our ability to love the people we love; our families, our children. It's in the appreciation of a beautiful forest, a mountain range, an art gallery, or a quiet leafy suburb. It's caring whether people get enough to eat, helping someone who's hurt themselves, and in working hard to give our children a better future. These are the things we live for. And to do any of that, we have to be soft. We have to be able to *feel*.

"Sure, we need to be tough sometimes to look after these things. And yes, sometimes we even have to fight wars to protect these things. But we are so busy defending our lives; we forget to take care of our reasons for living.

"I think we have enough tanks, don't you? I think we have enough guns in the streets, don't you? I think we have too many children going to bed hungry, don't you? I think we have too many good prisons but not enough good schools, don't you? I think we have too many polluters out there, ruining our precious planet, don't you? And I think it's time to cherish the men and women serving our country as our own sons and daughters, and never *ever* put them in harm's way unless it is a *clear* and *present* danger, don't you?"

She paused to let the rising crescendo from the crowd fill the arena. As arms and flags waved, she lost sight of Faith's face and turned her eyes out over the whole mass of people.

"As we escort President Madson out of the White House," she continued, "I think we should usher out the influence of greed along with him, don't you?' The people screamed their assent. "No longer will our Executive Branch of Government be influenced by large donors and special interest groups who line the politician's pockets with money and expect – correct that, *demand* favors in return. On my watch, I will do my best to ensure that this is a government for *all* people, not just *all the wealthy* people." Again, she paused to allow them to vent their agreement.

"And how about religion?" She picked up her thread again. "I don't know about you – but I've always liked the constitution. I like the idea of a constitutional government. And I think our founding fathers had the right idea when they enshrined freedom of thought and declared that an individual's religion is up to them. So when we unseat the current government, let's dethrone the Religious Right with them! This is not the Middle Ages, this is not the Inquisition, people's beliefs are a dialogue between them and God and no earth-bound government has the *right* to intervene!

"As much as my Faith means everything to me…" She sought out her daughter's face again and was rewarded with a wink. "My faith may not be yours, and I will never push my beliefs onto anyone. We will be a *constitutional government!*"

She waited for the applause to subside before going on. "I think the Founding Fathers were some of the greatest people to walk the face of the earth. Their insight in creating a democracy at that time in history was a positive paradigm shift second to none. But with that said, I think it's time for the Mothers to step up and be heard too.

"Women – we've given men sole control of directing the human race for the last two thousand years, and look where we are. We have stockpiles of weapons as far as the eye can see and a military budget that keeps growing as literally *millions* of children go to bed cold, hungry and illiterate. Does that seem right to you?"

The audience roared back, "No!"

"As the current administration develops strategies for its next tax cut to the wealthy, we have a whole continent dying from AIDS and Mother Earth screaming at us in the form of melted ice caps and intense hurricanes to stop polluting – does that seem right to you?"

Their resounding "No!" came in a single, giant voice.

"We need schools to be built and improved. We need the sick to be cared for through Universal Health Care. And we need children to be fed, cared for and to *know,* without a doubt, that they are loved. It does take a village! We are all connected and in this thing together – so it's time we started acting like it. We need to start taking care of the soft stuff, because staying soft when times are hard is the toughest thing in the world and the only thing that keeps life worth living. Deep down, if you really think about it, all the work that needs to be done right now sounds like women's work, doesn't it? So it's just as well we've got a woman to do it."

She stood smiling as the waves of applause buffeted her, voices screaming themselves hoarse. A slight incline of her head indicated she had finished. On screen, they saw her mouth the words "Thank you" but nothing could be heard over the crowd. Her eyes darted back to the spot where she had seen Faith, now empty.

Extricating herself from the throng of well-wishers, Samantha managed to slip out of the hall with its festoon of banners, balloons, and ribbons. Looking back at the scene, her eyes stung. Once the party had decided to back her, they'd done it with zeal. She felt like the tiny figure of a surfer atop a massive breaker, riding the strength, energy and love of so many people. Samantha turned around abruptly and found the person she was looking for shadowing her closely.

"Hi," she said.

Hope stopped just short of her. "Congresswoman," she said.

"Hope... I'm sorry."

"There's no need to apologize, ma'am," said Hope.

"Yes, there is. You've been my loyal supporter, not just my agent, and I was horrible to you when you tried to help me."

Hope stood in silence.

"Well...?" said Samantha hesitantly.

"Thank you," Hope whispered, "apology accepted, ma'am."

"Can I give you a hug?"

Hope hung back. "That wouldn't be very professional, ma'am." She replied.

"You're off duty for five seconds."

The two women smiled, then embraced.

"Ma'am?"

"Yes Hope?"

"What changed your mind?"

"A friend helped me to see who I was when I cut myself off from my feelings – and I didn't like that person. I looked at how this country has cut itself off from its feelings – and it's become cruel and vicious. It's been behaving as if it's okay to torture people, it's okay to let people starve, it's okay to blacken the sky with our filth and turn the forests to wastelands – and I don't think that's how we used to be. But I think since we cut off all the softness, that's who we've become. And we should be terrified of that fate."

Hope tightened her arms around her.

"And I don't *care* if this is unprofessional," added Samantha.

"Oh, I'm being professional," retorted Hope, her chin resting on Samantha's shoulder. "I'm watching your back right now."

Samantha stretched her legs the length of the sofa, wiggling her toes with contentment. Mid-morning sunshine streamed into her apartment, illuminating the rising steam of her coffee, making spring seem more a reality than a distant hope. For the first time since the primaries began, she was taking two whole days off in a row: a real weekend. Of course, she was watching the political shows, but television hardly counted as *work*... The current President was giving his reaction to her victory.

"Personally, I'm glad Congresswoman St. Clair won the primaries," he said. Samantha gestured at the screen and grinned. "...because her campaign over the next month will showcase everything that is wrong with her party and the liberal agenda. In contrast, it will display everything that is right with the Conservative movement. And once these two ideologies are put side by side in comparison, the country will overwhelmingly choose the fiscally responsible and morally superior Republican Party over the big-government, morally deficient Democrats. We can once and for all come to the conclusion that Right is right and left is history."

"You're an idiot!" called out Samantha happily. "Democracy without opposition? Pah! Impossible!"

"That this is a country that believes in capitalism and not big government handouts," he continued. "That this administration and the Constitution were built on God-fearing Christian beliefs..."

"Constitution and secular affiliation in the same sentence!" yelled Samantha, like a baseball fan coaching her team from the sofa.

"...and not the godless, sex-starved orgy-mentality the other party likes to display. The Conservative movement is the right direction for this country at the right time in this nation's history, and the elections this fall will only reinforce this belief."

"The hell they will! Bend over, Mr. President!"

The doorbell rang. She bounded from the sofa to the door and flung it open with a smile.

"James!" She bounced backwards in surprise. "This is a surprise." He looked taller and more languid than ever, in a cream linen suit over a shirt of pale pink. She was suddenly aware that she was clad in yesterday's make-up and her bath robe. *At least,* she consoled herself, *it's the short silk one and not the woolen one.*

He seemed even more taken aback. "I'm awfully sorry – I hope I'm not intruding – I heard voices..."

"Oh, that was just me." She grinned. "Don't worry...I wasn't talking to Faith – just to the TV... Come in."

He bent down, and from outside the doorway picked up a potted bush of red tea roses adorned with a large satin bow and a wrapped present. "For you," he said shyly. "I said I don't buy cut roses…but I found some in a pot, so it's okay… Oh, and this, as well!" He handed her the gift.

Inside, she untied the ribbons while he stammered on nervously.

"I really hope I'm not intruding – I just thought – well, I wanted to see you on a happy occasion, not just when you're upset. I didn't want you to only associate me with peat bogs, melting ice-caps, and crying your heart out – I'd rather you associated me with – uh – happy things… like…"

Samantha had unwrapped the present and was staring, astonished, at a new erotica novel.

"Like sex?" she said incredulously. She took a sip of her coffee to cover her confusion.

He went bright red, looking shocked. "No! I meant roses – I just picked up the book because I've seen some on your shelf and assumed you like them – but actually, uh, well – yes, that'd be nice too…"

She took another gulp of coffee, staring at him. In a fit of nervousness, she lowered the mug too quickly, splashing coffee down the front of James's clothing.

"Oh my God! Oh, James, I'm so sorry! Oh, no, your beautiful suit… And it's linen… Quick, get it off; if I wash it immediately, the stain should come out."

She stood, mortified, while he slid off his jacket and unbuttoned his shirt. His lips were tightly pressed together. He looked down at the splash of brown that had seeped the length of his trousers and began to remove them as well. As she studied his face, it began to dawn on her that his expression wasn't anger – he was trying very hard not to laugh at her, and obviously losing the battle. His resolve finally crumbled and he exploded with laughter, handing her his trousers.

"Zero to undressing in two minutes flat," he chuckled. "This is going far better than I expected."

ENJOY MORE TITLES
BY ALAN C. LYONS:

AVAILABLE NOW:

CROSS FIRE

COMING SOON:

THE RAY OF LIGHT TRILOGY:

BOOK 1: GODSPEED

BOOK 2: CRITICAL MASS

BOOK 3: REVELATIONS

FOR MORE INFORMATION
PLEASE VISIT:

WWW.ALANLYONS.COM